CARRIER

These are the stories of Carrier Battle Group Fourteen—a force including a supercarrier, amphibious unit, guided missile cruiser, and destroyer. And these are the novels that capture the blistering reality of international combat. Exciting. Authentic. Explosive.

CARRIER . . . The smash debut thriller about the ultimate military nightmare: the takeover of a U.S. Intelligence ship.

VIPER STRIKE . . . A renegade Chinese fighter group penetrates Thai airspace—and launches a full-scale invasion.

ARMAGEDDON MODE . . . With India and Pakistan on the verge of nuclear destruction, the Carrier Battle Group Fourteen must prevent a final showdown.

FLAME-OUT . . . The Soviet Union is reborn in a military takeover—and their strike force shows no mercy.

MAELSTROM . . . The Soviet occupation of Scandinavia leads Carrier Battle Group Fourteen into conventional weapons combat—and possibly all-out war.

COUNTDOWN . . . Carrier Battle Group Fourteen must prevent the deployment of Russian submarines. The problem: They have nukes.

AFTERBURN . . . Carrier Battle Group Fourteen receives orders to enter the Black Sea—in the middle of a Russian civil war.

W9-BRW-168

continued on next page . . .

ALPHA STRIKE . . . When American and Chinese interests collide in the South China Sea, the superpowers risk waging a third world war.

ARCTIC FIRE . . . A Russian splinter group has occupied the Aleutian Islands off the coast of Alaska—in the ultimate invasion of U.S. soil.

ARSENAL . . . Magruder and his crew are trapped between Cuban revolutionaries . . . and a U.S. power play that's spun wildly out of control.

NUKE ZONE . . . When a nuclear missile is launched against the U.S. Sixth Fleet, Magruder must face a frightening question: In an age of computer warfare, how do you tell friends from enemies?

CHAIN OF COMMAND . . . Magruder enters the jungles of Vietnam, looking for answers about his missing father. Little does he know that another bloody war is about to be unleashed—with his fleet caught in the crosshairs.

BRINK OF WAR . . . Friendly war games with the Russians take a deadly turn, and Carrier Battle Group Fourteen must prevent war from erupting in the skies. Little do they know that's just what someone wants.

TYPHOON . . . An American yacht is attacked by a Chinese helicopter in international waters, and the Carrier team is called to the front lines of what may be the start of a war between the superpowers.

ENEMY OF MY ENEMY . . . A Greek pilot unwittingly downs a news chopper, and Magruder must keep the peace between Greece and the breakaway republic of Macedonia. But what no one knows is that it wasn't an accident at all.

JOINT OPERATIONS . . . China launches a surprise attack on Hawaii—and the Carrier team can't handle it alone. As Tombstone and his fleet take charge of the air, Lieutenant Murdock and his SEALs are called in to work ashore.

THE ART OF WAR . . . When Iranian militants take the first bloody step toward toppling the decadent West, the Carrier group are the only ones who can stop the madmen.

ISLAND WARRIORS . . . China launches a full-scale invasion on its tiny capitalist island neighbor—and Carrier Battle Group Fourteen is the only hope to stop it.

FIRST STRIKE . . . A group of radical Russian military officers are planning a nuclear attack on the United States, but Carrier Battle Group Fourteen has been called in to make sure the Cold War ends without a bang.

HELLFIRE . . . A top-secret missile defense system being tested aboard the USS *Jefferson* accidentally targets Russia, igniting Cold War tensions once more—leaving Carrier Battle Group Fourteen to defend itself.

TERROR AT DAWN . . . Even as a raid on an Idaho militia compound goes horribly wrong—with deadly consequences—Carrier Battle Group Fourteen must face attacks from both Iran and North Korea, which may spark all-out war.

book twenty-two

CARRIER
Final Justice

KEITH DOUGLASS

J
JOVE BOOKS, NEW YORK

THE BERKLEY PUBLISHING GROUP
Published by the Penguin Group
Penguin Group (USA) Inc.
375 Hudson Street, New York, New York 10014, USA
Penguin Group (Canada), 10 Alcorn Avenue, Toronto, Ontario M4V 3B2, Canada
(a division of Pearson Penguin Canada Inc.)
Penguin Books Ltd., 80 Strand, London WC2R 0RL, England
Penguin Group Ireland, 25 St. Stephen's Green, Dublin 2, Ireland
(a division of Penguin Books Ltd.)
Penguin Group (Australia), 250 Camberwell Road, Camberwell, Victoria 3124,
Australia (a division of Pearson Australia Group Pty. Ltd.)
Penguin Books India Pvt. Ltd., 11 Community Centre, Panchsheel Park, New Delhi—
100 017, India
Penguin Group (NZ), Cnr. Airborne and Rosedale Roads, Albany, Auckland 1310, New
Zealand (a division of Pearson New Zealand Ltd.)
Penguin Books (South Africa) (Pty.) Ltd., 24 Sturdee Avenue, Rosebank,
Johannesburg 2196, South Africa

Penguin Books Ltd., Registered Offices: 80 Strand, London WC2R 0RL, England

This is a work of fiction. Names, characters, places, and incidents either are the product of the author's imagination or are used fictitiously, and any resemblance to actual persons, living or dead, business establishments, events, or locales is entirely coincidental.

CARRIER: FINAL JUSTICE

A Jove Book / published by arrangement with the author.

PRINTING HISTORY
Jove mass-market edition / November 2004

ISBN: 0-515-13849-5

JOVE®
Jove Books are published by The Berkley Publishing Group,
a division of Penguin Group (USA) Inc.,
375 Hudson Street, New York, New York 10014.
JOVE is a registered trademark of Penguin Group (USA) Inc.
The "J" design is a trademark belonging to Penguin Group (USA) Inc.

PRINTED IN THE UNITED STATES OF AMERICA

10 9 8 7 6 5 4 3 2 1

PROLOGUE

The American public, concentrating on the violent counterinsurgency operations of the Iraqi War, was unaware of other crises that were in the offing. Various governmental agencies, including military, intelligence, and law enforcement had become embroiled in other deadly situations that threatened the peace of the nation. These were real-life scenarios that had the potential of staggering devastation not only at U.S. facilities overseas, but also within the borders of the Continental United States.

Specially assigned men and women worked in clandestine haste as they struggled to defuse these disasters-in-the-making. The pressure and time limits of the various missions brought them more than their share of sleepless nights and deep depression. This acute anxiety was spurred on by the most feared emotional conditions known to the human race: uncertainty and a need to be quick and accurate to the nth degree.

Among the crises was a terrorist plot as merciless as the Oklahoma City bombing. This insidious scheme was moving into full activation within the borders of the United States. The originators of the outrage were not fanatical Muslims, but homegrown terrorists raging against what they considered government violations of their basic liberties. They harbored such fury that collateral casualties were not only acceptable, but considered beneficial to their cause. Their basic philosophy was that those people who were not with them were against them. No exceptions.

Another tragedy-in-the-making occurred when Iran began their own campaign of terror by using minisubmarines to attack the American fleet in the Persian Gulf. The American nuclear aircraft carrier *Jefferson* had been hit by a torpedo from one of these underwater craft. The torpedo's impact had caused massive damage that resulted in the death of one sailor and the wounding of fourteen others. Now U.S. Navy antisubmarine aircraft scoured those waters in an attempt to end the outrages, and bring a much needed stability to the area.

The third threat against the American way of life was hidden within a dangerous misconception. It was generally thought that the threat of World War III had evaporated with the collapse of the Soviet Union. The people in the First World were unaware that this comforting assumption was severely challenged on the Korean peninsula where American troops stood guard on the DMZ that separated North and South Korea. Spy satellites had detected evidence that Pyongyang's armed forces were moving up to concealed sites that looked straight across the neutral ground into American and South Korean defensive positions. What the electronics surveillance didn't reveal was that several elite North Korean jet fighter regiments and submarine squadrons were coordinating their own attacks with the ground forces. All these zealot automatons of Kim Jong Il—the man they called Dear Leader—stood in blood-lusting ranks, ready to roll across the 38th Parallel in addition to attacking the U.S. Navy in the Sea of Japan. If these intentions of the Hermit Kingdom weren't thwarted, the most massive catastrophe the world had ever known would murderously explode across Southeast Asia before engulfing the entire world.

CHAPTER ONE

United Nations Building, New York City
American office suite
Sunday, 15 September
1600 local (GMT −5)

Sarah Wexler, America's ambassador to the United Nations, looked across the conference room table at her assistant Brad Heaton and their unexpected guest. This was White House Chief of Staff Jim Dawson who had come in from Washington earlier that afternoon. His insistence on an immediate meeting was met with more than just a little resentment by the lady diplomat. Wexler's administrative plate was always filled to overflowing, and she detested interruptions that kept her from the myriad tasks awaiting her attention. But when the President of the United States sends a personal envoy, everything must be put aside.

The chamber where the trio gathered for the exchange of information reflected the ambassador's personality and preferences for interior decoration. No unnecessary frills or decorations adorned the place except for the American flag standing in a far corner. The furniture was plain but made of heavy, expensive mahogany, and the straight-back chairs had only the minimum of padding. This was undeniably a workplace, plain and simple. Wexler did not want the room to evolve into a social center where her staff would hang out during coffee breaks. This arrangement really didn't matter much since Wexler didn't allow conventional coffee breaks in any case. Her people were allowed to enjoy a coffee, soda, or snack at their desk twice a day at 10 AM and 2 PM while they continued laboring at their tasks. No work stoppage was tolerated.

Dawson had made the special trip up to New York for the meeting with Wexler because the President was unable to speak to her by telephone. He and the Israeli ambassador were huddled together at Camp David to discuss the latest cease-fire agreements, disagreements, and violations taking place on the West Bank. The Palestinians had already voiced their own outrage about various incidents, and now it was Israel's turn to give their side of the recent unhappy events. Between Muslim suicide bombers and Israeli incursions into Palestinian territory, the President had all he could handle keeping the situation from blowing up like a keg of gunpowder.

Wexler sipped from a cup of decaf coffee. She generally took in caffeine like it was a nutrient, but lately her nerves and temper had become frayed from all the problems arising from the homegrown militiamen out in Idaho. The wife and two children of an innocent farmer were killed by agents of the FBI during a bungled raid on their isolated farm at Bull Run. It had been worse even than Ruby Ridge and Waco because of the family's complete disassociation from any controversial groups. The tragedy had been a result of poor intelligence, quick shooting, and a resultant fire started from teargas canisters, trapping the family members in the house where they burned alive.

This domestic catastrophe went international when the United Nations ambassador from Iran brought the world organization's attention to the unhappy episode during a general session. After discovering every single detail of the incident in the *New York Times,* the ambassador put forth a motion that called for a multilateral peacekeeping force to be placed in

Idaho to prevent any more murders of innocent people. The vote went overwhelmingly against the United States as gleeful Third World nations, forgetting all the American aid they received, saw an opportunity to humiliate and embarrass their benefactor. The idea alone was enough to infuriate the American public, and the reaction had spurred another "Get-Us-Out-of-the-UN" campaign in which e-mails, phone calls, and letters bombarded the White House and Congress.

Wexler had been forced to use America's veto to prevent the action from taking place. It was the only thing to be done in light of the limited options, but it certainly didn't put America in a better light as far as the rest of the world was concerned.

"The President is of course devastated by the Bull Run incident," Dawson said as if he were reading Wexler's mind. "He's come down hard on the FBI. The mismanagement of the Bureau had to be addressed vigorously, since their incompetence brought nothing but grief. The effect on the militia was to garner them a great deal of public support. The dissident group remains as strong as ever. Maybe stronger. Needless to say, something effective must be done to bring things under control."

"Yes," Wexler said. "I believe that's why he chose Admiral Magruder to take over any further actions against the militia."

"Except I noticed that Magruder brought in the very same FBI agent who had been in charge at Bull Run," Heaton commented.

"The President agreed not to interfere with his choice of staff," Dawson said. "Of course that was before the aforementioned agent was chosen. But our Chief Executive kept his word." He turned to Wexler. "At any rate, Madame Ambassador, what is your assessment of any fallout at the UN regarding the veto of Pakistan's motion? The President is very interested in the situation. He wants to go after any particularly irritating Yankee-haters in the UN, and lean on them a bit."

Wexler finished her coffee before answering. "In my estimation the turn down of a multilateral intervention sets a precedent that will make the UN less inclined to send in future peacekeeping forces even during serious regional conflicts. In other words, an atmosphere of laissez-faire even in cases of local genocide seems to be growing among member nations. Thus, some of those who enjoyed sticking it to us may end up paying a very hefty price if any of their dissidents decide to topple a legitimate government or do a bit of ethnic cleansing."

"That will put more pressure on the U.S.," Dawson said. "If the United Nations fails to act when some local ethnic group is massacring old rivals, then we'll be expected to step in unilaterally, and put an end to the atrocities."

Heaton chuckled. "Isn't it amazing how the same people that love to hate Americans, expect us to rush in to expend our own blood and funds when local bad guys act up?"

"Well," Wexler said, "it appears to me that the problem in Korea is going to snatch a lot of attention away from Bull Run, anyway. There's a real possibility of World War III breaking out if that boiling cauldron isn't pulled off the fire. And the first nuclear attack will surely come from that short, little reprobate in Pyongyang."

"Reprobate?" Dawson remarked with a humorless grin. "That's a very kind way to refer to a criminally insane despot."

"Are you aware the people of North Korea refer to him as Dear Leader?" Heaton asked.

"I'm wearing my ambassador hat right now," Wexler said. "Talk to me about Kim Jong Il in a bar and I'll call him a murderous son of a bitch."

"Right," Dawson said. "Before I leave here, the President wants me to discuss the eight suggestions you sent him to cool down the rhetoric at the UN."

"Alright," Wexler agreed reluctantly.

"He has added another half dozen," Dawson said.

Wexler glanced at Heaton who pulled a notebook from his attaché case. The Madame Ambassador sighed. This was going to be one hell of a long meeting.

Militia safe house
Deer Crossing, Idaho
Monday, 16 September
1430 local (GMT −7)

Deer Crossing wasn't really a town. In reality, it was the proverbial wide spot in the road with a combination gas station and
convenience store, bait shop, small café, a quartet of modest
dwellings, and a half dozen abandoned buildings. The community was up in the Clearwater Mountains; isolated and known
only by a very few people who were mostly hard-core outdoorsmen. These were the sort of men who did not hunt as
much for trophies as to put food on the table.

One sturdy log building was set off from the rest of the settlement on the side of a steep slant of terrain that sloped up toward
even higher country. The location offered an excellent view of
the town as well as the only road that approached the place. In
other words, it offered a good field of fire for anyone desiring to
defend the place from attack. This was not just coincidence.
The building was the headquarters for an Idaho militia organization.

The interior of the structure was specially designed and laid
out to meet the needs of the owners. A kitchen, complete with
an army surplus stove and refrigerator, was capable of storing
and cooking enough food to feed up to a couple of hundred individuals three times a day.

Additionally, three more rooms were spacious and empty,
providing perfect places for tired visitors to bed down for extended periods of time. All the windows were barred to prohibit
intruders and flying teargas canisters; the light and power came
from a generator in the basement; and gas for cooking was sup-
plied through propane tanks. No telephone lines linked the
building to the outside—instead an efficient communications
system made up of a two-way radio and cell phones was available for contact with the outside world.

The only permanent resident in what was really a large two-
story cabin was Darrell Kent, an ex-paratrooper who was in his

late sixties. For most of his life Kent had been in excellent physical condition because of extensive outdoor activities and a devotion to exercise picked up during military service. But for the past several years his health was fading—not failing— just taking a slight downswing. He didn't smoke, but was de- voted to a meat-and-potato diet and generous slugs of Jack Daniels Tennessee Whiskey. Kent ended most days with a taste or two of ol' Jack before going to bed.

The former paratrooper was also a retired typesetter who had spent his entire working career as both a machine- and hand- compositor in small-town print shops and newspapers around Idaho. He worked with hot-metal type and had been saddened when the onset of computers took away a trade he had labored in for years as a certified journeyman. In his younger days, when not setting type, Kent spent most of his spare time participating in the activities of a militia unit known as the Continental Line. Because of his service in a parachute infantry regiment of the 82nd Airborne Division he was picked to be the unit's operations and training officer. Now, after the death of his wife and the mov- ing of all three of his kids to California, he took on the position as a full-time staff member. Hence, he lived in Deer Crossing, maintaining the safe house and all the paperwork of the militia. Because of his age, he now left active field ops to the younger men.

That Sunday afternoon was a special one for the Continen- tal Line. The organization had been approached by members of another militia group with a request for facilities and a cou- ple of people to participate in a special hard-ass operation. The safe house at Deer Crossing was offered as a shelter for the project. Kent was pleased to have such distinguished visitors. One was Frank Woods from the Old Dixie Militia Headquar- ters in Charleston, South Carolina; and the other was Jackson Carter son of the late militia leader Abraham Carter. The elder Carter had been a respected militia commander who was killed in an escape tunnel while trying to flee government au- thorities from a stronghold at Lands End, Idaho. The place had been under assault by retired Admiral Thomas Magruder's multiagency task force. Jackson himself had been wounded by a United States Naval Air Reserve Viking S-3 when the aircraft attacked the truck he was in. He and another man were hauling arms and ammunition stolen from a Montana Inter-Service Reserve Center to a secure location. The driver died, but Jackson was able to limp away to safety in spite of serious wounds.

The other two people who would be there were from Kent's Continental Line bunch. They were a pair of tough outdoorsmen by the names of Arnie Thompson and Earl Perkins. They worked as truck drivers, loggers, construction laborers, and other such jobs when they had the need for money. When not bogged down by making a living, they hunted, fished, and served the Continental Line as militiamen. Both had well-earned reputations as tough, fearless, and dependable. When the call for volunteers to participate in a special, risky operation went out, Thompson and Perkins enthusiastically stepped forward.

Now, as Kent stood off to one side, the four men sat around the kitchen table for a planning session. Road maps of the Continental United States and the state of California were laid out along with a schematic of Qualcomm Stadium in San Diego. A large parachute-kit bag sat on the floor beside Woods. He was an army veteran of Desert Storm and Desert Shield, and served on the national staff of the Old Dixie Militia.

Introductions had been made and a few beers consumed so with all the preliminaries taken care of, it was time to get down to business. "Okay," Woods said, "let's get the ball rolling here." He turned his attention to Thompson and Perkins. "Jackson already has the skinny on this mission. Here's what's going down in a nutshell: We're going to plant bombs at the Super Bowl in San Diego. The game will be played there on January 26."

Perkins counted on his fingers. "That's four months away."

"Right," Jackson interjected. "And you guys said you could drop out of sight for that long."

"What do you mean exactly by 'out of sight'?" Thompson asked.

"Just that," Woods said. "You'll be holed up here. I understand you're both divorced guys rooming together, right?"

"Yeah," Perkins said. "We got a small apartment over in Coeur d'Alene. We go off for months on jobs, so it won't attract no special attention if we're gone for a while."

"But we got to keep the rent paid up in advance," Thompson pointed out.

"That's alright," Woods assured him. "We got funds for that."

"We can take care of all them details later," Jackson Carter said impatiently. "We're here for a mission briefing. I want to start all the preps as early as possible."

"You and me are on the same wavelength," Woods said.

"By the way," Jackson said, "how're you gonna get tickets for the Super Bowl?"

Woods chuckled. "We already got 'em. Old Dixie is a big operation with lots of money and connections."

Perkins was impatient. "Let's get on with the briefing."

"Okay," Woods said. "We'll be using C-4 plastic explosive. The idea is to take it around to various rest rooms and plant it."

"How're we gonna get C-4 into the stadium with us?" Perkins asked.

"We'll carry it in by putting it in picnic coolers," Woods said. He had already anticipated protests, and he held up his hand in a calming gesture. "Yes! They do look inside containers at the entrances to keep alcohol and weapons and all that shit from being brought into the stadium. But what they're gonna see when they look in our coolers ain't gonna be blocks of C-4. Instead—" He reached in the parachute-kit bag and withdrew a couple of Blue Ice containers, dropping them on the table "—they'll see this." He grinned, saying, "Don't try to cool down your beer with these. We've emptied 'em out. They've been refilled with C-4."

"That's a great idea," Perkins said. "But won't stadium security be suspicious if the stuff in there ain't cold?"

"You'll have some real Blue Ice in the cooler, too," Woods said. "Don't worry. It won't hurt the explosives to get cold along with your sandwiches and soda pop."

"Wow!" Thompson exclaimed, impressed with the idea.

"We'll each take one level of the stadium, and make a round of a half dozen rest rooms and plant these babies," Woods said. "They'll go off during the half at approximately the same time—if you do things right—and you'll be back at your seats cooling it when the big booms start."

"What kind of timers are we gonna use?" Perkins asked.

"No timers," Woods said. "You'll use timed fuses already capped, and they'll have fuse lighters attached. We'll be able to get these in by concealing them under our shirts; taped to our manly bodies."

"What you'll do is carry your individual boxes into the rest rooms," Carter said.

"It sounds like you ain't coming along," Perkins remarked.

Woods interjected, "He's too well-known. They even got wanted posters out on him in post offices." He chuckled. "He'll prob'ly be on the TV. They'll feature him on *America's Most Wanted* just about any time now."

"Yeah," Carter said a bit proudly. "Anyhow, as I was saying, you'll go inside a stall, quickly stick the capped fuse into here." He pointed to the white plastic cap at the top of each ice block. "Pull the fuse lighter; set the whole thing behind the toilet on the floor. Nobody's gonna notice 'em there. They won't smell no burning, neither. Remember you'll be putting them things in a shit house. Then hurry around to the next rest room and so on, 'til all your bombs are in place. You meet back at your seats and wait."

"Is that gonna be worth the trouble?" Thompson asked. "Those stadiums are built solid with steel-reinforced concrete. Me and Perk have worked in California on construction jobs. They got earthquake regulations over there that call for structures to be able to stay standing after even the worst tremors. That much explosive in one place ain't gonna do a hell of a lot."

"Oh, it'll do plenty of damage," Woods countered. "Don't forget the thick outer walls will contain the energy of the explosion for a millisecond. All that power will head out the rest room doors into the corridors where dumbass football fans will

be buying their overpriced beer and hot dogs." He laughed.
"Pure fucking devastation, man!"

Carter chuckled, "I believe that's what is meant by the term
'collateral damage'."

Darrell Kent turned from the table, walking over to the cabinet where he kept the Jack Daniels. He pulled down the bottle
and poured a good stiff drink.

CHAPTER TWO

As far as Major General Chan Sun Lee of the Chinese People's Liberation Army was concerned, the North Korean people's military forces not only looked like hell, but smelled that way, too.

The stench of the Korean populace's favorite dish of *kimchi* was everywhere. The overpowering malodor of this fermented mixture of cabbage, onions, and fish generously seasoned with garlic, horseradish, peppers, and ginger clung to everything—including Chan's hair and clothing. His Chinese sense of smell was offended at even the slightest whiff of the dish.

The first thing he planned to do when he returned to his precious homeland was to take a hot steaming bath that a Japanese devil would envy. After a thorough soaping down, he would force himself to sit in the near-boiling water long enough to melt the smell out of the pores of his skin.

Chan was a short, thin, graceful man descended from a family who had been wealthy merchants and honored scholars in old China. Even though he was a staunch Communist and a professional soldier, his personal mannerisms reflected his ancestral traits. He was by nature orderly and clean, and he feared he would have to burn all his uniforms and buy replacements for those that now reeked of the odorous *kimchi*. He could only hope the district quartermaster general would provide him with a clothing purchase allowance based on the hardship of foreign service in North Korea. This should be a stipulation of assignment for advisors such as he, who were sent across the Yellow Sea to serve in the Workers' Paradise ruled by Kim Jong Il.

To make matters worse, he was convinced that his Korean counterpart Kim Sung Chien was a complete madman. One of the most difficult aspects of this assignment was keeping the DPRK officers under control. Their education and indoctrination under the absolute control of their leaders Kim Il Sung and subsequently his son Kim Jong Il had molded them into barbaric automatons. Kim, known nationally as Dear Leader, relied on brute cruelty, not intellectual sophistication to maintain his inherited power over the backward country. If the bumbling megalomaniacal North Korean leader was ever forced to flee his homeland and seek asylum in China, his lifestyle would change drastically. The Red Chinese government would not tolerate having a disgraced ex-head of state not earn his keep. Kim Jong Il would have to take a job, but his lack of intellect and reasoning power would bring him a lowly work assignment. The North Korean would end up as an inconsequential bureaucrat in some distant province. His most difficult task would be counting pigs and chickens.

Chan's Korean associate Kim Sung Chien was paranoiac with a big dash of self-importance. This mental condition made him as unstable as an enraged tiger. The short, muscular, and volatile Korean was a peasant brought up in the intellectually smothering confines of a totalitarian militaristic environment. A great deal of difference existed between him and Chan.

Besides contrasting personalities, the biggest source of conflict between them came from the fact that Chan's rank title in Chinese was *shao jiang*. This literally translated as major general. Kim's rank title in Korean was *sang-lang* with a literal translation as colonel general. Under normal conditions a colonel general did outrank a major general. However, the actual meanings of the titles were far from subtle. Chan's position as a major general in China far outranked Kim's position as a colonel general in North Korea when it came to staff or command responsibilities. The crazy, rank-happy North Korean People's Army even had three different ranks of marshal: *dae-jang,* vice marshal; *won-su,* marshal; and *dae-won-su,* grand marshal. And all those were ranked ahead of general officers. They actually had fifteen commissioned officer ranks against the Red Chinese Army's ten.

Now, sipping tea in his sparse office provided by a miserly North Korean government, Chan waited a bit apprehensively for Kim to arrive for their scheduled weekly strategy meeting. Kim was in command of the DPRK troops massed behind the DMZ, and he was anxious to give them the go-ahead to make an insane assault across the 38th Parallel. He literally howled his intentions at the reluctant Chan, since he was under orders to undertake no operational activities without the specific approval of higher authority. In truth, there were not enough men or material on the North Korean side of the DMZ to accomplish such a mission. But the North Korean colonel general did not accept this stark truth as he seethed in furious impatience to charge straight at the South Korean and American forces dug in there. Chan's disagreement with those plans was their biggest bone of contention.

In spite of the impending unpleasantness of Kim's visit, Chan smiled to himself. An aspect of humorous teasing actually existed even in these conditions. The Chinese custom of inscrutability drove the brash Koreans up the wall. Indirect refusals and illusive suggestions were completely lost on these inheritors of the Hermit Kingdom. It was the only amusement available to Chan in this unenviable assignment far from his home in Kunming.

A rap on the door interrupted his thoughts, and his clerk

stepped into the office. "Excuse me, Comrade Major General. The Korean comrade colonel general has arrived to see you."

"Very well," Chan said setting down his cup of tea. The sight of his faithful PLA clerk, clean and neat in his uniform, always reassured him after viewing so many slovenly Koreans. "Please ask the Korean comrade colonel general to come in."

When Kim entered, he walked to the chair in the corner of the room, grabbed it, and swung over to a position directly in front of Chan's desk. He sat down without being invited. "Well, Comrade Major General Chan? What has my illustrious Chinese advisor heard from his superiors?"

Chan smiled. "They have told me to do my best in helping our North Korean comrades."

"You really think I'm a bumpkin don't you, Chan?" Kim snarled.

"I think no such thing, Comrade Colonel General Kim."

"I ask you a question and you do not answer it."

"I am sorry, Comrade Colonel General Kim," Chan said. "I thought I had."

"You know well of my plans to conquer the South and drive out the American Imperialists," Kim snarled. "Yet just now you completely ignored the present tactical situation and instead addressed the general mission statement."

"A thousand pardons."

"Listen well! I have three divisions of highly trained, elite tank assault troops hidden in bunkers along the entire DMZ," Kim said. "And I am cleverly adding more soldiers and tanks to this number on a weekly basis. These forces are capable of smashing through the Yankees and their South Korean lackeys in less than two hours. Secondary troops will come in directly behind them to fill gaps in the ranks as the southern movement of our great storm rolls on."

Chan thought, *I fear there will be many, many gaps for them to fill.* But he said, "Your plan is most meritorious and I am sure your brave soldiers can accomplish what you demand of them."

"There you go again!" Kim yelled, leaping to his feet. "You answer my pronouncements like a poet describing a sunrise! You utter words, but you say nothing."

"I am regretful for my unpardonable failings," Chan said.

Kim leaned over the desk, glaring into Chan's eyes. "Do you know how it rankles me to stand here? To be in my own beloved country and be placed under the command of a Chinese foreigner! To be unable to serve my Dear Leader properly because a Chinese officer whom I outrank stands in my way."

"Your unhappiness saddens me, Comrade Colonel General Kim," Chan said, thinking *if it weren't for the Chinese volunteers who came here in 1950 to pull your yokel arses out of the mess you North Koreans were in, there would be American troops walking the streets of Pyongyang this very day. And we'll keep you from being defeated again in spite of your inborn stupidity.*

Kim sat down again, seething. "My comrade superiors have forbidden me to put my attack plans into operation without your permission. But I have a right to demand an explanation from you." He paused, taking a deep breath as he fought to bring his temper under control. "And don't preach to me about that damned American aircraft carrier again."

"An aircraft carrier is a floating airfield, Comrade Kim," Chan said calmly. "And at this very moment, there is one far north of the 38th Parallel in the Sea of Japan. That is the same thing as having it firmly established behind your lines."

"To the devil with that aircraft carrier!" Kim snapped. "I do not fear an aircraft carrier!"

Chan knew this was one of those rare instances when he had to speak directly. "If you launched your attack prematurely, the United States Air Force at bases in South Korea would act quickly and decisively. They would come at you with missiles and bombs from the front to support the American and South Korean troops. United States Navy aircraft from the carrier would come at you with missiles and bombs from the rear for the same purpose. Stealth aircraft would fly with impunity through North Korean skies from all directions."

"You have your officers with our brave air force," Kim said. "Why are they not leading them on an attack against that carrier?"

Chan thought of his friend Colonel Tchang Won struggling to get North Korean pilots up to par. "I am sure my comrades will know when the right moment comes for such an undertaking."

"Insults!" Kim screamed, leaping to his feet. "You insult our bravery and our determination to free the world for socialism!"

The Korean general picked up the chair and threw it against the wall. Then he went to the door and jerked it open, kicking a trash can on his way out of the office. Chan's clerk appeared in the door.

"Would you like some more tea, Comrade Major General?"

"Yes," Chan said almost serenely. "Thank you, Comrade."

Viking S-3
Persian Gulf
0610 local (GMT +3)

Lieutenant Johnny Dunbar eased back on the throttle and settled himself from the violent catapult action that had sent the Viking S-3 flying off the USS *Jefferson*'s flight deck. He kept the pair of podded TF-34 turbofan engines at just enough to maintain a gentle, persistent climb into the thin, hot sky over the gulf.

The S-3 Viking, called the Swiss Army Knife of naval aviation, was rated as the world's most versatile carrier-based aircraft. Its acoustic processing suite and ESM capabilities made it a superb surface surveillance and command-and-control platform. In addition to the APS-137 ISAR Radar and Forward-Looking Infrared Radar, it carried Harpoon antiship missiles, MK-46 torpedoes, and sixty sonar buoys. The versatile aircraft was operated by a crew of four—pilot, copilot, TACCO, and an enlisted SENSO specialist—in the performance of its missions.

Johnny Dunbar's crew was already scanning the various instrumentation that fed a constant flow of up-to-date information to them. Ed Flynn, the aircraft TACCO, leaned over and peered out the starboard window at the carrier disappearing in the distance. "The old girl is just about back to normal," he remarked to the enlisted technician who was ready to monitor the sonar buoys that would be scattered throughout the operational area.

The technician grinned. "Are you talking about Captain Bethlehem?"

"Let's not be disrespectful of our Lady Leader," Flynn said of their female commander Captain Jackie Bethlehem. He lowered his voice and leaned toward the sailor's ear. "Actually, I was talking about both her and the ship."

He went back to his position and addressed Dunbar over the intercom. "Well, Johnny old boy, let's go submarine hunting."

"Roger that!"

The aircraft settled on to the patrol vector, its sensory capabilities invisible and active.

USS Jefferson
0615 local (GMT +3)

Damage control had been working continuously and furiously all through the night as the various teams went to their assigned areas after the strike of the torpedo from the Iranian minisubmarine. The actual impact had been but a bit over four hours previously, but the well-drilled and disciplined crew was setting records for keeping the damaged vessel under control.

It had been 0157 exactly when the incoming torpedo launched from the small undersea vessel had been detected approaching the carrier. The alarms sounded throughout the ship, kicking everyone's adrenaline into high gear as they rushed to their assigned stations. The evasive turn began slowly as the rudders bit the water, but the maneuvering increased with additional help as the counter-rotation force from the two starboard steam turbines began kicking up speed. As the attempt to evade continued, Captain Jackie Bethlehem was on the bridge, her teeth clenched in anger. Her mind kept echoing one thought over and over.

Not my ship, godamn it! Not my ship!

The sound of the torpedo's impact was much less than the physical feeling that vibrated through the ship. The big carrier lurched hard to port, causing crewmen to stumble from the impact as items rolled off tables and desks. Bethlehem was aware that DCC was already on the job from their pronouncements and directions over the 1MC, and she fought the temptation to start taking over the action herself. The voices coming over the sound system were calm but terse with serious tones, and the sound of the verbal orders buoyed her confidence. These were her people; she had supervised the training of all onboard drills and procedures, and now it was time to let the crew show their stuff.

The angle of list steepened as shattered compartments were flooded by the invading seawater. But the watertight doors held and the foaming intrusion flooding belowdecks was kept at the absolute minimum. At the same time, all damaged electrical connections and waterlines had been rerouted.

After only a very few minutes, it became evident that the ship could still continue her mission. Unfortunately there had been a human price paid in the incident. Fourteen sailors were injured, and one of their shipmates was killed by an improperly secured watertight door.

Bethlehem thought about her crew's reaction to the disaster, happy they had demonstrated their collective skills. *Good job, people,* her mind spoke. Any following kudos would have to come later over the 1MC, or at subsequent award ceremonies.

Now, as this new day begun, the *Jefferson* was striking back. Aircraft had already been launched on ASW missions as well as attacks on Iranian shore batteries.

Tomcat patrol
0700 local (GMT +3)

The six aircraft had run an armed reconnaissance from latitude 28° to 32° along the Iranian coast where the previous

day's radar-guided surface-to-air missile attack had occurred.

The half dozen RIOs did more than study their scopes; they
glared at them in their eagerness to find a target to sic the laser-
guided Maverick missiles on. Unfortunately, the SAM sites that
had dotted the shoreline the day before were made stark by
their absence. Not even an eager Islamic fanatic standing on the
beach with a Stinger was in evidence.

The patrol leader's voice reflected the disappointment all
six aircraft crews felt. "Nothing on the beach, boys and girls.
It looks like they learned their lesson. Let's go home."

The aircraft arced gracefully as the folks in the backseats
picked up the vector for the *Jefferson.*

Viking S-3
0710 local (GMT +3)

"Got one!" the SENSO's voice came over the intercom.
"Solid."

"Take her to three-three-five," Flynn the TACCO said.

"Roger," Dunbar responded. "Three-three-five."

The Viking dipped in the turn to lose altitude as it settled on
the proper azimuth. Once again the technician's voice sounded
on the intercom. "In range."

Dunbar fought the attitude of the aircraft as the 518 pounds
of MK-46 torpedo was launched away. The sudden change in
weight and configuration affected the plane's attitude, and it
took both stick and rudder to maintain a semblance of decent
flight.

"We have a splash and she's going for the target," the
SENSO said. "Wow! She's doing more than forty knots."

"Just make a quick report," Flynn said. "Save the embell-
ishments for your sea stories."

"Aye, sir," the enlisted man responded. He spoke again almost instantly. "Contact! A hit! Target destroyed."

"Excellent," Flynn said. "You may now embellish."

"We got the motherfucker!"

"Well said," Flynn remarked with a wry grin. He spoke to Dunbar, "Let's make another run. This one may have a wandering buddy out here somewhere."

USS Jefferson
PriFly
0950 local (GMT +3)

Captain Jackie Bethlehem joined the air boss in his cramped quarters on the top of the island that offered a full view of the flight deck. She stepped gingerly into an area where she had no control or command status. During flight quarters, the air boss owned the flight deck and ten miles of all airspace around the carrier. Normally the captain wouldn't have intruded into Primary Flight Control, but things had slowed down as the last Viking S-3 was coming in on its final approach.

"That's the one that got the sub," the air boss said over his shoulder.

"That makes me feel a lot better," the captain said. "That should take the starch out of those Iranian bastards' skivvies."

Bethlehem had come to PriFly to get away from the crowded bridge and CDC for a while, but she was actually in a more compact group even if it were smaller. She stood back to stay out of the way as best she could while the busy air boss communicated with his many people as they happily wrapped up the final landing of the day.

Bethlehem had been stuck in her swivel chair on the bridge, monitoring the patrol flights, ASW activities, and—most of all—the progress being made by the damage-control teams for several long, harried hours. The captain had a few fond thoughts of the privacy and comfort that was available in her cabin. It was deliciously tempting to think of getting away by herself in the privacy and solitude available there. But her ship was in turmoil as it both recovered and reacted to the near disaster that had struck the night before. It would be a long time before she could stand down, and she sure as hell wasn't going to do it until things were back to normal.

Anyway, the emergency situation should last but three or four days more and plenty of strong Navy coffee was available to keep her running at top speed.

CHAPTER THREE

Kim Il Sung Air Base, North Korea
Wednesday, 18 September
1115 local (GMT +9)

The MiG-29's wheels touched down smoothly as Colonel Tchang Won of the Chinese People's Air Force came in for a landing after the morning's training operation. His charges—students in a special instruction unit—were all young North Korean fighter pilots. They had landed ahead of him and had already taxied to their parking positions in front of the six huge hangars occupied by this handpicked fighter regiment.

Tchang continued down the strip, turning off to steer to his own space marked with a large sign bearing a rather well-done replica of the Red Chinese armed forces flag. This banner was red with a yellow star in the upper-left corner. The Chinese characters of 8/1 were to the immediate right of the star. They were also in yellow, and signified the first day of the eighth month to commemorate the founding of the People's Liberation Army on August 1, 1927.

Tchang's Chinese crew chief and mechanic stood waiting for him as he came to a halt, cutting the engine. The two technicians had been with the colonel for more than ten years.

A strong rapport had developed among them, and most tasks could be accomplished silently, using old established habits.

By the time Tchang opened the canopy, they were flanking him on opposite wings to aid him in getting out of the aircraft. He struggled from the confines of his harness and parachute, gratefully standing up. He was happy to stretch his legs after two hours of a battering flight in simulated dogfights. Tchang took the thermos of hot tea offered him by the crew chief, and edged past the man to climb down the short ladder to the concrete.

He turned to gaze with a combined mood of affection and respect at the aircraft he had been flying. Tchang was one of those natural airmen who made piloting appear as if it were an innate, natural instinct of human beings. Other aviators described him as having "good hands", which was a sincere compliment within that hard-driven profession.

Tchang poured the tea into the combination lid and cup, drinking slowly as he savored the taste. At that moment, the only thing that kept him from erupting into a towering rage was the knowledge that his superior, Major General Chan Sun Lee, was having a much worse time than he on this wretched assignment to North Korea.

When Colonel Tchang arrived in the northern part of the Korean Peninsula six months before, he had been completely unprepared for what he was about to encounter. He had expected eager young pilots, ready to learn from an old veteran like himself; but instead he found a group of arrogant know-it-alls who figured they needed no instruction.

The North Korean pilots labored under the impression that they were the best in the world. This high regard for themselves did not come from comparing their flying skills with those of other national air forces of the world. They felt they were the best because they had been *told* so.

In reality, the North Korean People's Air Force's ability to defend its airspace was only marginal at best. Most of the fighter regiments were equipped with older MiG-17 and MiG-21 aircraft that had not arrived from Red China or Russia in the best condition for operational flying. The pilots had very few hours in the air because their commanders didn't want too much stress put on the aging aircraft. There was also a shortage of fuel, as well as outdated training doctrines and policies.

The North Korean pilots seemed to have taken the example set by their leader Kim Jong Il who was the son of the man the air base was named after. This little despot had not only convinced himself that he was to rule the world someday, but his egoistic antics and speeches had evidently rubbed off on many of his subjects. These of course, were the politically correct individuals who occupied the more privileged places of the national society. This included jet fighter pilots.

Tchang had been dispatched to North Korea to whip the best fighter regiment into a truly elite unit. A special gift of MiG-29s from Red China was provided as military aid to give this organization an edge. This model had been first flown in 1984, while the MiG-17s of all the other North Korean units were remodeled from the MiG-15 of 1950, and their MiG-21s had gone into service in 1957.

Tchang's own air force was a direct descendent of the Chinese PLA—the People's Liberation Army. When the Chinese Communists made their first bid for power in 1927, they attempted to implement the Soviet Union program of urging city workers to rise up against the established government through carefully planned demonstrations and strikes. Riots in the streets were the name of the game. But this tactic turned into a dismal failure in China rather than the victory won in Russia. Then a momentous decision was made to turn from the urban areas to the peasants in the countryside for the establishment of a Communist state. It was from this agrarian revolution that the People's Liberation Army formed their basic doctrine of strategy, organization, and tactics.

Mao Tse-tung, the Chinese leader with a priestlike prestige, told his army that the peasants were the sea and the soldiers were the fish; and everyone knew that fish needed the sea to survive. Rather than rob and harass the peasants, the PLA sought to bring them into the Communist fold. While bombarding them with propaganda, they also won their hearts by bringing them food and medical help. They even armed and trained the young men so they could defend themselves against government troops, bandits, and the mercenaries of warlords. But the most important thing the PLA gave the peasants was land. These vast tracts had been taken away from country landlords while the urban leaders huddled in the safety of the cities.

The impoverished farmers rallied to the red flag with a fervent dedication. These willing soldiers were numerous, and Mao Tse-Tung and his associate Chu The developed a strategy in which the walled cities were isolated and picked off one by one from the open country lately won by the Communists. All this led to the final victory of 1949 when Chang Kai-shek's Nationalist troops were driven from the mainland to Taiwan.

Tchang was shocked by modern North Korea where the peasants starved in drought conditions while the fat cats in the government and armed forces lived well in the cities and garrisons. It was laughable that the elite of this backward nation led by a little man who tried to make himself look taller with elevator shoes and a hairstyle worn sticking straight up, thought they were destined to rule the world. The North Korean leader further fed his ego by issuing nuclear threats.

If these weasels weren't brought under control, the entire Korean Peninsula would eventually be taken over by the Americans and South Korea. Contemporary diplomacy and political environments would prevent China from actively defending any attacks against the North Koreans, thus the leaders would have to take on the responsibility of keeping their territory.

But first, the vainglorious bastards would have to have some sense kicked into their thick skulls.

Now, the day's training flight completed, Colonel Tchang Won watched his crew chief and mechanic button down his MiG-29. He allowed himself the luxury of two more cups of the hot tea his crew had brought him in the thermos. He stuck it under his arm after removing his helmet, and strode over to the regimental headquarters building. This was where all post-op debriefings were given after the training flights. When he walked through the door the Korean pilots awaiting his arrival

immediately quieted down. All eyes were on him as he strode
to the front of the room. The young North Koreans were not
fond of this snooty Chinaman even if they admired his flying
abilities. As far as these heavily indoctrinated pilots were
concerned he represented a political system that was sinking
into the decadent traditions of the West. It was widely reported in all North Korean party publications that the Chinese government in Beijing was even encouraging private
enterprise.

Tchang stepped up on the platform in front of the assembly,
and turned to face his audience. His bad mood was not helped
by their smug expressions of self-satisfaction. *Well,* he thought
to himself, *it's time to take care of that.*

"Comrade pilots," he began, "I have more than twenty
years of service in the Red Chinese Air Force. I have three
thousand hours of flying that includes much time in the latest
aircraft gained during tours of duty and training in what was
once the glorious Soviet Union. I have flown every version of
MiG fighters in all possible weather and tactical conditions. It
is my honor to have been checked out in all models of the
Sukhoi as well as the Tupolev-128. Last year, I was further
honored by being allowed to earn certification in the MiG-29
with the Russian *Strizhi* aerobatic team at the air-technology
demonstration center in Kubinka. I have also flown with the
Vietnamese Air Force and the Cuban Air Force while attached
to active operational regiments."

He paused to pour himself more tea. The North Koreans
seemed puzzled now, their arrogance whisked away by a combination of curiosity and dread.

"However," Tchang continued, "in all my experience I
have never seen any poorer military flying than you demonstrated today." He could not afford the subtlety practiced by
Chan Sun Lee with the North Korean Colonel General Kim.
These were frontline fighter pilots and they had to be shaped
up damned quick if they were to evolve into a stellar fighter
organization. "If you were airline pilots you would have been
fine. Those who fly passenger aircraft operate alone, following

lackadaisical schedules and not bothering about other planes except to avoid colliding with them." He took a quick, angry swallow of tea. "But you are *not* working for an airline. You are military aviators!" He paused again, this time to let his words burn into their brains. "Your discipline was nonexistent. I saw nothing but individualism and showing off. Your formations were loose and disorganized with some going one way and others another. Your attacks, maneuvering, and breaking off were pathetic. So far I feel as if I'm wasting my time." He closed up the thermos. "The certificates of competency I must sign for this regiment are from my air force and must meet all requirements demanded of Chinese aviators. Therefore, I will sign none. *None!* Until you've earned them."

A cocky young pilot stood up. "Perhaps we would do much better under the command of one of our own senior officers."

Tchang's temper flashed. "I was one of a dozen candidates chosen for this mission by the high command of the North Korean People's Air Force. It was *your* senior officers who chose me! Do you criticize your leaders?"

The pilot's face showed the sudden surge of fear that coursed through him. He had just committed an offense that could well place him before a firing squad. He had criticized an action taken by ranking officers who stood between him and Dear Leader. The pilot quickly sat down.

Tchang stepped from the platform, walking toward the front of the room to continue through the crowd until reaching the door. He walked from the building and went directly to the pathetic quarters provided for him. He opened the flimsy door and stepped inside. The sight of the narrow bed with its thin straw mattress, the worn blankets, battered desk, and simple chair aggravated his already bad mood. After tossing his helmet on the desk, he carried the thermos over to the bed, and flopped down. He was so upset that even the thought of another cup of Chinese tea failed to soothe him.

Tchang's stomach growled from hunger. He could eat in the mess hall with the others, but that meant having to taste and smell the awful *kimchi*. The Chinese colonel preferred to cook for himself. Every morning he went to the kitchen to get a few rice balls and bits of vegetables, seasonings, and fish before they went into the *kimchi* pot. It wasn't long before the other Chinese followed his example.

Now, just as he began putting charcoal into the brazier, a knock on the door interrupted him. He turned angrily expecting to find the North Korean Air Force General Dai Yong. But when he opened the door, he was relieved to see that it was his maintenance officer Captain Song Hao. Song stepped inside and saluted.

"Good day, Comrade Colonel."

Tchang went back to his cooking. "How are you, Comrade Captain Song?"

"Perturbed, Comrade Colonel," the captain answered. "I am finding it more and more difficult to have the planes readied for each day's training flights. It pains me to see those magnificent MiG-29s so rudely treated."

Tchang turned and looked at him. "I do not want any aircraft taking off that does not meet the airworthiness standards of the Chinese Air Force. I do not care what our status is in North Korea."

"Understood, Comrade Colonel," Song said. "I have brought up this unpleasant subject only because the Korean Comrade General Dai was furious with me because I have deadlined a half dozen of the aircraft. When I mentioned that the North Korean mechanics are not quite qualified yet, he took it as a personal insult."

"The first thing I will do tomorrow is visit with Comrade General Dai," Tchang promised. "I will refer both him and his complaints to our Comrade General Chan in Pyongyang."

"A thousand thanks, Comrade Colonel," Song said. "I see you have lit your brazier."

"Yes, Comrade Captain Song. Please fetch your food from your quarters and join me," Tchang said. "Believe me, I can use some Chinese company after a day with North Korean yokels."

"That is a sentiment I share wholeheartedly with you, Comrade Colonel."

War Room, American Command Headquarters
5 miles south of the 38th Parallel
1900 local (GMT +3)

The war room had an impersonal, very cold atmosphere. The tables and chairs were arranged across the floor properly dressed
right and covered down like a well-drilled rifle platoon. A two-
foot-high, twelve-by-ten-foot raised platform was located at the
front of the chamber with a podium securely attached to the exact front center.

To the audience's left front was a white board with various
colored markers neatly arranged in a tray along the bottom.
To the right front was a bulletin board on which documents,
announcements, orders, and other necessary paperwork could
be tacked for quick reference by speakers. Between the white
board and the bulletin board was a 1:8 scale rectangular map
showing the DMZ operational area. On the wall to the left was
a map of the same scale that portrayed the entire Korean Peninsula. Each map had various colored pins stuck in it that stood
as indicators of the locations of military units. The blue were
for the good guys and the red stood for the bad guys in the
North. This, of course, was the American and South Korean
point of view. These were dispassionate symbols of organized
groups of men ready to slaughter each other when and if the
proper orders were given them.

On this particular evening, Lieutenant General Donald
Hamm, the commander of both the American and South Korean troops along the DMZ, was holding an impromptu intelligence briefing in that same war room. This quickly assembled
session was the result of a phone call to his quarters from the
sergeant major in the G-2 office. The Two-Shop, as the G-2
was informally called, was the intelligence section of the staff.

General Hamm was in the company of Lieutenant General
Chun Do, commander of the South Korean forces and the
deputy commander of the DMZ directly under him; and Commander Harry Robinson, United States Navy, who was the liaison aircraft-carrier officer off the USS *Lincoln* that was now
on station in the Sea of Japan. The speaker of the evening was

Colonel William Atkinson, Hamm's G-3 officer. The intelligence sergeant major had come along to assist in the presentation. Atkinson opened the meeting with an announcement.

"The latest satellite images of the DMZ have been printed out and analyzed," he said with a sense of purpose in his voice. "These two-hour-old findings are not routine," Atkinson said. He nodded to the sergeant major to dim the lights, and as he turned on the digital projector to throw up images on a screen he pulled down the front of the map. He aimed his laser pointer to the top of the photo, shaking the red dot at a road junction some fifteen miles north of DPRK lines. "The roads in this area are concrete as would be expected where rapid transport is desirable. You will notice the tracks of various vehicles off on the shoulders as well as indentations in the highway itself." He waited a beat then added, "Obviously, the quality of the concrete is rather poor. However, when compared with previous images, the wear and tear is much more than would be expected under normal conditions."

Since no-smoking rules did not apply to general officers, particularly to the commanding general, Hamm lit a cigar as he gazed at the pictures. "Colonel Atkinson, I've seen the reports from our ground observation posts that indicate that various types of North Korean vehicles have been leaving their positions on the DMZ and returning after a short time. Generally this implies routine trips for resupply or mechanical inspections. However, these latest activities appear to be more than normal maintenance procedures. In fact, there seems to be an increase in these rearward sojourns."

"Observe the following set of photos, sir," Atkinson said. He flipped the remote for another image. "Here is a two-platoon convoy of T-72 tanks headed north out of the DPRK operational area." An enlarged version of the same photo was flipped up. "The same eight tanks. Note the numbers on the turrets. Now—" he put up another photo "—the same tanks returning in the company of an additional four. A dozen tanks total rather than eight."

"Ah, yes," Hamm said. "I see the eight original numbers are displayed with four more. An additional platoon has been added to the convoy before they returned from the north."

"Yes, sir," Atkinson said. "This activity has been repeated no less than thirty times in the past sixty days in various numbers of additional vehicles. We are certain that a total of 144 additional tanks have been subtly added to the armored inventory in that particular section of the DMZ."

"Mmm," Hamm mused, "that's an additional regiment."

"These incidents have occurred at a total of twelve locations," Atkinson said. "Over seventeen hundred tanks have been brought in with others supposedly returning from routine maintenance procedures."

General Chun spoke through pursed lips. "That's a North Korean tank corps that has been transferred to the DMZ from other locations."

"Correct, sir," Atkinson said. "Now observe this next series of activities."

The observers watched photos that depicted the movement of infantry. The DPRK followed former Soviet doctrine of using motorized troops for their rifle units. However, the infantrymen pictured would ride so far in their trucks, then disembark to continue on foot. The vehicles would turn around and go back in the opposite direction.

Hamm exhaled a thick cloud of smoke. "That's normal procedure when there is a shortage of trucks. They went back to pick up more men, then they'll catch up with the others on foot. The troops on the trucks will unass the vehicles, then those that have been humping it down the road will take their places. That way the column keeps moving as fast as physically possible under those conditions."

"Yes, sir," Atkinson said, flipping up another photograph. "Now check the trucks as they return with the troops."

"Those bastards!" Hamm exclaimed. "A half dozen more trucks have joined the originals."

"Correct, sir," Atkinson said. "And those six trucks are filled with an additional seventy-plus soldiers." He ran through fourteen more photos, showing the constant addition of trucks and troops.

"Enough!" Hamm said. "I get the picture, Colonel." He

flipped some ash off the end of the stogie. "What is G-2's estimate of the increase of infantry?"

"An additional motorized rifle corps has now been crammed into the lines," Atkinson replied.

Hamm chuckled. "Did those dumb bastards think we'd fall for this crude ruse?"

"I had thought so, sir," Colonel Atkinson said. "On the other hand, maybe they want us to take note of their activities. In the past they've shown they'll be provocative unless we give them certain concessions and aid to relieve their economic problems."

Hamm shook his head. "In this instance, I don't think so."

General Chun interjected. "I am sure they are quite confident that they would fool us. The North Koreans have a sense of superiority brought about by decades of outrageous bullshit from Pyongyang. That is their Achilles' heel."

Hamm nodded his agreement. "But where are they hiding all those sons of bitches? They haven't shown up in the front lines where satellite pictures or our ground observation posts have picked them up."

"What else have they had to do for fifty years but continually expand and improve their facilities?" Chun said. "They have been planning this operation from the day the cease-fire was first signed back in 1953. They undoubtedly have tunnels like the Vietcong used in Vietnam. Of course this system would be much larger." He turned to face Hamm. "They are massing for an attack, Don."

"The shit could hit the fan just about any time," Hamm observed as he glanced over to the wall where the map of the Korean Peninsula was located.

Commander Harry Robinson, U.S.N., who had been silently drinking in the interesting intelligence, finally spoke. "Speaking as an aviator, it would appear to me that in the eventuality of an attack by the North Koreans, their entire side of the DMZ is going to have the hell bombed out of it. You have Air Force bases to the rear, and a mighty fine carrier with plenty of aircraft off the coast in the Sea of Japan."

"Well pointed out, Commander," Hamm said. "My head-quarters will take care of alerting the U.S. and ROK flyboys. As the liaison officer from the *Lincoln,* I take it you'll get hold of your shipmates. I want that taken care of ASAP."

"Aye, aye, sir," Robinson replied.

"Y'know," Hamm said with a wide grin, "I always get a kick out of that sailor talk."

CHAPTER FOUR

Magruder's headquarters
Lands End, Idaho
Thursday, 19 September
0915 local (GMT −7)

Admiral Thomas Magruder wasted no time in setting up a new headquarters at the Carter Compound in Lands End. This was a prize of war won in the successful showdown with the militia-man Abraham Carter and his operational group. Magruder admired the setup of the place, and concluded it would serve him well. After all, if it was good enough as a headquarters for a civilian playing at soldier, it sure as hell was good enough for a retired admiral of the United States Navy leading a special law-enforcement team formed through a presidential appointment.

The location was also convenient for action against future militia activities; and since the place was already in federal hands it didn't require any requisition of additional funds to occupy. The headquarters was a sturdy cinder-block building with a well-built barn a half mile away. This was where the militia-men had kept a truck filled with stolen weapons and ammunition that was supposed to be transferred to various places of concealment.

The terrain that stretched away from the compound was forested mountain country that had provided excellent cover for Magruder's sniper teams during the siege they laid to the place. The old flag officer, working with both Hank Greenfield of the FBI and A. J. Bratton of the CIA attached to his staff, wasted no time in preparing for the showdown. But he had to give the situation a chance to develop before deciding what tactics to employ in the operation.

Inside his fortification, Abraham Carter knew that he and his men stood no chance. Eventually the government agents would blow the place apart or starve them out. Either way, the militiamen were losers. But Carter was one of those wise individuals whose plans, even from the beginning of his antigovernment activities included a pessimistic slant. Contingency was his middle name when it came to organizing his operations. He always included alternate actions to meet unexpected situations. In other words, Carter was a serious believer in Murphy's Law, i.e., if anything could go wrong it probably would. In this case, his ace in the hole was a trapdoor in the floor of the building that led to a tunnel. The underground passage, although only big enough for one man at a time to wiggle through, opened up in the forest, offering a quick way to safety through the cover of the trees. Carter's son Jackson was also part of the escape. Jackson was tasked with driving the truckload of stolen weaponry out of the barn and onto a back logging road to a safe house. Unfortunately for Carter and the men who followed him through the narrow tunnel, when the truck passed over the excavation, it collapsed. The unlucky militiamen died under tons of crushing earth that pressed the life out of their bodies while filling their mouths and noses with suffocating dirt. It was a horrible, ignominious end to their rebellion.

Jackson Carter's own luck ran out on him, too. Within a very short time, his truck was hit by a missile from a Naval Reserve S-3 Viking aircraft that had been called in by Magruder to lend a hand in the siege. The vehicle spun and rolled in the explosion, spilling its cargo out along the road. The driver died, but the younger Carter was able to limp away from the scene.

The occupation of the compound had been quick and successful in spite of the presence of a pair of hostages. After the government agents broke into the place, they found the TV journalist Pamela Drake and her cameraman of ACN news, duct-taped to chairs where the militiamen had confined them. This indignity was foisted on the brash reporter just before the first teargas containers were fired into the building. Needless to say, she and her companion were stung and blinded in the chemical clouds, and didn't tape any scenes to show on the eleven o'clock news. In fact, as soon as they were safe from the militiamen, their initial relief at being freed was dashed when Magruder furiously demanded to know how they ended up there. Drake claimed her privileges as a journalist, and Magruder decided it wasn't worth the trouble of an investigation. But he refused to grant her any interviews just to show her how disenchanted he was with her conduct.

Later the government claimed a victory during a White House news conference, but Magruder knew that the loss of several men and the recovery of some stolen weaponry were not enough to put the militia out of business. They were a loosely strung organization, but had solid contacts with each other. This particular fight was far from over.

Now, in the cool air of early morning, Thomas Magruder, Hank Greenfield, and A. J. Bratton strolled aimlessly in a circuitous route around the compound. Some people in government and law enforcement had been shocked and dismayed when Magruder placed Greenfield on his staff. The FBI man had been in charge of the horrible fiasco at Bull Run, and had caught hell about it from the Bureau's higher echelons as well as the news media. But Magruder know from his own sources that Greenfield had been fed bad intelligence by his higher-ups. Instead of admitting their own mistakes, the FBI hierarchy passed the blame down. Magruder as a Navy man expected those in command to bear the responsibility when things went wrong, rather than pass reprimands down to their blameless subordinates. His respect lessened noticeably for the Bureau, but soared considerably for Agent Greenfield.

The three top men in the Magruder task force continued their ramble around the compound, happy to escape the claustrophobic atmosphere inside the main building. The trio soon fell into a discussion regarding the situation as it now stood, and what could be done about the Idaho militia elements that still posed a potential but serious threat. As things now stood, some very perilous possibilities loomed in the future.

They spoke slowly and occasionally, enjoying the sweet natural scents coming from the forest with its abundant stands of white pine. Magruder, with his hands clasped behind him, studied the ground to his direct front. "I wonder how long they're going to stay underground."

Greenfield replied, "Those bastards took one hell of a drumming. All the weapons and ammo they stole is now recovered. No one else from the group has come out in the open as of yet."

Bratton smirked. "If they're up and breathing, they'll be back with a vengeance. The only way to destroy the militias is to kill every goddamned one of them."

"I'm not cleared to solve my cases by murdering suspects," Greenfield said testily.

"Oh yeah?" Bratton sneered. "Do you want to talk about Bull Run?"

Greenfield turned to have a go at Bratton, but Magruder grabbed him. The admiral glared at the CIA man. "You don't have all the facts."

Greenfield laughed aloud without humor. "That's never stopped the CIA before."

"Now hear this!" Magruder snapped. "Both of you shut up. I won't stand for bickering on my staff."

Greenfield had disliked Bratton from the moment he met him. This was a government man who didn't have to play by the rules of law enforcement. No Miranda warnings to give; no Constitutional rights to observe; no personal liberties to fret about; nor any concerns about human life. As far as the FBI agent was concerned, the addition of Bratton to the team was like sticking them with a weapon that could go off at anytime no matter in what direction it was aimed.

However, Greenfield had to admit to himself that Bratton was not programmed to operate except in hostile environments. He was not even supposed to be taken off his leash within the boundaries of the United States. His turf was out in the mean areas of the world where no niceties of diplomacy or Western civilization were observed. The CIA had gotten him assigned to this particular operation by playing dirty tricks of insinuations and rumor-mongering to make the Homeland Security and Defense Agency look as incompetent and ineffective as possible. That included the FBI. Strong suggestions that the CIA should be brought into the HSDA mission clearly violated their charter, but they had been successful in breaking down convention by strong persuasive arguments presented to the President himself. Thus, here was A. J. Bratton, the quintessential CIA operative supervisor thrust into the midst of a domestic disturbance.

Another thing that bothered Greenfield about Bratton was his complete ignorance of their militia adversaries and what motivated them. He had no knowledge or interest in the fact that these were individualistic men who could not condone outside interference in their personal lives. Income tax, environmental issues, open land policies, regulation, deregulation, and a hundred other things that interfered with their lifestyle had finally reached proportions that infuriated them. Maybe it was true that they were carrying on traditions made impractical by the modern world, but most of them had established homes in isolated areas where they had hoped to be left in peace. They were constant in their anger; completely unlike many farmers and ranchers who decried government interference in good times, but bellowed for help from myriad U.S. agencies when things turned bad and the price of beef and crops nosedived. The militiamen wanted to be left the hell alone no matter what condition the economy was in.

Greenfield, having already suffered the consequences of being in law enforcement when things went horribly wrong, didn't want a cowboy like Bratton dragging him into another tragic situation.

The three reached the end of the compound and turned to

retrace their steps in their meandering stroll. Bratton really hadn't said much, and this bothered Greenfield more than if the guy had been ranting and raving. His demeanor was not one of quiet acquiescence to the situation; it was more like Bratton was simply waiting for the right moment to take action in an operation he had planned to implement from the very first day he joined Magruder's team.

Deer Crossing, Idaho
1015 local (GMT −7)

Darrell Kent, his mouth dry and sour from the previous night's whiskey, slowly organized a pot of coffee. The safe house wasn't equipped with a coffeemaker, so he had to turn to the old-fashioned method of using a percolator. He put an unmeasured amount of coffee in the brewing basket after pouring water into the pot, setting the whole thing on the propane-fed stove.

He turned on the burner then walked over to the kitchen table and sat down to wait for the brew to perk. Jackson Carter and his three companions had sat up almost the whole night drinking beer and playing penny-ante poker. Kent sat in for a few hands, but games bored him, and he'd retired to the kitchen for some solitary drinking. The only time he saw the others was when one or the other came in to get a few more cans of beer from the refrigerator.

The percolator began gurgling and he looked up, anticipating the welcome influx of caffeine he was about to force-feed into his system. Kent felt rotten, but the buzzing hangover behind his eyes wasn't the cause.

Darrell Kent was drafted into the U.S. Army in 1955. The Selective Service that called him to duty operated under an unrealistic and unfair system. They gave deferments to college students who were mostly from the upper- and mid-income groups, while pulling in young blue-collar men to take two years out of their lives without a chance for a postponement.

The fact that Kent was into the second year of a six-year print-ing apprenticeship did not earn him special consideration. The training he had to complete for his life's chosen work was not considered important enough to deserve special consider-ation before taking him into the army. That also included mo-tor mechanics, machinists, plumbers, carpenters, and myriad other trades. Never mind that a good number of the trades-and craftsmen worked at higher skill levels than many of the white-collar jobs that awaited college graduates. This im-posed class system did not recognize the young craftsmen's true value to the country. The inequity continued after their release from the service when the G.I. Bill for education was not provided for apprenticeships; but any veteran going to col-lege, even if majoring in something as irrelevant as art appre-ciation, was given funding.

Kent was disappointed that his training in printing was in-terrupted, but like most young men of the time he recognized his duty to his country and was proud to serve. Being an Amer-ican serviceman meant something to those youngsters who had grown up during World War II. In the days before commercial television, they saw images of the war at the movie newsreels. These depicted the fighting in both Europe and the Pacific, as islands were stormed by the United States Marines and Amer-ican infantrymen moved off the beaches of Normandy to head for Berlin. Celebrating Europeans welcomed the Americans who came to liberate them from Nazi oppression. They threw flowers, offered drinks, and the girls kissed the Americans who had driven the Nazis from their countries. The message was clear: American soldiers were good guys.

When the concentration camps were finally exposed, Kent sat shocked at the movie newsreel scenes of emaciated bodies stacked like cords of wood. He thought of his uncle George who was a paratrooper in the 82nd Airborne Division, realiz-ing that his uncle had risked his life in the massive struggle that brought a halt to such atrocities. It was because of his un-cle that Kent volunteered to be a paratrooper after he com-pleted basic training. He even ended up serving in the same 82nd Airborne Division.

The period of Kent's service of 1955–1957 was part of the time in history called the Cold War. During those years the young men in military service were in effect standing guard during their periods of active duty. They faced a serious threat from behind the Iron and Bamboo Curtains, where hundreds of thousands of troops in Communist armies were poised to launch savage attacks against the West. Massive ranks of infantry, tanks, artillery, and aircraft were poised to spread the tyrannical rule of their Soviet masters and subjugate the Free World. The only thing that stopped them was Kent and his comrades-in-arms who would have been part of a rapid and violent reaction to the invasion. The military planners in the Kremlin kept a check on their armed forces, knowing that victory would not be theirs whether it be in a conventional or nuclear war.

Darrell Kent did well in the 82nd Airborne. He made his way up to the rank of sergeant; a feat that was nearly impossible for a draftee. He was also picked to go with a special detachment to West Point in the summer of 1957 to teach the cadets combat skills in the field. This was an annual event in which only the best troopers were chosen. Kent taught squad tactics and patrolling during those three months, proud that he was possibly sending a few future generals along on their first steps of acquiring a thorough military education.

When Kent returned to Fort Bragg from West Point, his ETS was only a couple of months away. Both his company commander and first sergeant gave him a serious re-up talk, but he was done with soldiering. All he wanted was to get back home to Idaho and finish his apprenticeship. His girl Kathy was waiting and they planned to be married before the next Christmas.

The return to civilian life wasn't much of an event. He was surprised that a couple of people in his hometown hadn't even known he'd been gone. The young man also learned that he didn't get much respect for his military service anyway. He hadn't seen combat, and as far as a lot of people were concerned he had been just another Cold War serviceman playing at soldiering. No one took into consideration that if it hadn't

been for that particular generation of servicemen, the Warsaw
Pact Communist nations and the Red Chinese PLA would
have swept across Europe and Asia, then descended on America like hordes of drunken Huns. Kent especially resented the
snide remarks from World War II veterans who had served out
of combat in the rear echelons. He faced more danger making
parachute jumps in peacetime than they did in their administrative jobs in wartime.

A few years more drifted by and Kent's patriotism never
lost its edge. He was uncomfortable in big cities, finding that
the American values he had acquired over his lifetime were
not always recognized or practiced in crowded urban areas.
He preferred to work in small communities, and had many
friends among farmers and ranchers. He also liked to fish and
hunt, and many times went up into the mountain wilderness
just to get away from things.

He discovered that most people where he lived looked on the
Communist threat as very real and serious. Several groups had
armed and organized themselves to meet the potential of a Red
invasion. He eventually met some of those militiamen through a
man he worked with. The printer was a member of an organization called the Continental Line Militia. It had been named in
honor of George Washington's Army during the Revolutionary
War. When Kent signed up, they were glad to get him. Here was
an ex-paratrooper sergeant who had actually taught at West
Point. He was quickly appointed as the training and operations
officer on the staff. He had held the position ever since, supervising training while leading the planning staff that directed all
activities.

As time went on the Continental Line turned more political. It seemed there was a growing pressure from outside envi-
ronmentalists and government bureaucrats to change a lot of
things in the backcountry. Kent resented these intrusions as
much as anyone else, but sometimes the reactions of his fellow militiamen disturbed him.

The percolator gurgled to silence, and Kent got up from the
table. After pouring a cup of coffee, he took it into the living

room. The remnants of the poker game littered the place with filled ashtrays, empty beer cans, and food wrappers. He thought of the four young men asleep upstairs and what they planned to do. Collateral damage. Like in Oklahoma City. Innocent men, women, and children killed and maimed to make a statement of freedom from oppression.

Kent finished the coffee and set the cup down on the card table. He walked toward the front door, taking his cap off the wall peg. He went outside, got into his pickup and drove down to the gas station at the crossroads. After pulling up next to the public phone, he got out. He stood in thought for a moment, then went inside the booth to look up a number in the phone book. He dropped some coins in the slot and dialed the number he had found. The voice that answered was that of a young woman.

"Good morning. Coeur d'Alene FBI office."

CHAPTER FIVE

United Nations
New York, New York
Thursday, 19 September
1000 local (GMT −5)

The representatives of the member nations in the UN Assembly listened intently as Iranian Ambassador Mohammad Sayyad spoke tersely from the sheets of notes in front of him. They heard his discourse through earphones that brought numerous translations of the Farsi language to the multinational assembly as the irate man made his case to his colleagues.

All the members were highly educated, knowledgeable and experienced diplomats with years of service on the international scene. As professional ambassadorial representatives they instinctively maintained their composures in spite of the tone of the angry discourse. No reaction or emotion was displayed on their collective countenances as the passionate speech resounded through the communications system. However, there were some noticeable exceptions to the discreet politeness. A half dozen representatives of various Arab and Third World governments leaned forward in their seats, obviously delighted that the United States of America was getting its nose tweaked.

They looked at each other with near-impish grins of pleasure.

The American Ambassador Sarah Wexler leaned back in her chair, her arms folded across her bosom, displaying a look of utter disgust and disbelief. The woman was almost smirking with sarcasm as she shook her head in a display of absolute ridicule as Sayyad's voice rose and fell in his tempestuous expression of anger. Her aide Brad Heaton was in his usual chair to her left rear, taking notes. They had already been fully apprised of the current situation in the Persian Gulf, and a carefully prepared reply to the Iranian's tirade sat in a folder on the floor next to Wexler's chair.

Sayyad paused to take a sip of water then continued. "Furthermore, on September 15, aircraft from the American carrier USS *Jefferson* wantonly and without warning or provocation attacked defensive shore positions of the Iranian armed forces along our sovereign coast. These unspeakable outrages cost the lives of more than a dozen brave soldiers who had no idea their very existence on Earth was in imminent danger. Additionally, several innocent civilians who were fishermen peacefully going about their work were also martyred when their boats were sunk in further attacks by American warplanes. Our citizens who live along the coast fled for their lives toward the interior. We were forced to set up refugee camps to provide these frightened, brutalized people with food, shelter, and medical aid." He paused for effect and another swallow of water. "As if this was not enough, during the following two days other illegal and immoral sorties were flown by various types of fighter and bomber aircraft from that very same American ship. With all available targets already destroyed, the Iranian government can only conclude that the continuance of this war crime was designed to further terrorize our citizens. The Iranian government demands a cessation of these wanton acts and insists on a complete confession to the crimes, apologies for same, and that repatriations be paid to the Iranian people. We also accuse the American military and naval commanders who directed these outrages of being war criminals. We demand they surrender themselves for trial before a tribunal at the Hague." The next pause was to display a facial expression of sorrow combined with righteous indignation. "Thank you, ladies and gentleman of this august assembly for your most kind and understanding attention. The people of Iran are certain you will take the appropriate actions needed to rectify these aforementioned atrocities."

A smattering of applause broke out among the Arab and Third World groups. The Secretary-General, acting as chairman of the session, banged his gavel for order. "Does the lady ambassador from the United States of America wish to make a statement in regards to the speech by the chairman of the Iranian delegation?"

Now Sarah Wexler leaned forward to her microphone, turning it on. "Yes, Mr. Secretary-General. The lady ambassador from the United States of America *most certainly* does wish to make a statement." She picked up the folder by her chair and set it deliberately and slowly on the desk in front of her. She opened it and withdrew the report that Heaton had prepared in speech form from an official Pentagon document. "I refute almost everything that the ambassador from Iran has stated. However, I'll begin with something in which we are in complete agreement. Yes! Aircraft from the American carrier the USS *Jefferson* did fire on Iranian shore gun installations located on sovereign Iranian territory on 15 September last. This was done in retaliation for antiaircraft missiles fired at those same aircraft without provocation or legal intent from the aforementioned gun positions. And yes! The next two days those same aircraft returned to make certain that the shore installations were still out of operation and were unable to deliver any more sneak attacks endangering the lives of American citizens legally and properly serving their country in an operational area on the side of the Persian Gulf that is directly opposite from Iran."

The Arab nations were now bored with the situation, knowing that the American was no doubt correct in her reply. The Third World people, on the other hand, had become confused and a bit dismayed. Now it was the Iranians getting their noses tweaked.

Wexler laid aside the first page and picked up the second.

"Now I shall discuss our disagreements with the Iranian gentleman. Firstly, there were no fishing boats destroyed on any days of the incident. Our aircraft have very sensitive electronic sensing devices and no such watercraft were detected in the vicinity. However, on September 15th an Iranian naval vessel—a minisubmarine to be exact—attacked the carrier the USS *Jefferson,* firing a torpedo that struck her amidships. An antisubmarine aircraft immediately retaliated and sunk the submarine. On September 17, another Iranian submarine was discovered in the *Jefferson*'s operational area. This boat displayed hostile intentions and it too was sunk." Wexler glanced over at Mohammad Sayyad with a slight smile. "Perhaps the representative from Iran has confused the two submarines as fishing boats. The United States Navy did not. We also noted on satellite images that there are no signs of any refugee camps of any sort in the area. Thus, the camps set up to feed so-called refugees were either underground, exceedingly tiny, or nonexistent. I am a hundred percent positive it was the latter." Wexler's expression turned grim. "I say now that the United States will pay not one dollar, franc, pound, or any other form of world currency to Iran. Furthermore, we warn Iran that any more outrages on their part will result in serious retaliation from the United States. Such action will be launched without warning, and carried through to a final conclusion."

The Iranians showed their displeasure by getting to their feet and following Ambassador Sayyad from the chamber.

Tomcat patrol
Sea of Japan off North Korea
Friday, 20 September
0815 hours (GMT +9)

Lieutenant Commander Earl "Ski" Waleski looked out from his cockpit canopy to each side of his aircraft, noting that his two wingmen maintained their position without much difficulty. He had not laid out any specific course he was going to follow during the reconnaissance, so they had to keep a close eye on him and either respond to one of his laconic announcements of a change of direction or follow his turns. The RIOs, of course, didn't give a damn one way or the other. They sat in front of their scopes, dials, and switches monitoring the local environment electronically, unconcerned about the route.

His own RIO Lieutenant J.G. Pete Scarpati interrupted the boss's thoughts. "Seven blips, bearing three-three-seven, range thirty-five miles. And my IFF tells me they ain't friendlies."

"Roger," Ski acknowledged. He spoke to the flight. "I take it you guys have just picked up the targets at three-three-seven. They seem to be doing the same job we are today. Follow me."

"Wilco," Bill "Wee Willy" Frederickson said in his usual businesslike manner.

"Show me the way, Boss," came back Tom "Skank" Healey.

The flight eased over onto the proper azimuth, and Pete announced, "They've picked us up. Coming our way."

"Anybody got a lock-on?" Ski asked. After a pair of negative replies, he said, "Let's stay alert. At the first sign of a rude act, we'll return the compliment. Be prepared."

MiG-29 patrol
0817 hours (GMT +9)

"Those are American aircraft," Colonel Tchang Won announced to the six North Korean pilots arranged in a staggered left echelon to his rear. "This is not part of today's training mission. Undoubtedly they are on a routine observation patrol. Stay alert. Take care. Remember you do not carry live weapons. This is not a time for rash action."

Second Lieutenant Kim Hwan, three aircraft back from Tchang, sneered into his oxygen mask. He still chafed under the public admonishment he had suffered from Tchang at the last posttraining debriefing. His uncle, Lieutenant General Kim Sung Chien, had told him of the trouble he was having with the Chinese counterpart that was assigned to him by Dear Leader. The Chinaman was supposed to advise him on the activities of troops on the DMZ. According to Uncle Sung Chien, the foreign counterpart was timid and frightened of the Americans. As soon as the Yankees were properly whipped, the great Democratic People's Republic of Korea would turn its wrath on the People's Republic of China. Now Kim's own radar picked up the three blips of approaching aircraft. Americans were they? Cowardly running dogs of Wall Street! He decided to give them a good scare. After all, the Great Leader Kim Il Song had himself stated that the Americans had no heart for a fight. This was in the State's history books studied by every North Korean boy and girl.

Kim laughed as he locked on the lead aircraft and turned on the wing pod that simulated an air-to-air AA-8 Aphid missile.

Tomcat patrol
0816 local (GMT +9)

"We're locked on!" Scarpati shouted. "Launch imminent!"

"I've got the son of a bitch," Ski said at the same instant that he cut loose an AIM-120 missile. Just as it kicked off the wing, it was joined by two others from the flight.

MiG-29 patrol

"Break! Break!" Tchang screamed, cursing the idiot that was stupid enough to point a toy gun at people with real ones.

The squadron followed tactical procedures, but they were slow and sloppy. Kim's eyes were opened wide as his incoming-radar warning indicator showed three air-to-air missiles locked hard on his aircraft. Evidently the Americans did have a will to fight. He pulled a sharp turn, but they went with him. Now frightened witless and forgetting to spill out flares and chaff, his next maneuver was a violent loop followed by a steep dive before leveling off into a series of rolls. Nothing worked.

The explosions were simultaneous, and Kim's last sensation was a millisecond of brilliant heat.

Tomcat patrol

"Secure from attack!" Ski ordered. Something was wrong and all his gut instincts told him that the attack had been some sort of mistake or stupid reaction. The enemy was obviously breaking all contact. They had no hostile intent. "I want all three RIOs to write down their versions of this incident. Don't forget vectors, times, the whole nine yards. Something tells me that written reports will be required about what just happened here. And they'll go all the way up through the chain of command to the White House."

Skank moaned. "Oh, God! Our poor careers!"

Harpster, Idaho
1500 local (GMT −7)

The four men sat close together in the Denny's booth. Since this was the slow time in the restaurant, they were able to get a corner table without too much trouble. No words were exchanged as they waited for the waitress to bring the food. Only after she had served them and gone back to the kitchen, did they begin to talk. It was Darrell Kent who spoke first.

"I'm not a snitch," he said. "I want you to understand that."

"Sure, Darrell," Admiral Thomas Magruder said. "We consider what you're doing as the act of a good citizen. You'll be commended for it."

"Yeah?" Kent said. "I noticed you quickly arranged to have me on the inside when we took the booth."

A. J. Bratton interjected, "Let's get down to business."

"Let the man have a couple of bites for Chrissake!" Greenfield the FBI man snapped at the CIA man. This was no way to establish a rapport with an informant. "We're not on a tight schedule."

"Speak when you're ready, Darrell," Magruder said.

"I've been in the militia a long time," Kent said. "When I joined up we were organized to go into action in case of a Soviet invasion. World War III, y'know? We were keeping our soldiering skills and physical conditioning up to par so we could offer our services to the U.S. Army as insurgents with Special Forces. Later the thing got political."

Greenfield knew what was bugging Kent. Before he was going to talk, the man would be damn sure everybody understood exactly where he was coming from. This wasn't a guy who had lost his nerve or had turned on his friends for money. He also wasn't trying to cover his ass in case of arrests. The FBI agent said, "Yeah. That would have been a big help in any unconventional warfare operations against the Reds."

"I was a paratrooper," Kent continued. "82nd Airborne Division. I served in a parachute rifle company in the 325th Airborne Infantry Regiment. I had plenty to teach the guys in the militia."

Magruder liked Darrel Kent's looks. He had an open, near-handsome countenance under his thinning gray hair. His blue eyes were clear and looked straight at you without blinking. "Excuse me for asking, Darrel, but do you have a college education? You speak quite well."

"I studied grammar during my six-year apprenticeship," Kent answered. "I was a typesetter. Hand- and machine-compositor. Hot type. Linotype, Ludlow, and handset. We even used the old California job cases in some of the shops where I worked. Computers put an end to that. It was a fine trade with good people working in it."

"I'm sure it was, Darrell," Magruder said.

"They're going to plant bombs at the Super Bowl in San Diego," Kent said, setting down his cheeseburger. He wasn't hungry anymore. "They're staying in a safe house in Deer Crossing."

"Names!" Bratton commanded.

"The head guy is Frank Woods from the Old Dixie Militia in Charleston, South Carolina," Kent said.

"Yeah," Greenfield said. "We know of them."

"There're two guys from my outfit the Continental Line," Kent went on. "Their names are Arnie Thompson and Earl

Perkins. The fourth guy is Jackson Carter, but he's not making the trip to San Diego."

"Ah!" Magruder exclaimed. "He's alive."

"Yeah," Kent said. "He's alive alright. His father was—"

"Abraham Carter," Bratton interrupted. "We knew him, too."

"The reason Jackson Carter isn't going on the mission," Kent said, "is that they figure he's too well-known."

Bratton was tiring of the small talk. "How is this shit supposed to go down?"

"They're going to use Blue Ice containers filled with C-4," Kent said. "They'll bring them into the stadium in coolers."

"That makes sense," Greenfield said. "Stadium security will look inside the coolers and what do they see? Snacks with Blue Ice to keep them cold."

"Right," Kent said. "They're not going to use timers. Woods says lighters and timed fuses will be close enough. They'll set them in toilet stalls toward the rear where they can't be seen. They want them to go off during halftime."

"Godamn!" Greenfield exclaimed. "A lot of innocent lives could be snuffed out in a heartbeat."

"They're going to hit as many levels as they can," Kent said. "That's what I know now. I figure I can learn more as things develop. The game won't be played until the middle of January anyhow, so we've got plenty of time."

"Are you willing to testify about this in court, Darrell?" Magruder asked.

"Yes, sir," Kent answered. "But I'll have to leave the area afterward. I wouldn't last a week in Idaho."

"We can get you into the Witness Protection Program," Greenfield said, "but we'll have to change your identity and state of residence."

"No problem," Kent remarked. "My wife is dead and all my kids have moved to California."

"What's the exact location of this safe house they're using?" Bratton asked.

"It's in a little place called Deer Crossing like I said," Kent said. "It doesn't amount to much, but I can show you the exact location on a road map."

"Alright," Bratton said, turning to his notepad. He spoke aloud as he wrote it down. "Deer Crossing." He suddenly looked up. "How in hell are they going to get tickets to the Super Bowl?"

"They already have them," Kent said.

Magruder grinned. "They've got connections I wish *I* had!"

CHAPTER SIX

General Headquarters, People's Army
Pyongyang, North Korea
Saturday, 21 September
0915 local (GMT +9)

The heavy, gilded picture frame held an immensely enlarged portrait of Dear Leader Kim Jong Il. The oversized likeness dominated the front of the conference room by its size and bright colors. Surprisingly, the large chamber was luxurious by any standard. However, in North Korea it was not unlike a well-furnished and appointed condominium put into a slum apartment building.

It was obvious that the arrangement of the painting of the DPRK chief-of-state was done to please the height-challenged little man with the Napoleonic complex. The head was near the ceiling, glaring down in a stern expression of both threat and wisdom at whatever underlings would be gazing worshipfully upon it. However, the men in the room—Chinese Major General Chan Sun Lee and Colonel Tchang Won along with Koreans Colonel General Kim Sung Chien and Lieutenant General Dai Yong—ignored the picture as they sat around the heavy rectangular table centered in the heavily carpeted meeting chamber. They were well into the third hour of a session that had been most confrontational.

The sunlight streaming in through the large, narrow windows reflected off the four sets of epaulets adorning the officers' shoulders. Stars glittered from the surfaces of the devices, reflecting on the surrounding walls like a series of tiny mirrors. The obvious chairman of the conference was Colonel General Kim. He and General Dai wore black armbands to signify they were in mourning over the death of Kim's nephew Second Lieutenant Kim Hwan the day before. A state funeral complete with frenzied official mourners had been played over and over on the twenty-five hours of weekly television allotted to the public.

Government accounts of the event stated that the heroic young pilot had been blasted from the sky when two dozen cowardly American Imperialist naval aviators caught him in a dastardly sneak attack. Comrade Lieutenant Kim had been on a training mission in an unarmed MiG-29 over North Korean territory when the crime was committed. In spite of his skillful evasive maneuvering, he was unable to escape his attackers. There were too many of the foreign capitalist devils. In a final show of sacrificial socialist courage, Comrade Lieutenant Kim turned his fighter toward the enemy, diving into the leader's aircraft to keep the Imperialists from bombing ground targets where innocent civilians lived and worked. The surviving Yankees, frightened out of their wits by this brave act, fled the area before North Korean jet fighter regiments could be alerted for retaliation.

Colonel General Kim turned his cold eyes on Colonel Tchang of the Chinese Air Force. "You were the officer in command of the training mission, were you not, Comrade Colonel?"

"Yes, Comrade Colonel General," Tchang replied. "It was part of our overall schedule. Yesterday was the third cycle of that particular part of the program."

"Why so many cycles, Comrade Colonel?" Kim asked, his voice tinged with anger.

Tchang calmly replied. "Because the pilots had not yet mastered the objects of the lesson."

"Perhaps a superior master should have conducted the classes," Kim suggested.

Chan broke in angrily. "Comrade Colonel Tchang is among the top five pilots of the Red Chinese Air Force! He is an honor graduate of the Advanced Fighter Tactical Academy of the Soviet Union. He has trained pilots in Vietnam and Cuba who have gone on to become top-rated aviators in their own right."

Kim looked up in pleased surprise at this loss of control. It would seem the Chinese are not quite as inscrutable as they liked to appear. He decided to goad his counterpart. "Perhaps you have suggestions, Comrade Major General Chan. You seem so passionate on the subject."

"Of course," Chan said, his voice now lower and under control. "The young North Koreans are filled with zeal and ardor for the causes of international socialism, Comrade Colonel General Kim. It is possible that their learning is somewhat obstructed by that virtuous eagerness."

Kim clenched his teeth in anger at this missed opportunity of one-upmanship. The Chinese *sochul* Chan was obviously now back to his noncommittal ways. He had actually dodged the very direct question while complimenting the North Korean student pilots.

Lieutenant General Dai Yong, a flyer himself, decided to get to the bottom of things. "Why did you order an attack on three armed U.S. F-14s with simulated weaponry, Comrade Colonel Tchang?"

"I did not order such an attack," Tchang said. "I had already cautioned my students of the enemy's approach and ordered an immediate withdrawal from that airspace."

"You preferred to flee, Comrade Colonel?" Kim asked with a sneer.

"The patrol was unarmed, Comrade Colonel General," Tchang replied. "Comrade Major General Dai has just pointed this out. And I might add that this information is in a report filed on the incident. The young pilot turned on his simulator for reasons known only to him. Perhaps it was done in error."

Chan interjected, "Yes. Or perhaps his virtuous zeal over-rode his better judgment, and he intuitively turned to his aircraft's weapons array."

"Whatever the reason," Tchang said, "his action activated the Americans' warning systems exactly as fully armed ordnance would. They responded with aggression, believing an attack had been launched against them."

"Ah!" Kim almost spit out in his rage. "Are you now defending the Imperialists, Comrade Colonel?"

Once more Chan entered the conversation to take the pressure off his fellow Chinese officer. "I believe Comrade Colonel Tchang is critical of the American's display of low intelligence and cowardice, Comrade Colonel General. It is obvious that the actions taken by the late and lamented Comrade Lieutenant Kim frightened them. They undoubtedly urinated in their flight suits from nervous apprehension when faced with the righteous anger of a socialist pilot."

Once more Kim ground his teeth in frustration. The two Chinese officers were not going to get flustered enough to allow themselves drawn into his trap of deception. He had hoped for unwise statements from them that the room's recording system would pick up. If he could only get them to say what he wanted, they would be sent back to China and he could begin the next phase of his personal quest for North Korean glory.

Chan had had enough. He stood up and bowed slightly with a smile. "We thank our dedicated North Korean associates for their time and courtesy in providing this meeting. We must get back to our duties. Please excuse us. Thank you."

Kim and Dai watched them leave, then turned to each other. They, too, had to be careful about any statements they might utter. More than one senior officer had ended up in a death camp for careless or misunderstood remarks. Kim took a breath, then spoke in a pleasant voice. "I am reassured now that our Chinese comrades have our best interests at heart, Comrade Lieutenant General Dai."

"*Chamuro,* Comrade Colonel General Kim!" Dai cheerfully responded. "It is a relief to know everything is in order."

"Ne!" Kim said. "Now we can put our full concentration on expanding the glory of Dear Leader and our nation."

Tomcat patrol
Sea of Japan off North Korea
1030 local (GMT +9)

The three Tomcats made a sweeping turn to the left as their RIOs apprehensively monitored their instrumentation for signs of unfriendlies. So far, after a full hour of observation around the area where Ski Waleski and his team had retaliated to a lock-on, it appeared as if even the seagulls were avoiding the place.

Lieutenant Commander Fred "Loopy" Johnson sensed his backseat partner's concentration. Normally Glenda Simmons chatted like a schoolgirl while tending to her job. Loopy figured she had been the type of kid who did her homework with her stereo speakers booming about a yard from each ear. And earned a 4.0 grade point average doing it.

"Hey, Simmons," he said over the intercom system. "Are you awake back there?"

"Yes," she replied sarcastically. "But I'm doing my nails like any woman would under these leisurely circumstances."

"I noticed your lipstick was smeared a bit when you climbed aboard," Loopy said. "You might check that out, too." Simmons was notorious for her careless attention to makeup.

"I don't want to look too alluring," she shot back. "I'd feel bad driving you big boys wild with unrequited sexual depravity. You'd all be taking copies of *Playboy* into the head with you."

"There's a couple of guys in stores that might prefer *Playgirl*."

"Don't ask, don't tell," she intoned. "By the way, let's take a long, slow right turn this time. This part of the world is about as active as my dreary hometown on a Saturday night."

"Roger," Loopy said, beginning the maneuver. "I wonder what it was that Ski ran into when he was out here."

"Me, too," Simmons said. "It's funny as hell how they were

locked on but didn't receive any incoming. Everything shows the intruders were North Korean. MiG-29s to be exact."

"That's something new," Loopy said. "The latest intelligence buzz was that their best were MiG-27s."

"Maybe they got presents from somebody," Simmons said. "Anyhow, they were approaching with weapons systems turned on."

"That doesn't happen unless somebody is real serious about shooting a missile up your butt," Loopy said.

"Yeah—" Simmons' voice suddenly turned coldly professional. "SAMs. Directly below."

The RWRs had broken out in lighted blips as the entire patrol began sharp evasive maneuvers, spewing flares and chaff that littered the immediate area. A trio of what appeared to be telephone poles loomed up into the air. Suddenly the formation split apart in electronic confusion as dancing images from fluttering decoys drove their guidance systems to distraction.

"Hey, Simmons," Loopy said after the threat disappeared a bit slower than it appeared. "Where'd those babies come from?"

"Had to be a submarine," Simmons replied. "But there isn't hide nor hair of it now."

"Y'know," Loopy remarked, "I bet those North Koreans are just about ready to turn this part of the world into a nuclear cauldron. God! Millions of people would die."

"No doubt," Simmons agreed, thinking of the crowded population of the Koreas, Japan, and Red China. "They probably figure we're stretched about as far as we can go what with Iraq, Afghanistan, and Kosovo occupying most of our attention. So why not goad the Imperialists, hey?"

"You forgot the new missions in Africa," Loopy said.

"The only thing I concentrate on are these tubes and dials to my direct front."

"Good girl!"

"You're just a natural-born chauvinist, aren't you, Loopy?" Simmons said, irritated by the flippant remark.

"As well as a natural-born pilot," Loopy answered smugly.

USS **Lincoln**
Flag briefing room
1200 local (GMT +9)

It seemed strange to Commander Marianne DiLuca to be in the
room alone with the admiral. Usually her intelligence briefings
were held with the place packed with everyone including the
ship's captain, air boss, and myriad other attendees. She had
hoped that Harry Robinson could get a Greyhound hop from
the DMZ out to the carrier, but the liaison officer could not be
spared from General Hamm's headquarters. The potential of
serious developments kept him tied to the Army.

Admiral James Collier sat beside her in the row of seats directly in front of the podium. His aide had arranged for a
pitcher of iced tea and a couple of glasses; the admiral got up
and poured them both some of the cold brew. It was like him
not to ask if she really wanted a glass or, if she did, whether
she preferred sugar and lemon. He presented her with the drink,
then sat down again.

"How's it going, DiLuca?" he asked her.

"I'm staying pretty busy, sir," she replied.

"I know," he said. "I've been appraised that there's a real
strong potential that we'll be facing a rather serious situation
out here in our little part of the world. I wanted to discuss the
matter with you before we bring the others in on it."

She was flattered by his confidence in her. "Well, sir, there
are a couple of items we could discuss. The first is the matter
of one of our patrols shooting down a North Korean MiG-29
yesterday. Then a trio of SAMs was fired at a Tomcat patrol
this morning. Probably retaliatory for the loss of the aircraft.
The old Oriental loss of face syndrome obviously brought that
on." She fumbled in her folder and pulled out another commu-
niqué. "And I received this from Robinson less than a half
hour ago. He's our liaison officer with U.S. Army Headquarters at the DMZ."

"Yes," Collier said. "I'm well acquainted with Big Dog.
Let's discuss the situation about the shooting down of the MiG
first, shall we?"

"It happened at approximately a quarter after eight on Friday," DiLuca said. "It was a routine patrol under the command of Lieutenant Commander Earl Waleski. According to the reports, seven North—"

Collier interrupted. "Reports? Are you using the plural?"

"Yes, sir," DiLuca said. "There were four to be exact. One from Waleski and one each from the three RIOs involved."

"That'd be like Ski to cover his ass," Collier remarked. "I'm glad he did it. Were there any discrepancies?"

"No, sir. The incident began as a routine encounter with North Koreans that has happened countless times out there," DiLuca said. "Seven bogies turned out to be MiG-29s. That's something new. We didn't know they had any."

"I hope they're not being set up by Red China to do some mischief," Collier said. "That's the only place those MiGs could have come from."

"Yes, sir," DiLuca said. "Anyhow, our guys had just begun an evasive maneuver as had the North Koreans. Then suddenly Waleski was locked on for an air-to-air launch. He reacted to the hostile action appropriately as did the others. All three AIM-120s honed in on the guy's radar. The result was that one MiG-29 was destroyed. The bad guy's buddies evidently showed no indication of attacking. They continued on their way out of the area."

Collier sipped his tea. "That's a mind-boggler. The North Koreans are crazy as hell, but why would only one out of seven want to pick a fight?"

"Waleski says there's a possibility the guy hit the wrong switch."

"Yeah," Collier said. "They're dumb as hell, too. But Waleski did what he had to do. If he hadn't been such a cool customer, he would have taken off after the other six. I'll see that he gets a letter of commendation for not turning an unfortunate mishap into an all-out incident. Or war."

DiLuca smiled. "Waleski will be glad to get an 'at-a-boy', sir. I think his mind has been creating pictures of a court-martial."

"Alright," Collier said. "Now tell me about the SAM launch."

"The command pilot was Lieutenant Commander Fred Johnson," DiLuca said. "Again it was a patrol of three Tomcats. According to the report—only one in this instance—three telephone poles came up at them. They took the usual evasive action and dumped a skyful of flares and chaff. Nothing happened after that."

"What was the attack's origin?"

"Obviously from a submarine, sir," DiLuca said. "No surface ships were indicated on the radar. Four Vikings were launched to check out the situation but they returned with negative reports."

"Not surprising," Collier remarked. "I imagine the sub captain made a run for home right after taking his shots." He got up and poured himself another glass of tea, and topped off DiLuca's without being asked. "Well, all that info isn't particularly remarkable. Worrisome, yes, but we're used to worrying, aren't we?"

"We've got Robinson's report, sir."

"Now I detect some concern," Collier said. "Give me the gist of it. I'll eyeball the thing back in my cabin."

"Yes, sir," DiLuca said. "And get ready to worry. The North Koreans have been reinforcing their positions on the DMZ. It's serious, and has been going on for six months."

"Six months!" Collier exclaimed. "And we're just now hearing about it?"

"There's been some trickery, sir," DiLuca said. "Evidently it was so obvious it went unnoticed until all the data was brought together. Armored and infantry units have been snuck up into the operational area. It's estimated there's enough there now to start a very serious war."

Collier sank into thought. He knew the presence of the *Lincoln* was a thorn in North Korea's side. The carrier provided a very real threat of a double-pronged air assault on their territory if they misbehaved. However, if the buildup continued, the Reds would eventually be able to absorb plenty of punishment until knocking out the advanced air bases in the south. What was needed in the Sea of Japan was another carrier.

DiLuca interrupted his thoughts. "Will you need me for anything else, sir?"

"What? Oh! No, DiLuca," Collier said. "We'll have a full intelligence briefing this evening. 1900 hours."

"Aye, sir," DiLuca replied, getting up to leave.

Collier sat by himself, his mind racing with thoughts instinctively organized by habits developed over twenty-three years of U.S. Navy service.

CHAPTER SEVEN

United Nations
New York, New York
Monday, 23 September
1015 local (GMT −5)

Brad Heaton, sitting behind his boss U.S. Ambassador Sarah Wexler in the General Assembly, leaned toward her and whispered, "Déjà vu all over again, huh, Chief?"

"Tell me about it," she whispered back. "But, as our friends in the armed forces say, I'm really learning the drill."

The speaker at the moment was a gentleman by the name of Toon Sung who was the ambassador from the Democratic People's Republic of Korea. The others in the assembly sat back in their seats with silent sighs of resignation. They knew this would be another tirade against the United States of America; a favorite game of the international organization. The confluence of diplomats knew that after the angry dissertation had been delivered, the American ambassador would refute every single item; point by point, ad infinitum.

The boredom had set in solidly, even though Toon was less than five minutes into a speech in which he accused the United States of America of warmongering in the Sea of Japan close to the coast of his country. Namely that an unarmed MiG-29 on a training mission had been shot down by a patrol of three American Tomcat fighters off the carrier USS *Lincoln*.

Two days before, at ten o'clock on Saturday morning, Wexler had been unexpectedly summoned from New York to report to the President at Camp David. She barely had time to pack before the limousine had drawn up outside her apartment house in Manhattan to pick her up. She was hurried across town to LaGuardia Field where an unmarked government Gulfstream Commander waited for her. Wexler was flattered. Normally the aircraft was used for the unobtrusive transport of important people on vital clandestine missions that had to be kept from public scrutiny.

She sat alone in the passenger compartment during the flight south, gazing unseeing out the window. She was deep in thought, wondering what could have happened that triggered the summons from the nation's Chief Executive. Wexler could recall no incident out of the ordinary that would cause any great concern. Obviously, something had occurred outside the sight and hearing of the news media. Only the insiders with special access were in the know. And it was obvious that it was going to be dealt with somehow in the United Nations. Why else would she have been ordered to Camp David?

After landing at the airfield at Fort Lee, Virginia, she was whisked away in a Honda Odyssey van on a circuitous route that eventually ended up in the presidential compound. Her bags were taken to her cabin by a taciturn, husky young man in sunglasses, while at that same moment she was literally taken by the hand by the White House Chief of Staff Jim Dawson. The young man, totally dedicated to his job, had been awaiting her arrival. Dawson at least gave her a quick greeting, and escorted her to a building so far out of the way that she had never seen it before. Inside was a rather homey parlor where she was presented to the Commander-in-Chief.

The President greeted her with a curt, "How are you Sarah? Sit down, will you? We have some more difficulties with North Korea staring us in the face."

Wexler forced a smile. "Other than that, how are things?"

"About as bad as could be expected," the President said with a wink of forced humor. He nodded to the pair of short-haired gentlemen sitting nearby. "You know Kerwood Forester and General Feldhaus, do you not?"

"Certainly," Wexler said. She turned to the Air Force representative on the Joint Chiefs of Staff. "Hello, General Feldhaus."

Feldhaus, dressed in a sweatshirt and shorts, nodded to her as he raised a glass of scotch. "How are you, Madam Ambassador?"

"I am bursting with curiosity," Wexler said. "That's how I am." She looked at Forester, the Director of Operations for the CIA. "How are you, Ker?"

"Fine, thanks, Sarah," he replied, also lifting a glass of scotch. He was dressed the same as the general, and the tennis rackets next to their chairs showed how they had passed the earlier hours of the morning.

Wexler sat down, noting the rather early start in the day's drinking. Johnny Kalos, the president's valet/companion, appeared at her side with a cup of coffee. "I put a good shot o' Christian Brothers Brandy in there for you, Madam Ambassador. I recall it's your favorite."

"And from the looks of things around here, I think I'm going to need it," Wexler said to the Greek-American gentleman's gentleman. "Thank you, Johnny."

The President waited until he was presented with a refill of his skim milk, then turned his full attention to Wexler. "Sarah, I want to get you ready for Monday morning's session in the UN, as well as put you in the know on a recent, highly classified situation. One of our naval aircraft shot down a North Korean fighter in the Sea of Japan yesterday morning."

"Oh, God!" Wexler groaned. "I pray to God our people didn't instigate the incident."

"We're innocent," the President assured her. "But the North Koreans are taking full advantage of the situation."

Wexler took a fortifying sip from her cup and winced,

forgetting how generous Johnny was with the brandy. "What do they want to stir up now?"

"Well," the President said, "a first impression is that this was one of their provocative little gestures. The American patrol leader was locked on by a DPRK fighter for an air-to-air missile attack."

"Then it was indeed justified," Wexler said, wincing a bit after taking another swallow of her coffee. "Of course we'll have the usual bullshit to put up with when their Ambassador Toon takes the floor at the UN."

Forester interjected, "It's not really that cut-and-dried, Sarah. The North Koreans were a flight of seven MiG-29s. Only one showed hostile intent toward our people. When he was dealt with, the others broke all contact and headed straight back to their sovereign airspace."

Wexler shrugged. "Sounds like they were scared off."

"They outnumbered our planes seven to three," Feldhaus pointed out. "They had a distinctive advantage in the situation, yet broke it off."

Wexler nodded her understanding. "They sacrificed one of their own to force a showdown."

"If they did, then that guy was about the dumbest son of a bitch in the world," Forester said. "Or the others were playing a practical joke on him by not joining in after he made ready to attack." He finished off his scotch. "Neither one of those scenarios is likely."

"You're right," the President agreed. "What confuses me is that the MiG-29 is a new addition to their inventory, right?"

"Yes, Mr. President," Forester answered.

"Then why would they purposely sacrifice one on a ruse?" the President asked. "It would seem more practical to offer up an older airplane."

"Perhaps they wanted to get whoever gave them the MiG-29s pissed off, too," suggested Feldhaus. "I'm thinking of Red China. Or perhaps Russia through the Chinese."

"There are a lot of ifs, ors, and maybes in this situation," the President complained. He turned to Wexler. "Anyhow, earlier today, one of their submarines fired surface-to-air missiles at another Tomcat flight. It disappeared before we could retaliate properly. Our antisubmarine warfare efforts came to naught."

"That rather hasty act was a face-saving gesture on the part of North Korea," Forester said. "They wanted to make a show of retaliation. But only a show. They didn't really care whether they destroyed any of our aircraft or not."

Wexler hit the brandy-laced coffee again. "Now, gentlemen, this is really getting confusing. We evidently blew one of their airplanes out of the sky, so they shoot SAMs at us without caring about doing damage. That does not make one iota of sense."

"I have a theory that I've already discussed with the President," Feldhaus the veteran pilot said. "It's my professional opinion that the Korean flight was a training mission that went awry when some eager-beaver kid pilot turned on his simulated air-to-air weapons system as a joke. It backfired, and he got his butt toasted. They sent out a submarine the next day and waited for an opportunity to launch sea-to-air missiles at the first available American aircraft. Thus, they've now rattled their sabers."

"I don't see the point of such conduct," Wexler admitted.

"They're simply taking advantage of a spontaneous occurrence," Forester said. "Anyway, the North Koreans are world champion saber rattlers."

"Right," the President said. "This has given them an opportunity for a unique approach. It's common knowledge they suffer from an acute shortage of food—at least the common people are hungry—and they've been alluding to their nuclear potential in order to get handouts from us. They say they won't build a superbomb if we give them food, money, and other aid. We agree to pass over some goodies, and they behave for a bit. The next thing you know they announce their nuclear program is back in full swing. Then they ask for more pretty presents. It's been an endless cycle."

"Right," Forester agreed. "Now this new opportunity to display hurt feelings has dropped in their laps. They'll use it

to demand more help. They're beginning to lean toward petro-
leum and other fuel products."

"They've even gone so far as to make an elaborate feint of
building up their forces on the DMZ," the President said. "I
have to admit I was pretty worried when the first reports came
in from General Hamm at the DMZ. But the way the North
Koreans did it has been so crude and laughable that we've finally reached the conclusion it is more noise made with sabers.
In other words: All that movement of troops and armor was
for our benefit."

"Then you're not worried about an attack across the DMZ
into South Korea?" Wexler asked.

"Not in the slightest," Forester said in a tone of dismissal.
"But we want a subtle message sent to the North Koreans that
it's time to end the bullshit. Knock off the nuclear façade for
good, and we'll begin serious discussions about a five-year
plan of aid for them."

Wexler finished her coffee and brandy and set it down.
"I think I've figured out my part in this. At this Monday's
General Assembly, the North Koreans will lodge an official
complaint about their airplane being shot down. And they'll
probably say that we also attacked one of their naval vessels.
They can produce evidence that may not completely back up
their accusations, but will be credible enough to make us look
like we have a bit of egg on our faces. My job will be to admit
to the aircraft evidence, accuse their submarine of attacking
us, and then give a subtle hint that this shit about gifts for no
nuclear weaponry has got to be addressed in a serious and final manner."

The President grinned. "Bingo! The lady wins a cigar."

"I'd prefer to have my cup refilled," Wexler said, grinning
back.

The President looked over at Johnny. "Give the lady another one of those special coffees."

The North Korean UN Ambassador Toon Sung had been
droning on for more than an hour. Although he never repeated

himself word for word, he made his points at least a half dozen times before bringing his speech to a halt. The two points he emphasized during the talk were that American aircraft had attacked an unarmed training mission of the North Korean Air Force, and the next day they attempted to sink a vessel of the North Korean Navy.

The Arab representatives showed little emotion. Although they certainly were happy that the United States was once more the subject of accusations of warmongering, North Korea was worse than an infidel state. The people were atheists, and surely more damned by Allah than the Christians and Jews. No good Muslim would show outright support for such people whose eternal fate was to burn in hell for denying the existence of Allah. The non-Muslim Third World nations seemed confused by this lack of righteous indignation from their Arab friends, and the representatives thought the interpreters on the communications system may have missed a few subtle nuances during their translations.

The Secretary General banged his gavel to quiet the hum of conversation that had begun to build up. He turned his gaze to the American delegation with a look of resignation. "Madame Ambassador," he said, "does the United States of America wish to make a statement?"

"Yes, thank you," Wexler said. She cleared her throat and turned her attention to the notes she had scribbled during the flight back to New York on Sunday. "The honorable gentleman from the Democratic People's Republic of Korea has left out several important facts regarding the recent incidents in the Sea of Japan. First—and most important—the North Korean fighter airplane was shot down only after it showed hostile intentions toward one of our naval aviation patrols by aiming its radar air-to-air missile system at one of three of our aircraft during an encounter over the Sea of Japan. Secondly, American aircraft did not attack a North Korean vessel. Rather a North Korean submarine fired three sea-to-air missiles at an American naval aircraft patrol. In this latter incident, they missed unlike our own aviators did in the first incident."

Wexler paused, and turned toward Brad Heaton. The pair feigned a short intense conversation for a couple of minutes, before the Madam Ambassador turned back to her microphone and audience.

"The President of the United States is most distressed and disturbed by the incidents in the Sea of Japan. He has authorized me to inform this august body that he has summoned the Ambassador of the Democratic People's Republic of North Korea to confer with our Secretary of State for a more complete study of this unfortunate matter. It is hoped that arrangements can be made that will permanently prevent more of this unhappiness." With those few words, she had delivered her message before the UN. The President's instructions had been carried out to the letter. Wexler now folded her notes and looked up toward the Secretary General. "This is the final statement on the matter from the United States of America."

"So noted, Madam Ambassador," the Secretary General said, happily relieved by the shortness of the rebuttal. He turned toward the assembly. "Is there further new business to discuss today? Ah, yes. The chair recognizes the Gentleman Ambassador from Iceland."

Sarah Wexler and Brad Heaton both noted that North Korean Ambassador Toon Sung evidently liked what he heard and now sat impassively in his chair. The two Americans settled back to observe the proceedings that would continue through the remainder of the morning.

Militia safe house
Deer Crossing, Idaho
1400 local (GMT −7)

The building was quiet as Darrell Kent stood in the doorway of the kitchen looking out into the main room. Frank Woods and his three cohorts, Jackson Carter, Arnie Thompson, and Earl Perkins had cut open a dozen $3^1/_2 \times 6^3/_4$-inch Blue Ice containers and removed the contents. They were now wordlessly concentrating on packing C-4 back inside, molding the plastic explosive to fit.

Thompson finished his first one and placed the top half on it. "How much you figger one o' these weigh?" he asked.

"What you got there is about a two-pound explosive block," Woods said. "That's enough to blow a toilet stall into hunks o' shrapnel that'll shear off anything in its path." He chuckled. "The toilet itself is gonna add to the destruction. Porcelain shrapnel, man! Good as steel any day."

"Okay," Perkins said. "And you say a lot of it will go flying out the shit house door into the corridor where all them eager football fans will be buying beer and hot dogs, right?"

Carter looked up from his work. "They'll be hauling chunks of flesh out of the stadium more than whole bodies."

"Egg-zactly!" Woods affirmed. "It's gonna be hell on earth for about a split second. There'll be maybe another three or four beats before the moaning and screaming start." He looked up at Kent. "Hey, Darrell. Have your worked out the best route for us to take to San Diego? We're gonna drive down there."

Kent shrugged. "What's the rush? The Super Bowl isn't until January."

"Well, yeah, but we got to run a recon, don't we?" Woods remarked impatiently. "I got to make contingency plans and all that shit."

Thompson interjected, "You ought to let Darrell do that, Frank. He's our operations officer."

Kent shook his head. "I'm trained for infantry-type operations. Attack, defense, ambushes, patrolling, and all that. I'm afraid I'm a bit weak on planting bombs."

"That's okay," Woods said. "I got that shit covered."

"I can figure out the best way to get from here to San Diego, though," Kent said.

"Can you snap it up?" Woods asked. "I'd like to leave before the weekend."

"Yeah!" Carter exclaimed. "You guys want to spend a little of your time down there cruising them babes on the beaches before you come back, don't you?"

"Damn right!" Woods said. "There ain't any rules against getting laid, is there?"

"We don't allow that more'n three times a day in the Continental Line," Perkins joked.

Kent, not amused by the witless banter, walked across the room to the basement door that led to his office where he kept his file of road maps.

CHAPTER EIGHT

South Korea
The DMZ
Tuesday, 24 September
0900 local (GMT +9)

Lieutenant General Donald Hamm, overall commander of the American and South Korean side of the defensive zone, gazed through the battery commander's scope. The instrument was an old-fashioned model that he owned personally. It was set up purposely for his use on the site.

The general could see nothing across the DMZ other than North Korean fighting positions camouflaged in such a way that it was impossible to tell what sort of weaponry or troops they contained. The concealment was excellent as would be expected after a half century of being done, redone, and modified numberless times until a high degree of perfection had been attained. The one mistake made by the North Koreans as noted by some three generations of American and ROK soldiers, was occasional carelessness about not replacing the vegetation at the same time along their line of defense. The older covering would be faded while the other stood out stark and green. This gave away the exact positions of weaponry and emplacements,

although it did not reveal the manpower or ordnance hiding at
that particular spot. However, these areas had been carefully
mapped, and were included in the firing plans of all howitzers
and mortars on the southern side of the DMZ. General Hamm
stepped back from the scope. "I can't see shit."

His G-2 Colonel William Atkinson and Commander Harry
Robinson the naval liaison officer off the carrier *Lincoln*
grinned at him. Atkinson chuckled. "Sir, you've been coming
out here for almost a full year now, and you say the same thing
everytime you take a look over at the Commies."

"I just hope to see one of the little bastards scurrying
around," Hamm said. "I'd be happy to spot some North Korean
glance my way if only just to flip me off. It would make things
more personal; sort of add a human touch to the situation." He
laughed. "I bet I've gotten the finger more than once from soldiers on *this* side of the DMZ."

"No comment, sir," Atkinson remarked. "I wouldn't touch
that line with a twenty-foot pole." He gestured to the liaison
officer. "Care to take a look?"

Robinson walked up to the scope to check out the view. He
had been on this assignment for less than three months, and he
was still fascinated by the environment of ground combat.
These people lived within walls of earth and sandbags, not the
cold steel of naval vessels. Their creature comforts were mini-
mal and that included the necessity of having to eat field rations
with only occasional visits by mess teams bringing up hot
chow. The next time he heard some seaman bitching because
his eggs were underdone, he'd let the kid know how the other
half lived. Of course the sailor would probably say that was
why he enlisted in the Navy in the first place; to avoid sitting
in a foxhole and eating MREs.

"See anything, Robby?" Atkinson asked.

Robinson shook his head. "Nope." The army people had
taken to calling him Robby from the moment he reported in
for liaison duty. His call sign of Big Dog didn't mean a damn
thing to the infantry. After getting to know them, he was glad
they hadn't come up with something more colorful.

Hamm looked over at the nearby American troops standing

nervously around, giving the three officers wary looks. He
turned toward the commo trench that led back to the rear. "Let's
get out of the way. The last thing these guys need is a fucking
general and two field-grade officers hanging around making
them nervous."

The three threaded their way along the earthen gash that
had field telephone wire strung along the sides. It took ten
minutes of slow going before they reached the battalion command post where their driver and Humvee waited. The doors
were already open and waiting for them. Hamm took the front
passenger seat while Atkinson and Robinson settled in the
back. The driver, a clean-cut specialist from corps motor pool,
slipped in behind the wheel. The going was a bit rough until
they skirted past brigade headquarters and hit the macadam
road that led back to civilization.

Hamm set the mood as usual during the hour's return trip
to his headquarters. And he was somberly thoughtful. Even
the driver took extra care not to disturb the pensive general
with any unnecessary quick turns or abrupt changes in speed.
Hamm had plenty to think about. His request for reinforcements had been turned down by the high command in Seoul.
According to Atkinson, the 2-Shop down there was not concerned about the activities on the north side of the DMZ.
They considered it nothing more than a new spate of saber
rattling. The general was beginning to hate that term. It was
used over and over in intelligence summaries. Even the news-
hounds back in the States employed it in their endless broadcasts.

The cliché was acceptable back in higher echelon headquarters or Washington, or television, but when you faced the enemy
at close proximity like the young soldiers on the DMZ, the rattling of a saber—or the cocking of a submachine gun or click
of a bayonet onto a lug—was enough to send those proverbial
shivers up and down your spine. Especially when there were
thousands of good people who would die if things went horribly wrong.

The eighteen- and nineteen-year-old riflemen who manned
the positions along the DMZ would not have been fooled by

any saber rattling. They knew the score up there where they served. These were practical kids from blue-collar families, and Hamm identified with them. He had never been an enlisted man in the Army, having gone to West Point directly out of high school. But his late father had been a plumber in Cleveland, Ohio, and his older brother Stan now had a plumbing contractor firm back home. Stan, who had been one hell of a local football player during his days at Madison High, kept his business profits constant by successfully bidding on jobs in new construction projects out in the expanding suburbs. General Donald Hamm came from that working class of beer-drinking guys who cheered the Browns and the Indians, and worked at union jobs because they believed organized labor offered the working stiff a better deal. Union contracts were better than relying on the questionable generosity of profit-driven business executives. That choice was pragmatic not political, and they didn't trust politicians or corporate bigwigs any further than they could toss a Peterbilt truck. Sometimes, to Hamm's embarrassment, he felt there were times when soldiers shouldn't trust their generals, either. But Donald Hamm had always done his best for his people.

The general turned toward the officers in the backseat. "When was our last alert?"

Atkinson thought a moment. "Hell, sir! Just a week ago."

"We're going to have another one this week," Hamm said. He turned around to look out the windshield at the passing scenery. The troops would think it was chickenshit, but sometimes it was necessary to be tough on them for their own good.

Lieutenant General Donald Hamm was going to rattle his own saber.

USS Lincoln
1530 local (GMT +9)

The message left in Commander Marianne DiLuca's in-box was short and routine. It had been typed by a yeoman from a coded radio message sent by Big Dog Robinson from DMZ headquarters. DiLuca at first thought she would just file-and-forget the missive, but after reading it, she folded it neatly and put it in her trouser pocket for a visit to Flag Country. Things had been too crazy lately to take anything for granted.

Rear Admiral James Collier was going through personal mail that had just been dropped off by his aide. When DiLuca's arrival at his office was announced over his intercom, he dropped everything to invite her in. She stepped through the door with an apologetic expression on her face as she pulled the message from her pocket.

"I probably shouldn't bother you about this, sir," she said. "It's quite short, but you said if anything came from Big Dog I was to bring it to you immediately."

"Right," he said, reaching for the missive. "He's our only reliable eyes and ears over there with the Army. You sure as hell can't believe what you read in the papers." He chuckled sardonically. "And that goes for most of the summaries that come our way from the intelligence community." He quickly scanned the three lines of type. "Yep. There's not much to it wordwise, but there's a hell of a lot of meaning in it."

DiLuca shrugged. "He only states that General Hamm is pulling another full alert."

"So it would seem," Collier said. "But keep in mind that my illustrious colleague Hamm just called a full alert only last week. Why would you think he's having another in such a short time?"

DiLuca smiled. "Because he's a stubborn guy like you, sir. He doesn't believe the intel reports that say the North Koreans are simply strutting their stuff to get more handouts."

"Now that's why you're such a damn good intelligence officer, DiLuca," Collier said. "You're a born pessimist with a gloomy outlook on life. I just hope you don't lose that edge when you get promoted up to the higher echelons."

"I'll try not to, sir," she promised.

"Anyhow," the admiral continued, "I think I'll follow our army friend's example and jerk our own people's collective chains throughout the battle group." He thought about it a moment. "I believe I'll have General Quarters at exactly six bells in the midwatch."

DiLuca thought, *Oh, God! 0300 hours!* "Yes, sir. That'll get everyone up and running."

Collier raised his eyebrows. "Well! I certainly hope so, Commander DiLuca! That's the idea of General Quarters, isn't it?"

San Diego, California
1400 local (GMT +6)

"Jesus, Frank!" Earl Perkins in the passenger seat exclaimed. "You missed the fucking exit again."

Frank Woods banged the steering wheel of the Ford SUV with his fist. "I can't find my way on these godamn California freeways."

"Read the signs!" Arnold Thompson said testily from the back. "You can see the fucking stadium over to our left rear."

The trip from Idaho had been fine until they reached Interstate 5 in Portland, Oregon. Woods, used to driving in South Carolina, got turned around almost immediately, and they ended up getting off I5 and traveling back east on Interstate 84. That was an easy fix since all they had to do was turn around and head back toward Portland. Woods managed to stay on the right highway from that point on, and they zoomed south toward California.

Interstate 5 travels through sparse country in the northern part of California, and although things got a bit shaky going through the junction at State 99 south of Bakersfield, they made steady progress until they were in Santa Clarita. From there on they ran into Interstates 210, 405, 110, 605, and 710 in Los Angeles. The on-ramps, off-ramps, myriad of signs, diamond lanes, and merges drove Woods into a state of confused idiocy.

At one point they were in the San Gabriel Mountains; turned around west again; then south; then east until they were past

Pomona on Interstate 10. Once more they backtracked until they saw the familiar Interstate 5 South signs they were supposed to be following. They managed to stick to it through Orange County, then into San Diego County where they missed Interstate 8 East that led past Qualcomm Stadium.

Now they were heading back on Interstate 15 South. "Look at the godamn sign!" Perkins said. "It says stadium next right. Take the next right exit."

"Yeah!" Thompson said. "Next right means next right; not keep going straight until you run off the edge of the world."

"Gimme a break!" Woods snarled.

"Take the next right exit!" Perkins repeated.

Woods did exactly that and they ended up on Friars Road. They followed it as the stadium loomed up larger and larger. Thompson looked out at the parking lot. "They got something going on in there. Look! There's an entrance. Pull in."

Woods slowed and made a left through a gate. A sign with an arrow and the word PARKING caught his attention, and he turned and went down a row of cars until he found an open space. He pulled in and stopped.

"At last!" Perkins said. He jumped from the vehicle and treated himself to a stretch. After a glance around to make sure he was unobserved, he unzipped his trousers, and urinated on the car next to them. "Godamn California queer pinko bastard," he said with a satisfied grin. "A little good ol' patriotic American piss ought to do that Jap Toyota of his a world of good."

Thompson got out and looked over at the stadium. "It looks like they've got some sort of happening going on there. I see a bunch of booths and shit like 'at."

"C'mon, you guys, we'll check things out," Woods said. "We'll be going in Gate A on game day."

"There it is," Perkins pointed.

"I hope we get good seats," Thompson said.

Perkins laughed. "You dumb shit! What do you care? We're gonna blow the fucking place up. Remember?"

"Hey!" Woods said angrily. "Keep your voices down. Somebody might hear us."

They continued toward the booths until the aroma of chili

con carne wafted over to them. A few more paces and they saw the sign that explained everything.

SAN DIEGO COUNTY
ANNUAL CHILI COOK-OFF

"Look at the signs," Perkins said. "They're giving free samples. We can get something to eat."

"They're selling soda pop over at that booth there," Thompson observed.

"We'll worry about our stomachs later," Woods said impatiently. "Let's check the entrance we'll be using to make sure there ain't nothing over there that might cause a problem."

They took a roundabout route along the stadium, trying to look as nonchalant as possible. They found the gate and noted there was nothing unique about it. One simply went through it to the turnstiles, handed over his ticket, and headed for the proper seat with the stub in hand.

"We should park in this same area," Thompson suggested. "It's close to the gate. It might come in handy if something went wrong. Know what I mean?"

"Yeah," Perkins said. "We can get back out to Interstate 15 real quick." He was thoughtful for a moment. "So that Super Bowl is in January, huh? From the amount of trouble we had getting to this fucking place, I think we should leave Idaho around the first of November to make sure we get here on time."

"Watch your mouth!" Woods snapped. He didn't appreciate all the caustic comments he had to endure about his navigational abilities on freeways. "I'm a country boy, by God! I ain't spent my godamn life in the big city like these cocksucking Californians."

"I was just kidding, Frank," Perkins said. "Take it easy."

Woods calmed down. "Alright. Well, hell! Let's try some o' that free chili and get some soda pop to wash it down with."

The trio turned toward the booths, their appetites teased by the aroma of the pots of red simmering on barbecues. The cooks in the contest were more than pleased to pass out paper

cups filled with their homemade delicacies. The militiamen
went to a half dozen cook sites before they got their fill. By
then the judges in the event had made their decisions and were
ready to announce the winners.

The results didn't hold much interest for the three from
Idaho, and they returned to the SUV. Thompson was just about
to get in the vehicle when he stopped and gave the stadium a
long gaze. "That thing ain't gonna come down when that explosive goes off," he said softly. "It's built solid."

"Yeah," Woods said, "but think of the mess inside, huh?"

Perkins chuckled. "They'll have to take fire hoses to clean
all the blood and guts and shit off the walls."

"They'll have to work fast if they want to have things ready
for the baseball season," Thompson said.

The three got into the car to leave after Perkins urinated on
the Toyota one more time.

CHAPTER NINE

Kim Estate
Suburbs of Pyongyang, North Korea
Wednesday, 25 September
1900 local (GMT +9)

The evening meal dishes had been cleared and the two young housemaids on duty served coffee and chocolate cake a la mode to the three officers in Colonel General Kim Sung Chien's dining room.

His guests were Lieutenant General Dai Yong of the People's Air Force and Vice Admiral Park Sung, Commander of the People's Navy Submarine Force. All three were in mufti; wearing expensive sport shirts, slacks, and loafers ordered directly from La Haute Mode des Messieurs men's clothing store in Paris. Their choice of colors and styles might have been considered peculiar and ludicrous by Western standards, but in North Korea they were up-to-date and very, very chic.

Park gazed at his dessert in happy anticipation. "All this after three platefuls of *sanjeok*!" he said, referring to the main course of beef and vegetables. "You are a generous host, Comrade Kim."

"Komapseumnida," Kim said. "I am pleased you are enjoying yourself."

Kim's house was typical of the privileged elite of North Korea. It was a sprawling two-story domicile with all the amenities of the twenty-first century. These extraordinarily luxurious dwellings had been designed by an Italian architect hired by the State. He was paid hundreds of thousands of American dollars to create several models that all differed from each other in a most unsocialistic manner. The decors and furniture were also unique for each dwelling, and had been personally chosen by a London interior decorator. He also had received abundant compensation for his artistic services.

However, this exclusive building boom had come to a sudden and unexpected halt. This occurred when the money required for constructing more minipalaces for the nation's elite was no longer available. Funding that had once flowed into North Korea from the Soviet Union and Eastern Europe had dried up with the ending of the Cold War.

Kim was lucky to have been assigned this residence before the grants of money ended. His home boasted a half dozen bathrooms, eight bedrooms, a large dining hall, an immense kitchen with the latest appliances, central air-conditioning and heating, and a parlor that could easily accommodate up to fifty visitors. A staff consisting of his personal valet, a maid-in-waiting for his wife, a nanny for the children, cook, housekeeper, and a half dozen maids kept his household in order.

The three high-ranking officers had consumed several predessert courses without thoughts of the starving people in the countryside. Hard cash was for the privileged, not to finance programs to benefit common people. Lieutenant General Dai happily took a bite of his cake. "Swiss chocolate is the best, is it not, Comrade Kim?"

"Chamuro!" Kim agreed, then shoveled a huge piece into his mouth.

Park shook his head. "I must disagree, Comrades. The Dutch manufacture the best. I have a standing order with a firm in Amsterdam to send me at least ten kilos each month."

"Silcheui," Dai observed, "with this ice cream on it, you can't tell the difference anyhow."

The trio ate slowly, savoring the dessert along with the hot black Arabic coffee that added to the flavor. Kim's wife and children had discreetly withdrawn to a far part of the house to stay out of the way of the three men. This was customary when business was to be conducted. It didn't matter that a sumptuous meal preceded the serious part of the evening. The rest of the family dined on a simpler but equally sumptuous repast in the auxiliary dining room.

Dai's wife had gone off to the seacoast to a party villa near Hungnam to join her parents for a three-day vacation. The air force general looked for any excuse to get his spouse to go away. Mrs. Dai was the homely daughter of a high party official. This marriage, however unpleasant, had gotten the lieutenant general rapid promotion. Admiral Park's wife and children waited for him in their own palatial estate near the submarine base where he maintained his headquarters. As a sailor he was gone from home most of the time, and he enjoyed the brief stays he had with his children.

When they finished the final servings, Kim rang the bell. The maids appeared to remove the remnants. Dai stared appreciatively at the younger maid's shapely figure. She knew she was being observed, and she moved provocatively through her chore, casting seductive glances at the diners. This was a subtle way of letting them know she was available and willing. The young woman had learned quickly that the right sort of man could provide extra luxuries and necessities in her life in exchange for sexual favors. And without a doubt, these three men met that criteria. After she followed the older maid out of the room, Dai leaned toward Kim. "Have you tried that, Comrade Kim?"

"Of course!" Kim said. "That pretty plaything is most accommodating and enjoyable. She is a picture of loveliness when lying naked on a bed. If you want her, please feel free."

"My family is in Hungnam," Dai said. "Perhaps I will take her with me this evening to the Glorious Revolution Hotel off Victory Square."

"Enjoy yourself, Comrade," Kim said. "I will see that she is instructed to go with you and to please you."

"I have a bit of skirt at the Finance Ministry for when I cannot get home," Park said. He chuckled. "And another in the Bureau of Statistics. In fact, that is where half my chocolate goes."

"I have a little tart that's a stenographer at the central warehouse at the air base," Dai said. "I gave her a pair of rather expensive shoes some months back, but she says she prefers food. Especially canned goods."

"Ah, yes!" Park said. "That way they can ship it to their families out on the state farms."

"Well, I fear we must turn our attention away from pleasure," Kim said. "We have a most serious matter to discuss."

"Of course, Comrade!" Dai replied.

Kim got up from his chair and walked over to the sideboard. He took three Cuban cigars from the humidor, handing one each to Dai and Park while keeping the last for himself. They lit the stogies from a silver lighter Kim had purchased at the special department store for party bigwigs. This exclusive shopping center was on the top floor of the People's Assembly Building in downtown Pyongyang. Kim expelled a cloud of smoke, then looked at his guests.

"Shall we take a walk outside, Comrades? It is a beautiful evening."

"A wonderful idea, Comrade Kim," Dai said, getting up. "We will be able to enjoy the breathtaking view of our Motherland's open countryside."

"It will remind us of how fortunate we are to live here under Dear Leader," Park intoned.

Kim took his two guests out to the patio, and down the steps to the path that led away from the house. None of the three gave a damn about the view. The reason for the evening stroll was to get away from the recording devices that undoubtedly had been placed in all the rooms of the residence during construction. It was fine to extol their enjoyment of benefits as members of the party elite; such talk was a pronouncement of their appreciative loyalty to the regime. But there were other matters that needed discussing among them that evening, and it would place them in great danger if their intentions were discovered. They walked some twenty-five meters before Kim spoke again. When he did, his voice was tinged with bitterness.

"I have stood all I can of those Chinese *sochuldul!*" he spat.

"And I as well," Dai said. "It galls me to have a mere colonel dictate policy to me that directly affects my command. In truth, as long as he is here my own pilots belong more to him than me."

"I am in similar straits, Comrade," Kim said. "Chinese Chan is holding my troops on the DMZ hostage. Everytime I confront him, he goes into that maddeningly polite Chinese custom of always seeming to agree. Then he does just as he pleases even if it is in direct contrast to what he says."

Dai shrugged. "What can we do, Comrade Kim? Dear Leader Kim Jong Il has issued specific orders that the Chinese *pulangdul* are to be obeyed immediately and without question whenever they issue an order or even just a suggestion."

"I am fortunate in that the Navy has not been included in those programs," Park said.

Kim momentarily studied the sun setting in the west. "There is one point that Chan has made I cannot refute. The American carrier *Lincoln* remains dangerously close as long as she is out there on the Sea of Japan."

"I see your point," Dai agreed. "Her aircraft are a formidable threat if they coordinate their efforts with the American Air Force south of the DMZ. Together the Imperialist air commands could launch massive two-pronged aerial assaults against us."

"In my opinion, if the *Lincoln*'s capabilities are neutralized, we could attack southward with every chance of complete success," Kim said. "I am speaking of permanently ridding our peninsula of the Imperialists."

Now both Dai and Park knew why they had been invited to dine with Kim that evening. The evening's meeting was the result of earlier conversations among them. Over the previous year it had become obvious they agreed on many things.

Dai took a final drag off the cigar before tossing it away. "My aircraft could be used to engage the carrier's aviation squadrons, could they not, Comrade Kim?"

"Accordingly, my submarines could destroy the carrier itself," Park remarked. "Would that fit into your desires?"

Kim nodded and finished off his stogie, grinding it under his heel. "And with my troops' attack against the Americans and South Koreans coordinated with your efforts, we would win a glorious victory for the Motherland and Dear Leader."

"Ah!" Dai exclaimed. "But would Dear Leader order such an attack?"

"I fear Dear Leader has been receiving some very bad advice," Kim said. "This is amply evidenced by our being subordinated to Chinese visitors. Dear Leader is satisfied with frightening the Americans into giving us material support. He does not wish to provoke an all-out war, Comrades."

"Then we would have to move on our own volition," Dai said uneasily. "Such a thing is paramount to disobeying Dear Leader." A lifetime of subjugation under tyrannical rule while benefiting from the system made such an action near unthinkable to the career military Communist.

Kim gave the air force general a bold glare. "Do you hesitate, Comrade Lieutenant General Dai Yong?"

"It gives me pause to think," Dai admitted.

Park interjected, "I do not hesitate, Comrade Colonel General Kim Sung Chien. I feel such an action would benefit our country and set it firmly on the path for our destined glory. Dear Leader would heap praise and rewards upon us for our bold stroke against Imperialism. Our victory would be his victory."

This last statement gave Dai courage. He smiled and spoke loudly. "I agree with this action without hesitation."

"I must tell you something, Comrades," Park said, carefully picking his words. "On orders from my command headquarters,

I was required to engage an American plane with sea-to-air missiles from one of my submarines. My crew fired one salvo of three, then dove deep and made a silent withdrawal from the operational area. It would seem attacks against the *akmadul* are not completely out of order."

Dai was further encouraged. "Then we should be able to launch our attacks without immediate disapproval from Dear Leader. Quick successes would make him smile with pleasure and pride."

"We will have to be careful, however, Comrades," Kim cautioned them. "There are others who would betray us to Dear Leader out of jealousy if they heard the task we have set before us."

"That is true," Dai said. "It will take a great deal of coordination and planning on our part. We cannot let even a single subordinate know about what we really wish to do."

"Yes, Comrade," Park said. "I suggest we hide our preparations within our training programs. In fact, we could openly organize maneuver scenarios to accomplish such a series of coordinated attacks among the People's Army, the People's Air Force, and the People's Navy against a simulated enemy. This would involve carefully coordinated air, land, and sea exercises. It would appear aboveboard and imaginative to those who observed the preparations for the operation."

"I suggest a joint training conference at Armed Forces Headquarters tomorrow," Kim said. "We can begin composing our operation plans immediately."

"Agreed!" Dai and Park exclaimed simultaneously.

"Ah!" Kim exclaimed. "Now I wish we had brought more cigars with us."

"It would be better to have scotch whiskey to toast our endeavor," Park stated.

"*Ankokjong!*" Kim exclaimed. "Let us return to my house to do exactly that. Subtly of course."

"Of course," the other two agreed.

The trio retraced their steps back to the mansion.

Militia safe house
Deer Crossing, Idaho
Thursday, 26 September
1400 local (GMT −7)

Frank Woods, Arnie Thompson, and Earl Perkins had returned
from their San Diego trip at three o'clock in the morning after
a continuous drive that went on for a bit more than twenty-four
hours. The only stops made were to fill their coffee thermoses
and to get hamburgers and French fries to go. Thompson and
Perkins, extremely disenchanted with Woods because of his
inability to follow road signs, had done all the driving.

When they finally arrived in Deer Crossing, they pulled off
the road in front of the safe house, and took the driveway around
to the back. Thompson and Perkins stumbled out of the vehicle
and into the house, leaving their luggage in the van along with
Woods. The exhausted duo wasted no time in going straight to
their bunks for much-needed rest. Woods continued sleeping
peacefully in the backseat as he had done most of the trip. He
finally awoke at sunrise and went inside where he found Darrell
Kent and Jackson Carter fixing breakfast.

Now, in the middle of a cool afternoon, Thompson and Perkins
came downstairs where Carter, Kent, and Woods were talking
quietly while enjoying some cold beer. Kent looked at the pair
and nodded toward the kitchen. "Why don't you guys fix your-
selves something to eat?"

"I'm still too tired," Thompson said.

"Me, too," Perkins remarked.

"You should've let me do some of the driving," Woods said.

"Oh, yeah?" Thompson retorted. "If we had, we'd still be
out there somewhere looking around for the right road."

"I'm a plain ol' country boy, by God!" Woods said defensively, sticking to his oft-repeated cliché. "You set me out in
the middle of the woods and I know 'zactly where I am every
damn minute of the time. Or you could put me out in the middle of a desert or in the frozen North. I'd get along just fine.
I ain't used to all them roads coming in together with one

crossing over the top of the others, and signs all over the place."

"All you gotta do is read a fucking road map," Perkins snapped. "I don't know how you got along having to read military topography maps when you was in the Army."

"What the fuck do you know about the Army?" Woods asked. "Neither one o' you dipshits has spent a single day in the military."

"Maybe not," Thompson admitted, "but we can sure as hell read a map." He pointed to Kent. "Darrell right there—an ex-paratrooper of the 82nd Airborne Division—taught us how in the Continental Line."

"And how to use compasses *and* maps for land navigation," Perkins added.

Jackson Carter finished his beer. "You guys cool it, okay?"

Kent was slightly amused by the quarreling. He looked at Woods. "What outfit were you in when you were in the Army?"

"Armored, by God!" Woods answered haughtily.

"Yeah?" Kent said. "Armored infantry, armored artillery, or tanks?"

"Well—" Woods hesitated "—I was in a maintenance battalion."

Fucking motor pool scum, Kent the former parachute infantryman thought to himself.

Carter decided it was time to change the subject and get the trio to talking about their bomb plot. "So! What did you guys find out in San Diego?"

Woods was glad they could talk about the mission. "Looks good, Jackson. We found out that the gate we'll be using offers parking near an exit that will get us on the freeway real easy and quick."

"They had a layout of the stadium outside there," Thompson said. "It looks like we'll each pick a separate level, then start going from rest room to rest room planting that—" He laughed "—Blue Ice."

Kent nodded. "Okay. What are you going to do when the stuff goes off?"

"Nothing," Woods said. "I thought it'd be best if we just sat there until most of the crowd starts moving toward the exit."

"We'll be good little citizens and wait to see what stadium
security tells us to do," Thompson said. "Once we're outside,
we'll go to our car and leave."

"I'm gonna drive," Perkins said. "That way we can get directly on Interstate 15 and turn north when we get to Las Vegas."

"It's gonna be a piece of cake," Woods said confidently.

*You guys aren't going to be in your stadium seats more than
a minute before you'll be yanked out of there,* Kent thought, but
he said, "Yeah. You have this all worked out like clockwork,
guys. It should be quite a show."

Carter stood up. "I'm gonna get another beer. Anyone else
want one?"

Viking S-3
Sea of Japan
Thursday, 26 September
0715 local (GMT +9)

The ASW aircraft turned on the correct vector, its crew of four
feeling the pressing kind of fatigue that makes the eyes ache
with dryness while a dull stiffness settles between the shoulder
blades.

The pilot spoke to the TACCO over the intercom. "Harry,
can't you find anything out there?"

"Sorry," came the reply. "Things are as quiet as the grave."

The copilot spoke his own thoughts out loud. "I wish something would happen to make all this work worth the effort. I
hate to be driven to complete exhaustion for no good reason."

"Yeah," the pilot said. "Like any aviator, I want to log thousands and thousands of flying hours, but I'd hoped to have my
entire career to do it. Right now, it looks like I'm going to
reach that goal sometime in the next three days."

Benson, the enlisted SENSO, broke into the conversation.
"What the hell's going on anyhow? The admiral's laying this

shit on us hot and fast, and isn't giving us any reason for it. What's he got on his mind?"

"Hell, Benson," the pilot said. "Why are you asking us?"

"Because you're fucking officers," Benson replied.

"Watch your language, buster," the TACCO chided half-heartedly.

"Yes, sir," Benson said. "Old habits are hard to break. I was halfway into my second hitch before I discovered 'fucking officer' was two words."

"I'm so tired I don't know whether to laugh or chew your ass out," the pilot said.

The USS *Lincoln* had been running General Quarters and Flight Quarters for the past forty-eight hours. The multicolored shirts on the flight deck worked themselves ragged launching and recovering aircraft while the people in PriFly forgot what the term "a full-night's sleep" really meant. A myriad of orders and counterorders were coming out of the TFCC in a steady stream. The people in the CDC, who responded to the instructions coming their way at a fast and furious pace, swore their instrumentation was only minutes away from melting into a mass of liquid glass, plastic, and smoldering transistors from all the input. Tempers flared between equals while superiors took their frustrations out on their subordinates in the atmosphere of hurry up, move faster, and do it all over again.

One sailor expressed the general thought when he muttered aloud, "I feel sorry for anyone that picked a fight with us right now. We'd eat the bastards alive."

CHAPTER TEN

Kim Il Sung Air Base, North Korea
Monday, 30 September
0800 local (GMT +9)

Lieutenant General Dai Yong sat alone in the corps operations room studying the manning table posted on the wall next to his desk. This was a simple list of units of the People's Air Force in carefully arranged boxes that indicated command and staff coordination among the various squadrons and regiments. This geometric design represented pure naked power, capable of inflicting incredible mass destruction within a very short time span. This was especially true if such an onslaught was done as a sneak attack. Dai, Colonel General Kim, and Vice Admiral Park had spent the entire weekend huddled together with their individual staffs to organize a supposed training exercise they had dubbed *Chakjon Wonsukapda Yong*—Operation Avenging Dragon.

At that very moment an entire fighter fleet consisting of an elite division of MiG-21s and a brigade of MiG-29s was only scant hours away from readiness for full operational sorties. Each MiG-21 division consisted of three regiments divided into a dozen squadrons of twelve operational aircraft each;

while the MiG-29 brigade had two regiments of six squadrons. This was a total of 216 aircraft. Dai knew that the USS *Lincoln* had roughly twelve Tomcats and thirty-six F/A-18 Hornets in their fighter inventory.

However, he was not only concerned with those four dozen naval aircraft, but also the Vikings and Seahawks dedicated to antisubmarine warfare. They would have to be considered as important as the fighter and attack aircraft if Comrade Vice Admiral Park's submarines were to be protected in the undersea portion of the operation. The actual sinking of the USS *Lincoln* could only be done by a spread of torpedoes launched from the DPRK undersea boats. It was hoped the ASW squadron could be destroyed while parked out on the flight deck.

Dai, Kim, and Park agreed that Dai should dispatch four fighter regiments against the *Lincoln* during the initial phases of the operation and two along the DMZ. This would mean 144 aircraft against the *Lincoln*'s forty-eight; odds of three-to-one in the North Koreans' favor. Once the aircraft carrier was neutralized, he could turn the rest of the regiments inland to support Kim's ground assault. Park's submarines would stay out on the Sea of Japan to contest any reinforcements the Imperialists might send there. In Dai's studied opinion, the lightning-fast offensive they planned would hardly leave the Imperialists time to react quickly enough to stop the onslaught. Especially when the South Koreans who had suffered under the heel of the Yankees since the end of World War II, would rise up in a spontaneous gesture of gratitude and joy to greet the invasion from the north. With the yoke of oppression lifted from their shoulders they would drag their running-dog leaders from the palaces and tear them to pieces as well as lynch American soldiers who fled south from the battles.

Dear Leader Kim Jong Il would enter Seoul with the residents lining the streets, shouting their joy at his arrival. Flowers would be thrown at the ranks of North Korean soldiers parading down the main avenues before turning south to continue Operation Avenging Dragon to the farthest tip of the peninsula. That was where the frightened Yankees would huddle and beg for mercy in the final phase of the campaign.

Dai turned his attention back to the operational lists he had been studying. No step in the procedure of planning and execution was too small to be considered insignificant; even when outnumbering one's enemy with overwhelming odds, everything had to be reviewed and analyzed over and over.

North Korea
The DMZ

The lines of soldiers stretched from the ammunition trucks parked just outside the tunnels all the way to the T-72 tanks that sat in neat rows deeper in the interior of the shelters. The men passed wooden boxes of 125-millimeter shells, 7.62-millimeter machine gun rounds, and 12.7-millimeter antitank ammo down to the armored vehicles for distribution and loading.

The activity was well-organized, and each container of munitions swung along from man to man in a steady rhythm without interfering with the loading on either side. As soon as one tank company had received its quota for one weapons system, the job was switched to the next. Soldiers whose muscles cramped from the heavy two-round crates of the 125-millimeter cannon ammunition were immensely relieved as the smaller cans of 7.62 bullets appeared in their line.

The tank commanders supervised the stowing of other equipment, including rations and personal gear aboard the armored vehicles. All gas tanks had been topped off the evening before, and this regiment as well as the others along the entire length of the DMZ would be ready to roll when the word was given to them. The preparation hadn't taken a lot of time since all past and present units along the DMZ had been performing even the most routine of duties on high states of alert for a half century.

Down in the infantry regiments, the riflemen were fully equipped with enough ammunition and rations for three days. Behind these foot soldiers, their comrades in the heavy weapon support units now carefully reviewed the maps and firing plans that plainly showed the designated targets within the American and South Korean positions. Each heavy mortar had the traverse, elevation, and charge numbers noted for a marching barrage that would rain down on the Imperialists. These rolling explosions of fire and shrapnel would drive the enemy from their front lines and follow the fleeing dogs of the Imperialists, leaving a wide path of dead and wounded.

Chongjin Submarine Base
North Korea

The patrol schedule for Vice Admiral Park Sung's submarine command had been sharply altered on special orders from the admiral himself. This was all done under the guise of Operation Avenging Dragon. The supposed training operation began with all crews on liberty being called unexpectedly back to their boats for a complete fitting-out prior to being dispatched to their operational areas. As soon as they left port, those already on duty were summoned to return for a replenishment of supplies.

Park had no nuclear submarines. His twenty-one boats were all diesel-electric with a top speed of 13 knots on the surface. They carried a load of fourteen torpedoes that could be dispatched from either six forward or two aft tubes. These vessels were all Chinese and North Korean built to old Soviet specifications. The admiral had no delusions about their capabilities, but if he dispatched all twenty-one in seven squadrons of three each, enough would get through to sink the Imperialist carrier *Lincoln*. The survivors would be numerous enough to seriously hamper any American reinforcements brought into the Sea of Japan. After three days, Operation Avenging Dragon would be over as far as the DPRK's navy was concerned. It would be up to the army and air force to continue the fight down the peninsula.

Admiral Park would have liked to add his three Whiskey class subs to the underwater armada, but these boats transferred from the Soviet Union in 1974 were unserviceable; except for the one used for training. The other pair had been cannibalized to keep the last one operational.

At any rate, Park's intelligence data informed him that the USS *Lincoln* had six S-3B Vikings and four SH-60 Seahawk helicopters for ASW. Each one would have to get two of his submarines to render the fleet ineffective. But no doubt Comrade Lieutenant General Dai's MiG-21s and MiG-29s would knock a good many of those out of the sky.

Park expected fifty percent casualties in the least, but the death of the American carrier was a sure thing.

Harpster, Idaho
1315 local (GMT −7)

Darrell Kent parked his pickup in the IHOP parking lot, and walked toward the entrance. The last meeting he had with the FBI had been on the opposite end of town at the Denny's. He figured the change was because they did not want to become too familiar a sight around the area. That was a good idea since small-town people are notoriously nosy about strangers. And word might get back to the local militiamen who would be very curious about the unknown men he had been seen meeting.

Kent stepped inside and a smiling hostess walked up to him. "Smoking or nonsmoking, sir? Or would you prefer the counter?"

Kent glimpsed Charlie Greenfield and A. J. Bratton sitting in a corner of the restaurant. "I see my friends waiting for me. Thank you." He walked down the line of booths and slid in beside Bratton. "Good afternoon, gentlemen. Where's your friend?"

"Got hung up at the office," Bratton said. Actually, Admiral Magruder was back in Washington for a special Homeland Security briefing.

Greenfield nodded to him. "How are you doing, Darrell?"

"Fine, thanks."

The lunch rush was over, and it was but a moment before a waitress appeared to take his order. Kent asked for a short stack and coffee. As soon as the young woman left, he said, "I could have given you the information I have over the phone."

Greenfield nodded. "Yeah, Darrell, but it's a good idea we get together from time to time."

"Yeah," Bratton chimed in. "It gives things a personal touch."

They didn't bother to discuss business until after Kent was served, and the waitress was assured they were all set. Kent poured some maple syrup over his pancakes. "Those three guys got back from San Diego real early Thursday morning."

"Did they have anything interesting to say?" Greenfield asked.

"Just that they reconned the stadium," Kent said. "They said it was Qualcomm Stadium not San Diego Stadium. That surprised me."

"Lots of corporations are paying big bucks to get their names put up on arenas and stadiums," Bratton said.

"It was the Jack Murphy Stadium a long time ago," Greenfield said. "I was stationed at the San Diego office for a couple of years."

"Anyhow," Kent said, "there was a chili cook-off going on, so they didn't attract any attention when they walked around the place. They said they'll be entering and leaving on the north side. Mentioned something about getting away from the scene on Interstate 15 North after the incident." He chuckled. "The guy Woods kept getting lost on the freeways, so Arnie and Earl took over the driving."

"Woods must be a dumb bastard," Bratton said.

"The three of them together aren't exactly the Harvard faculty," Kent commented. "And that includes Jackson Carter."

"They worked out a pretty good plan for setting off explosives in the stadium," Greenfield said.

"Yeah," Kent agreed. "You have to remember that those guys are all hunters and fishermen. They have a certain animal cunning about them. But don't expect any really brilliant moves on their part."

"Yeah, you're right," Greenfield said. "Anyhow, we should pick them up right away."

Bratton shook his head. "Let's get them at San Diego. We know what seats they're going to be in."

Greenfield shook his head. "No. Since Darrell agreed to

testify against them there's no reason to hold off. We can get all of them in one swoop over there at Deer Crossing."

Bratton frowned. "Yeah, but—"

"I said we'll pick them up right away over there at Deer Crossing," Greenfield insisted.

Kent noticed Bratton's face redden with anger. He quickly figured out that Greenfield outranked him in their organization, and the guy didn't like it one bit. "Should I go back?"

"Yeah," Greenfield said. "We won't move for a couple of days or maybe even a week. They might get spooked if you suddenly dropped out of sight."

Bratton looked at his watch. "I got to check in with my office." He pulled a cell phone from his coat. "I better go outside. They'll never hear me on long distance from inside here."

The CIA operative got up and walked slowly through the restaurant. After getting outside, he went to a spot near the road that offered some clearance in the mountains around them. He quickly punched in a number, then waited for an answer.

A voice responded, "Slo-mo."

Bratton spoke clearly into the phone. "Execute. Execute. Execute."

He punched SWITCH-OFF on the menu, then went back to join his companions and finish his lunch.

General Headquarters, People's Army
Pyongyang, North Korea
Tuesday, 1 October
0930 local (GMT +9)

The overnight rain had drifted away slowly, leaving heavy clouds over North Korea's capital city. The weather matched Major General Chan Sun Lee's mood as he sat in his office. Even a cup of Chinese green tea failed to lift his spirits as he stared at the dismal scene outside the window. His dark thoughts were interrupted by the polite rapping on his door by his clerk.

"Comrade Major General," the man said, sticking his head in the office, "Comrade Colonel Tchang has arrived."

"Excellent!" Chan exclaimed, feeling better. "Please show the comrade colonel in."

Colonel Tchang Won stepped into the room and saluted sharply. "My most cordial greetings to you, Comrade Major General."

"And mine to you, Comrade," Chan said. "Please sit down. Shall I have a pot of tea brought in?"

"That would be most considerate of you, Comrade Major General," Tchang replied.

The clerk had already anticipated the need for tea, and appeared with a steaming pot under a candle burner on a tray. Several rice cakes were on a saucer. He sat the items on Chan's desk before making a discreet withdrawal from the office. Even though Chan outranked Tchang, he was the host and Chinese manners and protocol required that he pour the hot brew and serve the delicacies. Only after a few sips and bites had been taken, did Chan get down to business.

"Well, Comrade Colonel Tchang. What brings you over here from the air base?"

Tchang leaned forward, his voice instinctively lowered. "My training program has been interrupted by a special interservice training exercise of the North Koreans."

Chan looked toward the ceiling and pointed upward to signal a reminder that recording devices were planted in the room. "Ah! That is most interesting, Comrade."

"Yes!" Tchang said. "Our North Korean comrades are most keen about keeping their military skills at the highest level. It has been such a great pleasure to act as their humble instructor." As he spoke, he took his notepad out of his pocket and scribbled some characters on it.

"I feel the same as you," Chan said, taking the notebook for a quick read of the message.

Live ammunition loaded on all aircraft.

He slid the notebook back. "The North Korean comrades seem to be undertaking a specific task in their exercise scenario."

"I wish to respectfully request that you report this undertaking to our superiors in China," Tchang said. "I am sure the news of an elaborate training operation will convince them of the great success of our endeavors here." He scribbled on the page again, sliding it over.

Chan spoke enthusiastically as he said, "Perhaps we will be promoted, Comrade Colonel." He perused the notebook, reading what Tchang had written.

MiG-21s and MiG-29s directed to fly to position now occupied by U.S.A. carrier.

"In fact," Chan continued, "I shall send a message through our embassy this very day." He pulled the pages from the notebook and put them in the burner under the teapot. "More tea, Comrade?" he asked as the pieces of paper curled and burned in the small flames.

"Yes," Tchang replied. "Your kindness is most appreciated, Comrade Major General."

CHAPTER ELEVEN

South Korea
American Command Headquarters
Wednesday, 2 October
0630 local (GMT +9)

Lieutenant General Donald Hamm, red-eyed and irritable from lack of sleep, glared across his desk at Colonel Dan Drummond his quartermaster general. The senior supply officer awkwardly hung on to an armload of paperwork as he faced his boss.

Drummond was as tired as Hamm, and he had also been constantly traveling back and forth between the rear echelon and the DMZ. Drummond's buttocks and thighs ached from climbing in and out of his Humvee as well from having to take countless short walks and jogs between his vehicle and various headquarters, warehouses, and command posts. Drummond had also exhausted three motor pool drivers in his ceaseless journeys. To make his situation worse, he had just delivered a G-4 SITREP that infuriated his commanding general. The colonel always felt unappreciated serving in the overworked quartermaster department, and those frustrations had reached the boiling point. He'd often heard the old army saying "I'd rather have a sister in a whorehouse than a brother in the Quartermaster Department." Drummond's resentment of the traditional put-down was running high at the moment.

Hamm barked, "Godamnit, Dan! The United States Army still has contingencies for emergencies, does it not?"

"Yes, sir," Drummond answered in a hoarse voice. "And they are set aside only for those particular situations that we can classify as emergencies or which the upper echelons consider emergencies."

"Well, by God, isn't running short of supplies a fucking emergency?" Hamm roared. "It seems to me it should be!"

"Under certain circumstances it is an emergency, yes, sir."

"Alright then," Hamm said calmer. "We are running short of fuel and field rations right in the middle of a field-training exercise. Now that ought to be the exact criteria that will justify those higher echelons to issue us extra goodies. So what you do is this: Get on the horn with one of your contacts upstairs and tell the son of a bitch to send us some gas and chow."

Drummond's vexations peaked. "Godamnit, sir! I can't—"

"Or better yet," Hamm interrupted, "have one of your NCOs get hold of a buddy up there. Sergeants are notorious when it comes to bypassing SOPs and regulations."

Drummond gritted his teeth. "There are procedures, General, and I—"

"What procedures?" Hamm yelled.

"Sir," Drummond said stubbornly, "I have to put in all my requisitions ahead of time for each quarter. I base those requisitions on your instructions. You scheduled one FTX for this quarter and we are now well into our third. Consequently we are short of fuel, and the MRE stocks are just about exhausted. Troops that would normally be enjoying nice, hot Class-A rations in mess halls are now sitting on their asses in the mud consuming the last of our MREs."

Hamm leaned back in his chair and crossed his arms over his chest. "If we were under attack by the North Koreans—which we may well be soon—higher headquarters would send us the necessary fuel, bullets, and eats that we would need, correct?"

Drummond sensed the fatigue in his general's voice, and realized Hamm was as frustrated as he. He calmed down a bit and patiently replied, "Sir, we are not under attack at this moment. And as you recall your very own words during the last session in the War Room, the Pentagon does not expect us to be. They read the latest activities of the North Koreans as no more than gestures to get diplomats to the bargaining table." He paused, then delivered the words necessary to end the general's argument. "I have to prepare a report to that same Pentagon to explain why I have used up my supply quotas ahead of time. They are not going to be pleased with the message."

"Shit!" Hamm said, leaning forward once again. He knew that meant some nosy people would soon be underfoot to get to the bottom of his decision for extra training exercises. This was to be expected after the seriousness of his INTELREPs had been downgraded by the Doubting Thomases in the Pentagon. It was well known by the brass back home that he neither believed nor trusted decisions made in Washington. Hamm had a well-earned reputation for being a maverick, a troublemaker, and a hard head.

It was times like these that he wished he had opted for a plumbing apprenticeship with his brother when he got out of high school instead of going to West Point. He didn't speak for a few moments, and when he did his voice was barely above a whisper. "Alright. We'll stand down." He looked up into Drummond's haggard face. "Sorry, Dan. I was pissed off and you were the nearest whipping boy."

"Hell, I'm used to that, sir," Drummond said. "I'll try to get as early a delivery as possible to replace the stuff we've almost used up."

Hamm grinned ruefully. "I make your job twice as hard as it should be, don't I?"

"Yes, sir," Drummond answered candidly. "You sure as hell do."

"Well," Hamm said, "do the best you can on the reissue.

I still feel we're about to get a hell of a lot of heat from North Korea."

F/A-18E
15 miles off the port side of the USS Lincoln
0700 local (GMT +9)

Lieutenant Commander Gene "High Roller" Erickson eased out of the racetrack formation of circling aircraft after PriFly informed him to make his approach for landing. He flew in an exact opposite direction of the *Lincoln*'s course, losing altitude as he followed a path that ran parallel to the carrier's port side. The tailhook, flaps, and landing gear lowered as he began a calculated turn. He timed it perfectly and came out of the maneuver about three quarters of a mile behind the flight deck. Now he was ready for one of the hairiest experiences in military aviation, i.e., a controlled crash onto a vessel at sea, otherwise known as a carrier landing.

"Hey, High Roller," came the LSO's voice over Erickson's earphones. "The deck is green, baby."

"Bring me in, Steamboat," Erickson replied. The LSO was Larry "Steamboat" Chaffee; one of his best friends.

"Call the ball," Steamboat said.

Erickson could see the meatball's amber light with a row of green lights. "Roger, ball." Their illumination told him he was on the correct glide slope.

He came in smoothly, hitting the deck as his tailhook snagged the number three arresting cable. The Hornet came to an abrupt halt two seconds later, and Erickson winced under the restraints of his harness. As usual he felt as if his eyeballs were going to be plastered against the HUD. This unpleasantness was followed by the procedures of being freed from the hydraulically operated constraint, then taxiing under the direction of a blue-shirt plane handler to a place for an ordnance inspection and parking.

When Erickson hopped down to the deck he was met by his plane captain, a grumpy thirty-year-old first-class petty officer named Monger. The short, balding man who seemed to be perpetually in the need of a shave, gazed at the pilot with a heavy-lidded, morose expression.

Erickson nodded to the normally taciturn man and asked, "How was my landing, Monger old man?"

"Not too bad," Monger allowed.

That made Erickson's day complete. In the plane captain's way of expressing himself, "not too bad" was a superlative compliment that could only be surpassed by an award of the Navy Cross. The LSO would also grade his performance on the approach and landing as well as which arresting cable his tailhook snagged. Today's exercise would get a high grade, but that didn't mean as much to Erickson as to what Monger thought of his flying ability.

After turning in his gear, there was enough time before the day's debriefings for Erickson to sneak to the special place on the 0-3 Level where he had numerous rendezvous with a young computer technician named Cynthia Walker. She was a perky twenty-year-old female nerd with red hair and freckles. Erickson knew she had a big crush on him, but these get-togethers were not of a romantic or sexual nature. They only saw each other in the compartment used by the crew to send e-mails home. Cynthia showed her special affection for him by allowing him access to the computers outside of normal hours. It was a big violation of the ship's general regulations, but it was important to Erickson that he get certain messages sent at particular times.

Now, standing there on the 0-3 level, Cynthia gazed worshipfully up into the handsome pilot's eyes. "Do you have a message to go out today, sir?" she asked.

"Yeah," he said, looking around to make sure no one was taking special notice of them. "It's for my Uncle Stumpy in Vegas again."

"You must be very fond of your uncle," Cynthia said. "You send him a lot of e-mails."

"I have a great affection for him."

She glanced down the passageway to make sure the coast was clear, then opened the door. Erickson went straight to a computer already turned on and waiting for him. After logging in and calling up the e-mail send screen, he began typing immediately.

Dear Uncle Stumpy:
I said a prayer to Santa Anita for my safety like you advised. I flew at a thousand feet today for three minutes for the ninth time. I was a winner. I hope to do as well tomorrow.

> Your nephew,
> Gene

Cynthia, in a combined mood of curiosity and social ineptness, read the message over his shoulder. "That doesn't make sense. In fact, none of your messages make sense."

"I know, but Uncle Stumpy will understand what I mean," Erickson said. He stood up and walked to the door. "Thanks a lot, Walker."

"Oh, sir!" she said happily. "I'm just so glad to do you a favor."

Erickson walked toward the squadron ready room as Cynthia watched him depart. She did not know that Uncle Stumpy was Stumpy Maggiore, Erickson's bookie in Las Vegas, and the real meaning in the message was to bet a thousand dollars on the number three horse in the ninth race at Santa Anita to win the next day.

When Erickson arrived at the ready room, he found the other pilots already assembled. Their collective mood was downright jovial. "What're you guys grinning about?" Erickson asked as he slid into a seat.

"No Flight Quarters tomorrow," somebody called out in glee. "The pressure is off."

"No kidding," Erickson remarked. "What happened?"

A nearby pilot looked up from the magazine he was reading and said, "It seems we're close to finishing off our allotment of fuel for this period."

"I can believe that," Erickson replied. "And I think we might be lagging on our maintenance schedule, too. There wasn't any reason for all this extra activity that I know of." He settled back to wait for the squadron operations officer to show for the debriefing. He closed his eyes and thought of the bet he had just placed, subtly crossing his fingers.

Kim Il Sung Air Base, North Korea
1230 local (GMT +9)

The ancient Soviet Li-2 transport of the Red Chinese Air Force lumbered through its approach, yawing and pitching as the pilot aligned it with the runway. Less than a minute later, the aircraft hit the concrete hard, bounced up, then slammed down again before the props were reversed and brakes pressed to slow its forward progress.

Colonel Tchang Won of the Chinese People's Air Force winced at the poor performance. "We can see why that comrade was not chosen for fighter training."

"I sincerely hope he is a smoother aviator while in the sky," Major General Chan Sun Lee remarked.

"He had better be," Tchang frowned. He glanced over at his maintenance officer Captain Song Hao. "Make a note of his piloting skills during the flight back to China. If he performs poorly I will turn in a report on him."

"Yes, Comrade Colonel Tchang," Song replied.

The three officers and their entourages stood bag and baggage, watching the old airplane roll toward them. Orders had arrived that same morning instructing the Chinese contingent in North Korea to return to their homeland within hours.

Tchang took an opportunity for a quick smoke. As he lit up, he glanced toward Chan. "I meant to ask you, Comrade Major General, what was the reaction of the North Koreans at our abrupt return to China?"

Chan smirked. "They expressed their disappointment at the unexpected termination of our tour of duty."

Tchang lowered his voice. "Were they suspicious of the reasons behind the action?"

"Of course," Chan answered. "But what could they say?"

"I was especially curious about what Colonel General Kim might think," Tchang said.

Now Chan chuckled. "He was at the DMZ, and still is, I presume. I wish I could see his face when he learns we are gone."

This departure was to be taken quietly and as unobtrusively as possible. This was in direct contrast to their arrival in North Korea when the North Korean People's Army Colonel General Kim Sung Chien and his colleague North Korean People's Air Force Major General Dai Yong met them complete with staff officers and an honor guard. There had also been a half dozen little flower girls who presented bouquets to the arriving Chinese delegation.

Now, standing alone on the windy runway, they watched dully as the transport continued its slow taxi from the runway toward them.

USS **Lincoln**
Erickson's quarters
1300 local (GMT +9)

High Roller Erickson's roommate had gone home on emergency leave after getting the word that one of his kids had been hit by a car. The injuries weren't life threatening but the prognosis for the youngster was grim with the possibility of the boy being confined to a wheelchair for the rest of his life. Consequently, Erickson had the quarters all to himself. He was sorry about the young boy's injuries, but the solitude he now enjoyed was positively delicious.

Erickson's mail lay on his bunk awaiting his attention. A package and four letters were strewn across the blankets. He ignored the parcel, frantically searching through the letters until finding one from Stumpy Maggiore. This was what he'd been waiting for. He ripped it open and found a money order in the amount of twenty-five hundred dollars. A short note in the envelope informed him that the two races he had handicapped at the Caliente Racetrack in Tijuana had come in winners just as he gambled on. Now he didn't feel so worried about the thousand he had just bet at Santa Anita.

Erickson turned his attention to the remaining letters. One was from some woman in Panama City, Florida, he could barely remember, wanting to find out when he might come back through that part of the country again. She made a few allusions to missing him and the romance they had shared. The second missive came from his sister who brought him up-to-date on the latest family news. The third was from an elderly aunt in Minnesota. The old lady's letter informed him she had cooked up a batch of *krumkakke* and would mail it the next day. He immediately turned his attention to the package, his mouth watering with thoughts of munching a few of the Norwegian rolled wafers before sharing them with his friends in the wardroom. But the parcel was not from Aunt Katrina. Instead, it was from the Anchor Book Publishers in Norfolk.

He had submitted a manuscript a year earlier to them. It was a book he had written, titled *A Naval Aviator's Book of Fighter Tactics.* He had composed a manuscript in which he spelled out his ideas and opinions on the best way to deploy fighter aircraft in combat. They had accepted his proposal for publication, and he had heard nothing from them since. Inside were twenty copies of the book and a check with a thousand dollar advance on royalties.

Erickson laughed to himself. The unexpected boon covered his latest bet; and he wasn't going to let anyone have as much as a single bite of a *krumkakke* until they promised to buy a copy of his book.

CHAPTER TWELVE

Deer Crossing, Idaho
Militia safe house
Wednesday, 2 October
0340 local (GMT −7)

The explosion was beyond massive. The sound, concussion, and resultant debris of the detonation whipped both upward toward the mountaintops and downward into the flatlands and valleys. This force rolled unimpeded in successive waves that followed each other at microsecond intervals of invisible concussion. This merciless curtain of naked energy ripped apart buildings; shredded limbs from trees; and disintegrated human beings into microscopic bits of charred bone, flesh, and organic tissue.

The explosives that provoked this manmade holocaust had been quickly but expertly placed around the two-story cabin belonging to the Continental Line Militia. Blocks of M2 Tetrytol explosive had been set off by timed electric blasting caps. Although the detonation velocity of 23,000 feet per second was slower than that of composition C4, the intensity of dangerous fumes left after the explosion was much heavier. Forty-pound charges had been planted on all four sides of the cabin, blowing inwardly, then expanding rapidly upward and outward to the extent that even the gas station and convenience store down at the road crossing had been obliterated.

Jeff Taylor, a seventy-year-old loner who lived in a battered, ancient Airstream trailer some five miles from the origin of the blast, had been knocked out of his bunk by the force of the explosion. Cups, saucers, pans, ammunition, canned food, and his two hunting rifles rained down around him from shelves and wall hooks as his domicile rocked crazily on it airless, decayed tires. The physical pressure passed through like a blow from a giant unseeable sledgehammer, leaving him sprawled in the midst of the mess for a full minute before he could move. When he managed to sit up, his hearing was nothing but a dull buzzing. Jeff struggled to his feet, and staggered outside through the door that now hung by one set of hinges. He wore only the long johns he'd first put on a month before, and he paid no mind to the sharp rocks bruising his bare feet.

"Who's there?" he shouted crazily, his voice high-pitched with a fear that made him irrational. "Godamn your eyes! What the hell did you do?"

His own voice was barely picked up by his punished eardrums, and he could hear nothing of the natural debris of rocks, limbs, and dirt clods that rained down around him. Jeff was a grizzled old man, skinny and strong, with unkempt hair and a tangled beard that gave evidence of his previous week's menu. He coughed dust through his toothless mouth, and tried to spit. A scratching on his leg caught his attention, and he looked down to his frightened bird dog Benny. The animal was obviously whining though Jeff couldn't hear the sound. Benny was all right, but had been shook up as much as his master.

The dog followed as the oldster went back inside to dress. After getting into his plaid shirt, Levis, and boots, Jeff grabbed his cap and left the trailer, heading for his pickup. Luckily, the only debris on the old vehicle was dust, though a large tree limb lay not quite ten yards away. Benny accompanied his master, trotting ahead to the passenger door to wait to be let into the vehicle. This was their usual practice, and both dog and man wanted to get the hell out of there as quickly as possible.

The trip down the mountain to the highway was done through a maze of thick, floating dust and fluttering light debris that was now settling to the ground from the higher altitudes. Jeff drove slowly down the curving road in case a tree might have fallen across the way. A few minutes later he reached the highway, turning toward Deer Crossing.

When he reached the site of what had been the small settlement, he slowly eased on the brakes and came to a stop. "Oh, my Lord!" he hissed under his breath. "Looky there, Benny-boy."

The dog dutifully gazed through the windshield, hoping to see a bird or animal in the headlights. There was nothing to interest a canine mind, but Jeff's human one was shocked into disbelief.

Deer Crossing no longer existed.

A crater filled with splintered trees extended from just up the mountain, down across the highway, and went another fifty yards beyond the other side. Jeff got out of the truck, and he and Benny walked up to the edge of the excavation and continued to stare at what the headlights of the pickup revealed.

They were still standing there a half hour later when the first Idaho State Police car rolled onto the scene.

Department of International Relations
Beijing, China
0730 local (GMT +8)

Major General Chan Sun Lee walked down the corridor of the four-story building, appreciating the difference between Chinese architecture and that of North Korea. He knew full well that the interiors of China's official buildings did not match the amenities and furnishings of those in the West; but compared to North Korea, they were monuments to luxury. But best of all, there was not the slightest odor of *kimchi* in the air.

His escort was a smartly dressed young woman who obviously belonged to one of the many staffs that made up the elite handpicked Department of International Relations. Her short skirt showed off well-shaped legs, and her hairdo and makeup looked like something out of an American fashion magazine.

Chan could remember some thirty years before when his people wore nothing but Maoist uniforms and caps. This garb made them appear as a mob of unthinking automatons, moving without thought through their heavily regulated lives. In those days, they all took great care to see that their *Little Red Books* of Mao Tse-Tung's philosophies were visible, sticking out of their left breast pockets. That was where one's heart was, and the fact the *Little Red Book* pressed against that significant part of the anatomy further enhanced the appearance of complete devotion to The Cause.

His rather pretty female escort's Western style of dress with that skirt just above her knees would have been considered reactionary back in the bad old days when the Gang of Four ran China during the Cultural Revolution. The Red Guards, made up of zealous youths, would have grabbed this young lady and dragged her off to the authorities. Her unhappy fate would have been what thousands suffered in those days; years of life-shortening labor in a penal camp set up for punishment and reeducation.

They came to a door with frosted glass, and stopped. It bore no name or title. The woman opened the portal and gestured to Chan to enter. When he stepped inside, the door was closed behind him and he found himself gazing across a desk at a bald, middle-aged gentleman. When the bureaucrat stood up, he revealed his short stature and slight build. He smiled politely. "I am so pleased to meet you, Comrade Major General Chan. My name is Tung."

"How do you do, Comrade Tung?" Chan asked. He was not surprised that his host went no further in identifying himself. Many parts of the Chinese People's Government were secretive, as much from old habit as for security reasons.

"Please sit down, Comrade Major General," Tung said. He waited until Chan settled himself before he retook his own seat. "May I welcome you back from North Korea?"

"Yes. Thank you," Chan replied. "I am most pleased to have returned to my native land." He noted the man was a typical

Chinese government official who conducted his business without a portfolio, manila folder, or even a single sheet of paper showing on his desk. Everything was kept locked away and hidden from even the most casual visitors.

Tung said, "We are interested in the meaning behind the messages you sent from Pyongyang last Tuesday. The first day of the tenth month to be exact."

"I considered them urgent," Chan said.

"As do we, Comrade Major General. Please elaborate."

"My colleagues and I have been training and supervising various branches of the North Korean People's Army and Air Force," Chan said. "They proved to be uncooperative and rude toward us."

"That is typical of the North Korean comrades," Tung remarked. "They are not well versed in good manners or subtlety."

"My own counterpart was Colonel General Kim Sung Chien who commands his nation's forces on the DMZ," Chan said.

"Ah, yes," Tung said. "Kim. A most disagreeable fellow, is he not?"

"You seem to know a lot about him, Comrade Tung," Chan said. Normally, he would not have made such a personal, direct remark, but he felt secure behind his rank of major general of the People's Liberation Army.

"I am well acquainted with a number of important individuals in North Korea," Tung said. "From your messages, I assume that certain actions of Colonel General Kim alarmed you. Would you be so kind as to explain, please?"

"The comrade colonel general was most anxious to launch an attack against the American and South Korean troops along the DMZ," Chan explained. "He wanted nothing less than to liberate South Korea and unite his country into a single sovereign nation under his leader Kim Jong II."

"Mmm," Tung said. "That would not be in the best interests of China."

"It would also be directly against the orders given me from our high command," Chan said. "For those reasons I reported his conduct and attitudes."

"You will be pleased to know that certain people in the highest echelons of our government were very appreciative of your devotion to you nation's policies, Comrade Major General."

Now, Chan knew he had received some excellent marks for his unpleasant tour of duty. He wanted to share the glory. "I would like to state that Comrade Colonel Tchang Won of our Air Force was also suspicious of the North Koreans. In fact, he was in my presence last Tuesday when I sent the messages you mentioned."

"We are also well aware of Comrade Colonel Tchang's devotion to duty," Tung said, reaching into his desk drawer and pulling out a large envelope. He opened it, and pushed the contents over to Chan's side of the desk. "This is the complete report you submitted concerning your stay in North Korea. Would you be so kind as to read it? Please feel free to make any additions, alterations, or corrections you believe are necessary. Thank you."

Chan reached into his inside pocket and withdrew his pen. Now he knew for sure that his reports had not only pleased certain people in the upper levels of the government of the People's Republic of China, but the contents were taken very seriously. Some sort of action was in the offing. And it would not please the North Koreans. Chan could not help but grin in delight.

USS **Lincoln**
The Admiral's cabin
1000 local (GMT +9)

Lieutenant Commander Gene Erickson had taken quite a walk. He'd been called out of the ready room, climbed several ladders to the CDC, the TFCC, and down the corridor to the door of Rear Admiral James Collier's cabin. He took a deep breath, swallowed nervously, then knocked on the panel.

"Come!"

Erickson stepped inside the large room and snapped to attention, rendering a sharp salute. "Sir! Commander Erickson reporting to the battle group commander as ordered."

Collier sat at his desk in the office section of his quarters. He returned the salute. "Grab a chair, Commander Erickson. Make yourself at home."

"Thank you, sir," Erickson replied as he sat down. He could not fathom the reason why the commander of the carrier battle group would summon him. Then he noticed that a copy of his book *A Naval Aviator's Book of Fighter Tactics* sat in front of the admiral.

Collier picked up the thin volume. "A friend of mine at Anchor Books in Norfolk sent this to me. I just got it today." He shoved it over. "How about autographing it for me?"

"Aye, aye, sir," Erickson replied. He dutifully scribbled his name inside the front cover, and handed it back.

"So!" Collier said. "It appears we have a famous author aboard, hey?"

Erickson grinned. "I don't know about being exactly famous, sir. I doubt if they'll make a movie of the book."

"Well, maybe not," Collier said, "but I had a chance to peruse it quickly. Frankly, I found your theories interesting." He glanced at the book. "So you suggest we form up two F/A-18s into a single team, do you?"

"An F/A-18*E* and an F/A-18*F,* sir," Erickson said. "They should be formed into an operational team. The single seater 'E' is flown by the team leader. The 'F' is the wingman with the RIO keeping watch over both aircraft during combat operations. That leaves the pilots free to concentrate on available or assigned targets."

"Do you mean in both air-to-air and air-to-ground situations?"

"Yes, sir," Erickson said. "This allows the leader to concentrate on shooting bad guys down, knowing that he's being watched over by a wingman and his backseat partner using his radar."

"How would you organize a squadron under that concept?" Collier asked.

"Basically you form up two of those teams into a flight of four aircraft," Erickson continued. "The senior 'E' pilot is the flight leader and calls the shots for the entire flight." He leaned forward as his enthusiasm for his pet theory made him talkative. "So there're six flights in each squadron. When they're all together, the squadron leader is in command. He can maintain control or break them down anyway he wants. One independent team with two under his command. Or vice versa."

"That means his own team and another, right?"

"Yes, sir," Erickson said. "I see the squadron divided this way. There is the Command Team made up of the squadron leader and his wingman. You marry up the Alpha Team and Bravo Team under that Command Team. Then the Executive Team is made up of the executive officer and his wingman. The Charlie and Delta teams are under him. Or you can mix and match the organization to fit the current situation."

Collier pushed a piece of paper and a ballpoint pen across the desk to him. "Make a diagram of some examples, Commander. That's kind of hard to follow when the concept is a vocal presentation."

Erickson worked out several configurations to deal with various enemy formations and directions of attack. He spent a full ten minutes at the task before he finished. "Here you go, sir."

Collier silently studied the combinations. "All sorts of possibilities here," he mused. The admiral opened his book and scanned the chapter on tactics. "Okay. According to your book and diagram, the flights can be broken up any way that is desirable, but the teams always stick together."

"Yes, sir!" Erickson said. "If you check out my tactics and maneuvering chapter, you'll see I've worked out all the possibilities that a squadron, flight, or team might encounter in combat."

The admiral spent a few minutes more checking the chapter. When he finished, he looked up. "What about ground attacks? You said you covered that, too."

"Last chapter, sir," Erickson replied.

"I take it you don't consider ground attacks very important, hey, Commander Erickson?"

Erickson shrugged. "I'm not gonna shit you, Admiral. I consider myself a fighter pilot. Even if I'm given a ground attack mission, I leave the carrier a fighter pilot, then go into a ground-attack mode. As soon as that ordnance is expended, I'm a fighter pilot again. Pure and simple."

Collier closed the book and leaned back in his chair to study the aviator who sat across the desk from him. He saw a Scandinavian-American, six feet tall, athletic build, light brown hair, and blue eyes. He also noted an aggressive intellect backed by plenty of physical courage. "I tell you what I'm going to do, Erickson. I want you to form a flight. Pick another F/A-18E and two more FA-18Fs to go with your own aircraft. You'll be the flight leader. We'll run a few training exercises and see how things go."

Erickson smiled. "May I pick whomever I want, sir?"

"Certainly."

"That might piss off my squadron leader," Erickson said.

"What rank is your squadron leader?" Collier asked.

"He's a commander."

"And what rank am I?"

"You're a rear admiral, sir."

Collier leaned forward. "Enough said. Go organize your flight."

Department of International Relations
Beijing, China
1730 local (GMT +8)

Tung hand delivered Major General Chan Sun Lee's altered report directly to his superior. Chan had done some editing within the body of the document as well as scribbled a few lines in the margin. An entire paragraph of summary was written at the bottom of the last page.

The office chief, Wang Cho, a veteran of the diplomatic corps, carefully read the five pages, then turned his attention to Tung. "This is shocking."

"I agree, Comrade Wang," Tung said. "I fear that North Korea has become a millstone around our necks in this sea of international relations."

"They are obviously planning some mischief," Wang said.

"If things go bad, they will look to us to pull them out of whatever mire of stupidity and disgrace they have created for themselves. I do not wish this to happen."

Tung well understood the meaning of that last statement. Wang had just quoted a direct order from a very high official in the government.

"I do not wish it to happen, either, Comrade," Tung said, indicating his readiness to obey without hesitation. He carefully added, "But I fear there is little hope to reason with Chairman Kim Jong Il. If he has made up his mind to attack American forces on the Korean Peninsula and in the Sea of Japan, there is nothing we can do to stop him."

Wang turned to gaze thoughtfully out of the window for a few moments. Tung knew enough to stay quiet while his chief considered the dilemma. Finally, Wang looked back at him and spoke.

"Contact Mr. Tshek."

Tung smiled and stood up. "An excellent suggestion, Comrade Wang!"

CHAPTER THIRTEEN

The Oval Office
Washington, D.C.
Thursday, 3 October
0130 local, (GMT −5)

John Tshek sat alone in a chair alongside the office wall, gazing at the cleared top of the desk used by the President of the United States. The only thing showing was a pen and pencil set, looking much too simple for the leader of the Free World.

In spite of the early hour, the Chinese gentleman was impeccably dressed in a made-to-order Italian beige suit. His shirt was handmade and even the monogram on the pocket had been stitched by hand. A large diamond ring adorned his pinky finger, reflecting the light from the wall lamps around the room, and a diamond-studded Rolex watch, big and heavy, entwined his left wrist. Tshek's personal grooming was also of the highest order, and he looked as if he were about to walk into an ultrafashionable social event. His hair was styled longish, and swept back without a single strand out of place. This impeccable appearance matched the neatly clipped moustache draped around his small mouth. Tshek's manicured hands were almost dainty, and he had his arms folded across his chest in a dignified manner that gave the look of both power and wisdom. The man had a natural classiness, and his appearance gave ample evidence of his great wealth.

As he sat alone in the office, he continued to give his attention to the President's desk, vaguely wondering what discussions and decisions might have taken place across the heavy piece of furniture the day before. Were orders issued that would affect thousands of people? Perhaps a budgetary change went into effect that would create or delete jobs in some particular American industry. Could it be that a bill affecting the civil rights of particular groups of people was signed into law? A Constitutional amendment might have been formulated and sent into the system. Or maybe it was just a humdrum everyday routine from start to finish that meant little more than to maintain standards and practices already in place. If the day had been uneventful, this new one yet to dawn would put a bit of spice in things.

John Tshek, née Tshek Kaai, was born into a wealthy Chinese family in Hong Kong. Now he was a naturalized American who had adopted an English Christian name with his award of citizenship. He took his new nationality seriously and felt a great deal of personal pride in having become a citizen of the United States of America. The nation's drive and energy matched his own highly competitive intellect. Tshek was hard driven and shrewd in business to the point that he was more than willing to bend, if not break, a rule of ethics now and then. But his love for America was steadfast and true; and he would rather die than betray the nation that had accepted him as one of its own.

He was forty-four years old and had business interests that operated out of New York City, Washington, Hong Kong, Beijing, and Taipei. Tshek, despite his family's wealth, was a self-made man, having established himself as a successful international businessman who dealt in the import and export of goods between North American and Asian markets. His job title was that of the Chief Executive Officer of Oriental and Occidental Commodities, Limited. The company was listed as

OrOcCom on the New York Stock Exchange, and the organization's stock earnings kept the NYSE reports from slipping
too low even during bad times. When it came to the selling,
buying, and trading of manufactured goods, Tshek had the
ways and means of dealing that went beyond normal customs
and tariff controls. Anytime someone asked Tshek what profession he was in, the pleasant little man with a large sense of
humor would reply, "I am in show business. I do a big balanc-
ing and juggling act."

However, only a very few select people were aware that his
commercial skill and acumen spilled over into the delicate in-
tricacies of international diplomacy. He was known to several
national governments as a shortcut; a convenience; a jack-of-
all-trades who had the contacts and the innate qualities to
solve delicate and indelicate problems in a polite and most
clandestine manner.

This early-morning meeting in the Oval Office would be
the third for him in the last twelve hours. The first had been at
the Embassy of the People's Republic of China where he had
been summoned almost desperately. When he arrived, he sat
with a special envoy lately arrived from Beijing who engaged
him in a deeply troubling conversation. At the end of that session, Tshek returned to his own office in Bethesda, Maryland,
and placed a telephone call to invite a particular undersecre-
tary of the United States State Department to visit him in the
usual place at the earliest possible moment. He impressed the
need for haste, telling the man this was a most important and
perilous matter. A grave and growing problem had emerged
full-blown that would affect the security of not only the
United States of America, but the entire world.

The gentleman who responded to this urgent summons
knew John Tshek well. Horace DeVoss was one of those career
diplomats who had just about seen it all. This tall, thin, unim-
posing Yale graduate with a Ph.D. in American History, had
made international deals in locales as diverse and different as
government palaces in Europe to one particularly memorable
time in a thatched hut where he faced down half-civilized guer-
rillas on the wild frontier between Colombia and Venezuela.

This latter activity resulted in the release of an international party of archaeologists who had been held hostage for more than a year.

DeVoss was in bed when he received Tshek's call at a few minutes past midnight. After the short exchange, he came fully awake. He did no more than comb his hair after dressing, then went back to the bedroom to see if his wife Gretchen had awakened. She knew he had been called out on government business and had slipped back into sleep. She was used to such interruptions in their night's rest, and had long ago dispensed with suspicions of clandestine love affairs that were rampant in the upper echelons of Washington society. She mumbled a sleepy response to his good-bye, and he smiled to himself as he looked fondly down at her in the shadowy room. Almost thirty years of marriage existed between them. Their children were off in college; the oldest boy at DeVoss's alma mater, the youngest at the Massachusetts Institute of Technology, and the girl was at the excellent School of Journalism at the University of Missouri. Yet Gretchen still looked like the willowy young beauty he had married those decades past. At least to Horace DeVoss she did.

He went down to the apartment building garage to get his Lexus. The drive to Tshek's office building took a bit of time, and a half hour passed before he turned off Highway 355 into the industrial complex where the CEO's business was located. The main office building and the warehouse complex were pale yellow under the light standards that surrounded the place. DeVoss was well-known by the security staff, and was expected. The two guards on duty signaled him through the gate to the VIP parking section. Another security man met him, and escorted him up to see the boss.

When DeVoss walked into Tshek's personal headquarters he was surprised as always at the austere appearance of the place. For a dandy and a fancy dresser, the Chinese-American businessman kept the simplest of offices. The chairs were plain wooden fixtures; and the cheap desk appeared to be no more than a large shellacked crate with drawers built into it. Not one picture or other decoration adorned the walls. It was also typical that Tshek had no refreshments to offer. After a quick greeting, he launched into his presentation to DeVoss.

The session had been short but intense as DeVoss absorbed the intelligence given him. He made instantaneous analyses, judging each tidbit of information revealed to him. After Tshek had passed on everything he knew, the American diplomat made a quick call to a most special phone number.

Now Tshek continued to sit alone in the Oval Office while De-Voss was elsewhere in the White House conferring with the Powers That Be. Although Tshek had the patience of all Orientals, his desire for a cigarette was putting him on edge. He was an incessant smoker who ran through some three packs a day. The President of the United States absolutely forbade smoking within the areas where he worked or visited. That pretty much made the room Tshek was now in a smoke-free environment. Tshek fondly patted the silver cigarette case in his inside jacket pocket, craving a nicotine fix from one of the small tobacco-filled cylinders inside. The brand was *Sigara al Malik,* and the gold-tipped smokes inside cost five dollars each. Even John Tshek the wheeler-dealer couldn't find a better price.

The side door opened and the President walked in, obviously only recently awakened, yet looking alert and concerned. Behind him in file, paraded Horace DeVoss and the White House Chief of Staff Jim Dawson. The latter gentleman had also been rousted from bed, and his rumpled appearance indicated he had dressed while still half asleep.

Tshek stood up and bowed to the President. "I wish you a good morning, sir."

The President shook hands with the businessman, then signaled everyone to sit down. He settled behind his desk, leaned back in the chair, and spoke directly to Tshek. "What the hell is going on, John?"

"The government in Beijing is most concerned about North Korea, Mr. President," Tshek said. "They have information from several responsible members of their own military indicating that an attack appears to be imminent on an American aircraft carrier in the Sea of Japan. This is to be coordinated with an invasion of South Korea through the DMZ." He paused a moment to let the information set in. "I was called to the Red Chinese embassy a few hours ago, where they passed this information on to me. They are very disturbed about the situation, and urgently requested that I visit Mr. DeVoss with the intelligence they garnered."

The President looked at Dawson. "Who've we got in the Sea of Japan?"

Dawson answered, "The USS *Lincoln*. Part of a carrier group commanded by Rear Admiral James Collier."

"Thank you, Jim," the President said.

Tshek continued, "The plan is for North Korean units to cross the DMZ en masse after the aircraft on the carrier are neutralized. It is reckoned that the North Korean Navy's submarine flotilla will have to be brought in on the operation. It is to be a surprise attack."

The President thought a moment, then commented, "I am most curious who in their military discovered this plot?"

"A general officer of the Army and a colonel of the Air Force," Tshek said. "They were both assigned as advisors to the North Korean Armed Forces. One was at the general headquarters of the People's Army; while the colonel was attached to an operational fighter regiment."

"A fighter *regiment*?" the President commented. "I don't believe I've heard that term before."

"It comes from Russian military terminology, Mr. President," DeVoss explained. "It is their equivalent of our fighter wing."

"Yes," Tshek said. "The Chinese colonel of whom I spoke was in command of a training program involving fighter pilots. He reported noting that live ammunition was being loaded onto both MiG-21 and MiG-29 aircraft for what was supposed to be a training exercise."

Dawson gave the President a serious look. "Remember those intelligence reports from the DMZ? They reported massive troop reinforcements along the line there."

"I recall, Jim," the President said. "And I also recall that after a high-level meeting with some very well-informed people, a decision was reached that the North Koreans are stirring up trouble to get our attention again. The nasty little bastards need more handouts to keep their people from starving to death."

"Excuse me, Mr. President," Tshek said. "All indications are that this is not a feint or a bluster. The North Koreans are fully armed and organized to deliver a decisive blow in that part of the world."

"Do you have any facts or figures?" the President asked.

Tshek reached into his jacket pocket and pulled out the papers passed to him at the Red Chinese embassy. "These include more than locations and numbers of personnel and lists of ordnance and equipment, Mr. President. The exact units of the North Korean Army and Air Force are listed. Also a summary of their submarine inventory and capabilities. All up-to-date as of twelve hours ago." He added, "The Chinese have prepared this report especially for you."

"I am indeed flattered," the President said, taking the ten-page packet to begin a slow, careful read. "The Chinese have much to lose if the DPRK runs amok."

Johnny Kalos, the president's gentleman's gentleman, showed up with coffee, sugar, cream, and cups on a tray. The bachelor servant had permanent quarters in the White House. He sat the refreshments on a sideboard at the far side of the room. After wordlessly serving the four men, he withdrew, knowing that only a very serious problem would have prompted this very early morning get-together. The coffee was gratefully consumed, adding a bit of perk to minds fatigued from lack of sleep.

It was a bit after three when the President finished studying the document. "It would seem our Chinese friends do not want to become actively engaged in this situation."

"Indeed, Mr. President," Tshek agreed. "The Red Chinese want to move into the future smoothly and effectively. The recent space launch of their first astronaut is ample proof of this."

"They are hampered by past relationships with North Korea, are they not?" the President asked.

"True, Mr. President," Tshek said. "Beijing's relationship with Pyongyang is very sensitive."

"I understand," the President said. "Do you have anything to add to this?"

Tshek shook his head. "It is all there, Mr. President."

"Well done, John," the President said. "Once again you have proven your worthy devotion to your new country. As the nation's leader, I thank you."

Tshek was pleased and flattered. "I am happy to be of service." He understood the hint of dismissal, and stood up to return to his office. "I take my leave by your kind permission. If you desire anything else of me, Mr. President, please do not hesitate to let me know."

After the diminutive Chinese man left the office, the President turned his attention to Horace DeVoss. "What is your assessment of this information?"

"It is authentic, Mr. President," DeVoss answered without hesitation. "I recommend immediate preparation and a quick warning to the North Korean embassy that we are on to their game."

Jim Dawson shook his head. "This is more posturing. And by that, I mean the Red Chinese not the godamned North Koreans."

DeVoss frowned. "Are you implying that the Red Chinese are doing no more than just making this up?"

"I sure as hell am!" Dawson said.

"Why would the Chinese start this sort of rumble?" the President asked.

"It takes pressure off them," Dawson explained. "If we don't help those crazy bastards in North Korea, the Chinese will have to increase their own aid to the assholes. And it's costing them plenty now. Besides, the Red Chinese don't want that insane little fucker Kim Jong Il to keep working toward creating nuclear weapons. But they don't want to openly step in there and tell him to stop. There's no doubt that if Kim got pissed off at them, he would stick a hot warhead on top of any rocket he's got now and shoot it over to the Chinese mainland. That would fuck up their fledgling space program for sure."

DeVoss was alarmed. "But this is a brand-new situation. I'm sure of it."

"I understand your concern, Horace," Dawson said. "But believe me, we've been over and over this. We've had the latest intelligence reports and put everything through a pretty brisk ringer. Kerwood Forester the director of Operations for the CIA along with General William Feldhaus of the Joint Chiefs of Staff were in on this. Every single bit of data has been analyzed and squeezed until it's been milked dry and spread out for a full view."

"I reiterate!" DeVoss exclaimed. "This information is only hours old, and it's from the Red Chinese Embassy."

"The point is well taken, Horace," the President said. "However, I am not going to overreact to this situation. I'll see to it that orders are issued to the carrier battle group in the Sea of Japan and the troops along the DMZ to ratchet up their alert standing."

DeVoss swallowed nervously. "Is that all you're going to do, Mr. President?"

"That is all," the President replied.

CHAPTER FOURTEEN

USS Lincoln
Flag briefing room
Sea of Japan
0500 local (GMT +9)

Commander Marianne DiLuca, intelligence officer, stepped into the briefing room with a near apologetic expression on her face. Admiral James Collier looked up from the seat he occupied and nodded her a somewhat friendly greeting. "I had some coffee brought in," he said.

"I appreciate that, sir," DiLuca said, a bit disgusted with herself for feeling uneasy about requesting a private meeting with him. The commander knew she had no reason to be nervous since she was obeying the admiral's direct orders to the letter. She glanced around. "This room seems empty with only the two of us here."

"Yeah," he agreed, thinking that if a giant corporation had a conference room that size, the executives would feel they were in a broom closet. "It's strange not being crowded, isn't it?"

"Yes, sir," DiLuca said. "Close quarters is generally status quo aboardship even at an early hour like this." She got down to business. "I received—"

Collier interrupted. "Get yourself a cup of coffee, DiLuca. Nothing so instantaneously catastrophic is going to happen that will prevent you from enjoying an intake of caffeine."

"You're right, sir," she said. "Nothing catastrophic." She poured herself a mugful, then settled down in the chair next to the admiral's. "Sir, we've—"

"For Chrissake, DiLuca!" he exclaimed. "Take a swallow! Hell! Take two swallows!"

"Aye, aye, sir." She obviously and carefully put the mug to her lips and took two generous gulps. "There we are, sir. Two swallows."

"Good. No more. No less. Two swallows as I ordered," he said nearly laughing. "Now what do you have to tell me?"

"We've been ordered to go on a special alert," DiLuca reported. "I received an intelligence summary a half hour ago that indicated an unsubstantiated report of the possibility of a potential attack from North Korean aircraft and/or submarines."

"Mmm," Collier mused. "Unsubstantiated. Possibility. Potential. Those are not exactly words that make one think that the shit has really hit the fan, are they?"

"No, sir," DiLuca said. "But you wanted me to notify you the minute any sort of report came in with any indication of North Korean hostile actions."

"I certainly did," Collier said. "I assume that the word has been passed through the battle group."

"Yes, sir," DiLuca replied. "At this very minute, as a matter of fact. I was chosen to bring the information to you since I was coming up here anyway."

Collier stood up. "Care to accompany me to the CDC? I think I'll have a chat with the tactical action officer about putting this entire battle group on General Quarters until further notice."

"Yes, sir," DiLuca said. She reached for the mug to finish off the coffee.

"Let's shake it up, DiLuca," Collier said sternly. "We don't have time to dawdle over coffee, y'know."

"Aye, aye, sir."

Carrier Battle Group

The Redcrown vessel in Collier's battle group was the guided-missile cruiser USS *Terral*. This was the closest vessel to the carrier, and had the primary responsibility for coordinating the air defense of the group.

The remainder of the group—a guided-missile destroyer, a frigate, and a replenishment vessel—were spread out some sixty to a hundred miles distance from the *Lincoln*. Collier's command was vastly understrength in that he had no submarines and was short a destroyer and another guided-missile cruiser. More urgent needs in the Persian Gulf had stripped his command, and the Sea of Japan was rated at a much lower priority level. Even though the Iraq War had been won and was now in the deadly throes of a land counterinsurgency struggle, those vessels had yet to be returned to their rightful owner. Pointing out this shortfall to high command would have been a waste of time. The top echelons would have angrily reminded Collier that they damn well knew where each and every ship in the Navy was located, and they would move them around when they felt such action necessary.

Each time Rear Admiral James Collier received news of the North Koreans acting up, he felt like the proverbial man who showed up at an ax fight without an ax.

This shortage of personnel, equipment, and fighting ships put long, unrelenting periods of pressure on the command. In case of a heavy attack, the self-defense arsenal of Phalanx Close-in Weapon Systems, Sea Sparrow missiles, and Rolling Airframe Missiles would be much less than desirable. They would have to be employed wisely and sparingly, with no margin of error or delay. Another factor was the human element. It required extra manpower and hours to be prepared and ready to respond to hostile actions by bad guys. The men and women required to command and work aircraft, vessels, and ordnance had physical and emotional limits irregardless of their devotion to duty. They had already been through a long series of alerts and exercises and the routine was now starting up again.

The air wing aboard the *Lincoln* was not in such bad shape. With their fuel inventory at a minimum level, it appeared as if it would not be feasible for Flight Quarters during the upcoming new period of alerts. Aside from routine patrols, their only requirement was to be ready to go into action immediately in case of real trouble rather than the simulated kind.

The pilots spent their time in the ready room, catching up on their reading. More than a few perused High Roller Erickson's book on fighter tactics. The author himself preferred the *Daily Racing Form,* and concentrated on odds, horses, and jockeys as he handicapped the morning lines of racetracks from Hong Kong to Britain. When he finished picking the best horses, he would have to contact Cynthia Walker about sending another e-mail to his Uncle Stumpy.

Deer Crossing, Idaho
1000 local (GMT −7)

Pamela Drake and her new cameraman showed up at the disaster area in a van rented at the Boise airport the evening before. After a delay in finding out where Deer Crossing was, they finally got on the road earlier that morning. The cameraman drove with a heavy foot per Drake's orders, and her impatience to get to the scene of the explosion had netted them two speeding tickets from the State Police.

The cameraman, an eager young nerd named Dewey Turnbull, had replaced her other guy after he opted to take a vacation. The last time he'd gone out with Drake he'd spent a few frightening hours as a hostage of militia outlaws under attack by the FBI. He had no desire to see what other misadventures she might possibly lead him into.

The story of the explosion was no longer breaking news, but Drake wanted to let the usual flurry die down to clear the decks for some very serious digging. She was an innate journalist; sensing deeper and sinister backgrounds in what seemed to be cut-and-dried situations. It had been announced that inexpert bomb-makers had crossed the wrong wires or pulled some other bonehead stunt that resulted in a catastrophic explosion in a known militia headquarters. To her, this seemed too pat and convenient an explanation of the event. Something was lurking beneath the surface, and Pamela Drake was determined to dig it up.

Shreds and remnants of human remains had been discovered in the crater and debris in the immediate area of the detonation, and it was thought that three to eight people may have been inside the large militia cabin when the accident occurred. Three destroyed houses farther down the road toward the highway contained the remains of eleven identifiable corpses and pieces thereof. These proved to be the proprietor of the filling station/convenience store and his wife; the owner of the bait shop and his brother; a retired couple who had moved into the area from Pocatello; and a truck driver, his wife, and three children. Their remains had now been placed in caskets that awaited funerals and burials. One wag employed by a mortuary noted that if all the shredded corpses were put together, they would fit nicely into a single $12 \times 18 \times 6$-inch shipping box.

The mess had been cleared from the highway and it was now open for the normal traffic flow that was light on even a relatively busy day. Drake and Dewey walked around the area where the filling station and convenience store had been located. He took a few shots with the camera, slowly panning across the area to show the complete devastation. Next, they crossed the dirt street to where the residents had lived and died. Drake decided this was an excellent opportunity to begin her narration. She picked a good spot that showed the now-stacked remnants of the structures where eleven people had died. Dewey got her looking good in the viewer, then nodded.

"Three—two—one," Drake said. "Behind me is what is left of the little settlement of Deer Crossing, Idaho. It was once a peaceful locale; a jumping-off place for hikers and hunters who would leave their vehicles parked behind the convenience store across the street before beginning treks up into these beautiful mountains to enjoy the great outdoors of scenic Idaho. But farther up the community's one street—" she gestured with a nod of her head to the right "—stood another structure; a building that served as a gathering place for madmen. These misguided paranoids were bent on the destruction of the American dream, and within those walls they planned their crimes and built their bombs. And like the terrible atrocity committed in Oklahoma City, decent people were not spared. But these bunglers also suffered when they were caught up in the unpredictable justice of chance and circumstance. Their bomb blew up in their faces." She paused for a moment. "Cut. We'll do another later, Dewey."

"That was really good, Pam," Dewey said.

"Well, it wasn't too bad," she allowed. She glanced up to the source of the explosion. "Let's get some shots up there."

They ascended the hill, following the remnants of the street that was bordered with debris that had been bulldozed out of the way during the futile search for survivors. When they reached the site of the militia safe house, she stopped, then laughed aloud.

FBI agent Charlie Greenfield, squatting beside a technician turned around at the sound. He stood up and gazed at Pamela Drake without smiling. "I wondered how long it would be before you got here."

Drake grinned. "Guilty conscience?"

Greenfield's temper flared. "About what?"

Drake immediately regretted the remark; it sounded like she was referring to the tragedy at Bull Run. "Poor joke. Sorry. I was alluding that perhaps you FBI types had something to hide here."

He shrugged. "Sorry to disappoint you. We're just taking the time to substantiate what happened. And to whom. We're still running across pieces of human remains around this cabin site."

"You're not continuing to work for Magruder, are you?" Drake asked.

"Yeah," Greenfield replied. "It looks like we're going to be a going concern for a while."

"I figured you guys had wrapped up things back there at Land's End."

"Actually we did," Greenfield said. "This is the last hurrah, then we're closing up shop."

"Will you make a statement for me?" Drake asked. "On camera, of course."

Greenfield shook his head. "Sorry. You'll have to contact Magruder. We're not allowed to chat with the Fourth Estate on our own."

"How about off the record?" she persisted. "It might point me in the right direction."

"No." He studied her for a long moment. "Why are you out here anyhow? This is old news now. In fact, I don't think I've seen anything on television or in the newspapers for a day or two."

"I just want to check things out," Drake said. "That's all."

Greenfield didn't believe her. "You didn't come all the way back to Idaho just to check things out."

"Sure I did," Drake said defensively. "Remember I was a hostage at Land's End. Damn it! I have a personal interest in this militia bit."

"If you've received some tips, you'd better let us know," Greenfield warned her. "And don't try to fall back on that journalistic privilege bit. This is a terrorist case, and the new home-defense laws are harsh when it comes to hiding information."

"Relax, Charlie!" Drake said. "God! You're all set to throw me in jail, aren't you?" She calmed down. "Can't you give me any information at all?"

"I already told you that we're simply verifying what obviously happened here," Greenfield said. "That's all I've got to say."

"Okay," Drake said. "Thanks. But I'd like to get some shots of this scene."

"We'll get out of your way," Charlie said.

Drake turned to Dewey. "Are you ready?"

"As always, Pam," he replied. "Are you going to have a spiel?"

"I'll do a voice-over later," she replied.

Dewey hefted his camera up on his shoulder, and began

taking in the crater where the two-story cabin once stood. The ragged excavation was empty except for churned dirt along the sides. The full depth was now undeterminable because of dirt that caved in after the explosion. There had also been a rain that washed a good deal of mud down toward the bottom of the gigantic hole.

"Enough, Dewey," Drake announced. "Let's get back to the van."

They walked back down toward the highway. Dewey glanced at her and asked, "Are we going back to Washington today?"

"If we can get a flight," Drake said. "Shit!"

"What's the matter?"

"I just figured I'd find something extraordinary, y'know? I really felt that there was something here that needed digging up."

"Nothing ventured, nothing gained," Dewey intoned.

As they approached the highway, Drake noticed a police car had pulled up next to the van. The star insignia on the door identified it as the Joseph County Sheriff. A tall, rotund lawman with a protruding stomach stood at the front of the vehicle eating a sandwich. Drake stopped and studied the man from a distance. Her instincts told her this was a lawman that did his duty with fists and billy clubs. She smiled and winked at Dewey.

"C'mon!" she urged. "That's somebody I want to talk to."

They hurried down toward the large man who caught sight of them. He was surprised to see any newspeople. As the pair drew closer he was pleased to note the woman, while not a young babe, was a babe just the same. He smiled at her.

"Howdy."

"Hello, Deputy," Drake said.

"Actually I'm the sheriff," the man said pleasantly. "Sheriff D. W. Doss of Joseph County, Idaho, at your service, ma'am."

"I'm Pamela Drake of ACN," she replied. "I wondered if you would let me interview you."

"Sure!" he said. "I've seen you lots on the television, Miss Drake. I should've recognized you straight off."

"I am so flattered!" Drake said with a big smile. "Before we go in front of the camera, I'd like to ask a few preliminary questions about this incident."

"What incident?" he asked.

This is a live one, Drake thought. "About the explosion that made this mess."

"Oh! *That* incident," Doss said. "Sure. Go ahead and ask me anything you like. But I got to be truthful with you, Miss Drake. I didn't do no investigating. The State Police done all that, and later they called in the FBI."

"But you were on the scene, weren't you, Sheriff Doss?"

"Oh, yeah," he said. "I hung around. I tried to stay out o' the way, but I was concerned because I knew the folks that died here. The reason I came up today was because I been thinking about them. I used to have my lunch here a lot at the café. I guess I was feeling a little sad, so—" He showed what was left of his sandwich, then shoved it in his mouth. "—that's what I'm doing today. Having an early lunch at Deer Crossing."

"So you just hung around as you say?" Drake asked. "Did you pick up any tidbits of information?"

"Nothing much," Doss said. "This wasn't like the usual stuff I deal with. Generally I get cases where one feller gets mad at another and shoots him, and you know who it is. Same in a stabbing. No mysteries like on television. This explosion was complicated. When the FBI got here, they went through every spec of dirt from the highway here right up to the middle of the mountain where the cabin was."

"I guess there isn't a lot you can tell me," Drake said.

"To tell you the truth, there really ain't," Doss said. "I don't think I'd be very interesting for the TV viewers."

"You never know," Drake said, keeping the conversation going to make him talkative. "You didn't really get a chance to learn a lot, huh? That's too bad."

"That's right," Doss said. "Except for one thing. The explosion came from outside the building. Not inside."

Drake displayed no emotion as she coldly calculated the exact meaning and all the implications of what Doss had just said. She asked in a calm, almost bored way, "Was it the State Police who discovered this?"

Doss shook his head. "It was the FBI. The guy's name was—" He reached in his shirt pocket and pulled out a worn notebook. He didn't speak again until he flipped through the pages. "—Greenfield. Charles Greenfield."

"I see," Drake said. "Charles Greenfield."

"Yeah," Doss said. "You should speak to him. As a matter o' fact, I think he's still around here someplace." He turned and walked toward the patrol car door. "I have to get back to work, Miss Drake. I was real pleased to meet you. Sorry I wasn't more help."

Drake smiled sweetly. "That's alright, Sheriff Doss. I may see you again." She waited for him to walk around the car. "Oh, Sheriff!"

He stopped and turned. "Yeah?"

"I just had a thought," she said. "Would you be willing to do me a favor?"

Doss grinned. "I'd be right happy to."

"It would make my report a little more interesting if you made a statement about the explosion being outside rather than inside the militia cabin."

He was hesitant. "Well—"

"The investigation is all wrapped up anyhow," Drake said. "And you'll be seen on TV all over the country on the national news. Just like all those other sheriffs who get interviewed about big cases in their jurisdictions."

"I suppose there's no harm, Miss Drake."

She got them positioned with the scene of the explosion in the background. As soon as Dewey's camera was rolling, she made the intro, then turned to Doss. "Is there anything in particular you can tell us about this disaster, Sheriff Doss?"

"Yes, ma'am," Doss replied with a serious expression on his wide face. "It was discovered that the explosion was outside the militia building instead of inside of it."

"That's most interesting, Sheriff," Drake said.

"Another thing I just remembered is that there was four explosions," he said. "Not just one."

It took all of Drake's willpower to keep from reacting

outwardly to this unexpected revelation. She calmly asked, "Four explosions instead of one?"

"Yes, ma'am."

"What investigative agency discovered this startling fact?"

"It was the FBI, ma'am," Doss said. "They was the ones that figured that out."

Drake led on with a few innocuous questions, getting the sheriff to mention the names of Charles Greenfield and A. J. Bratton on tape. Then she brought the interview to a close. "Thank you, Sheriff D. W. Doss of Joseph County, Idaho."

"Don't mention it, Miss Drake. I got to get back to my office now."

She waited until Doss drove off, then turned to Dewey. "Let's get back to the motel. I need to get on the phone to alert the network about this story." Now she smiled impishly. "And I have to call in a few favors owed me by three or four politicos in Washington."

CHAPTER FIFTEEN

F/A-18E patrol
Sea of Japan
Friday, 4 October
0730 local (GMT +9)

Lieutenant Commander Gene "High Roller" Erickson was the lead plane in a formation of three with Lieutenants Benny "Peanut" Lemmons and Charlie "Tight Lips" Fredericks following him.

They were in a classic old-fashioned "Vic" formation with Lemmons and Fredericks spread out to Erickson's left and right rear respectively. Erickson, always the tactician, liked to experiment with different aircraft arrangements while out on patrol. It not only broke the monotony, but gave the pilots some expanded experience in maintaining their places in various configurations. The "Vic" was a basic World War II antibomber formation favored by the RAF, and Erickson used this patrol to consider its usefulness in mounting a concentrated attack during intercept operations. He had taken his two wingmen through some mock attacks, and after several maneuvers, concluded that his idea of combining a modern jet one-seater with a two-seater fighter would be superior. Modern aerial combat was more widespread and faster than the old days. It was a matter of efficiency of numbers. Too many aircraft in a formation was like an old Western sheriff taking an oversized posse to track down a lone bad guy. They would get in each other's way.

The three pilots, like others on patrol that morning, were glad to be off the carrier for a while and actually earning a living. The rest of the *Lincoln*'s crew had been standing watches, practicing emergency drills, and living a life of hell in what seemed to be a perpetual state of General Quarters. The aviators didn't have much to do, spending most of their time in their cabins, the ready room, or the wardroom. Their frantic flying schedules had been suspended in order to conserve fuel until the next resupply. They were in the way when they were out and about from their living areas, and the resentment shown them by the rest of the crew though silent, was so unsubtle and blatant that it might as well have been shouted out loud. Sometimes the glare of dozens of angry eyes is more effective than bellowing insults.

To make things worse, they eased their boredom by hanging around the plane captains on the hangar deck during maintenance and repair. This bugged the hell out of the aviation machinists and electricians who didn't appreciate having nosy aviators looking over their shoulders as they worked. The chief petty officers were also irritated because they liked to keep most of their nefarious activities to themselves. These intrepid individuals did whatever was necessary to get the job done efficiently and correctly. They were capable of lying and stealing to meet these ends. This was particularly true when it came to switching parts between airplanes.

Now, as the patrol continued its assigned duty, Erickson went the route of the waypoints, going off autopilot now and then, steering manually to break the monotony. He was a man easily bored, which was one reason he never opted to leave the Navy and get a cushy job on an airline. Flying out of a metropolitan hub to some distant city and back again was his idea of redundant hell. He also thought making those bothersome "This is your captain speaking" announcements would be especially irritating. Of course there were cute female

flight attendants for company during those long, dreary eve-
nings and nights in hotel bars and rooms between flights, but
even that couldn't match the exciting life of a naval aviator
launching from and landing on aircraft carriers.

"High Roller!" Lemmons commoed. "We got bogies at
one o'clock."

"Alright," Erickson replied. His eyes dropped to his right
DDI, and he saw the blips on the air-to-air radar in the RWS
mode. He eased onto a direction toward the bogies. "Jesus!
There're twelve of 'em."

"My IFF says they're bad guys," Fredericks said.

"Mine, too," Lemmons cut in.

"King, this is Prince Bravo," High Roller Erickson said
raising the carrier. "We've got twelve bandits, closing fast."
He didn't bother with giving their exact position at that point.
The glowing cathode ray tubes in the CIC would do that automatically.

"Prince Bravo," came back the reply almost instantaneously. "Do not engage. Return home."

"Roger," Erickson said, disappointed, but not surprised.
The operational area in the Sea of Japan was not considered a
war zone. "Alright, guys, we're going to run for it. Let's play
like we're the Blue Angels."

He pulled back on the stick and went into a half loop
with Lemmons and Fredericks sticking with him. When they
reached the top, Erickson made a quick stick adjustment by
pushing it forward for an instant, then rolled to 180 degrees to
return to an upright attitude.

"I'm in somebody's radar," Erickson reported. "My RWR
is going crazy. You guys break and we'll see about dividing
those bandits up. I have this tingling feeling that they're looking for trouble."

While Lemmons and Fredericks split off, High Roller Erickson made some sharp turns to port and starboard. He could
tell only one of the bandits had zeroed in on him, and the guy
was dead serious.

"I see him, High Roller!" Lemmons said. "The son of a
bitch is a MiG-29. He's closing fast."

Several thoughts rushed through Erickson's mind. The MiG-29 could hit Mach 2.4 under the right conditions versus his Super Hornet's 1.8. That gave the bad guy an edge. The sudden loud-pitched buzzing on his alarm told him a missile had been launched his way. Erickson kicked into a g-pulling, pain-in-the-guts turn, spewing chaff and flares. He couldn't outrun the missile, but he could sure as hell outturn it if the defenses didn't draw it off. A few quick turns and changes in altitude on his part would keep him going until the bandit missile used up all its fuel. Unfortunately this worked to the shooter's advantage. The bad guy had used this opportunity to close in, working into a favorable position for another launch.

Erickson acted from instincts developed initially during his training at Pensacola. These reflexes had been further honed during hours of operational flying, and a memorable stint in the Top Gun Program at the old NAS in Miramar. He broke in the direction of attack, cutting the angle between him and his opponent. The guy quickly overshot High Roller Erickson who reversed his direction once more, moving across the other's flight path. He did the same thing two more times, then inverted and dove, righting himself with the North Korean dead ahead in his radar. Erickson pulled the trigger.

The Aim-9 Sparrow missile left with a physically discernible *thunk,* and climbed and turned as it closed in. Erickson always hated that part of a launch. It appeared as if the missile was going to fly off to parts unknown. They always arced, and from the pilot's angle appeared to be looking for Albuquerque, New Mexico, rather than the target. But this one, like the others, was on the beam. A splash of orange and black showed the hit.

"Give me a hand, godamnit!" came Frederick's voice. "I got three of these sons of a bitches on my ass!"

Erickson's eyes were glued to his radar as he swung the Hornet into a steep turn to port. Within a couple of moments he picked up four blips. Three were closing in on Fredericks, working to lock in on him.

"Launch!" Frederick said. "I got a launch on me! Another! Godamnit!"

"Evade, Tight Lips!" Erickson said, even though he knew that was exactly what his buddy was doing. He hit his afterburner, heading for the conflict. "Hey, Peanut! Where the fuck are you?"

"I just cleaned up my own problem, High Roller," Lemmons answered in a confident voice. "I'm on my way."

"I'll lead the way in," High Roller Erickson said. His eyes stayed glued to the four blips circling his scope. Suddenly one of them disappeared. "Tight Lips! Did you get one?" There was no answer. "Tight Lips!" He turned to his IFF and got no signal back. The three survivors were all bad guys.

"High Roller," Lemmons said. "I see a chute. He's ejected."

Erickson was relieved, even though the North Koreans had broken contact and were heading away from the area. "Let's give search and rescue a vector."

"We've got more company, High Roller," Lemmons said. "Jeez! Look at all them blips!"

"Let's give 'em some grief, Peanut!"

He was relieved they were now a formation of two aircraft. This was a hell of a lot better than a Vic where the third aircraft was a supernumerary in modern air combat. The lead pilot and his wingman made up a traditional team of two that went back as far as World War I. Two of Germany's greatest fighter aces in that conflict, Oswald Boelcke and Max Immelmann, had quickly learned that a pilot by himself is plagued by various blind spots of observation. Having one partner covering your ass neutralizes that deadly disadvantage without the confusion when there are too many friendly aircraft around. Boelcke's forty victories and Immelmann's fifteen attest to the accuracy and practicality of their theory. Boelcke died when he collided with a fellow German's aircraft; Immelmann lost his life when a defective interrupter gear caused him to shoot off his own propeller.

Erickson was on the left and Lemmons the right in a combat spread as they closed in on the two bandits approaching them in a like formation. High Roller Erickson, ever the tactician, had worked out a ploy he called Split-and-Divide. This would work fine in this case, since they had evolved out of a BVR situation after a few minutes. To the naked eye, the enemies appeared to be small but rapidly approaching dots.

"Peanut," Erickson said. "Split-and-Divide. Now!"

They turned to their respective outsides, then suddenly cut inside on the bandits' line of flight, Erickson the higher of the two. The enemy quickly reacted by also turning outside to meet the double threat. At this point High Roller and Peanut traded opponents, passing each other to engage the MiGs. Each ended up on their targets' sixes, close enough to go to their M61A1 20-millimeter guns.

The G's pressed against Erickson as the turn increased, but his aiming reticle was easing closer and closer to his desperate opponent. Finally the device was over the MiG-29, and High Roller Erickson held on, teeth clenched until the IN RNG appeared on his HUD. He gave the trigger a second-and-a-beat pull sending between one hundred and fifty and two hundred rounds into the target. The North Korean aircraft shuddered, then exploded. Erickson pulled back on the stick, then rolled over to an inverted position before straightening out.

Lemmons was having a bit of trouble maintaining his firing position on his opponent. After a few moments, he switched from the gun to his AIM-120 ordnance. When he was locked solidly on the target, he cut loose the fire-and-forget missile, then dove away, rolling to the opposite direction of his flight. The MiG-29 was no more. Lemmons checked the radar. Once again he and Erickson were approaching another enemy duo coming at them in a combat spread.

"Do you see 'em, High Roller?"

Erickson replied, "Roger that, Peanut. It looks like it's going to be one of those busy days. Let's do a drag on these assholes."

The two carrier pilots concentrated on only one opponent this time. Both headed for the aircraft opposite them in an apparent head-on attack. But this time Lemmons broke to the right, drawing his man toward him. At that point, High Roller Erickson feinted left, then also made a sharp run to the right, away from the second bandit, working himself into the position he wanted.

Lemmons made another right maneuver, causing his man to whip back in a nearly opposite direction, heading for what seemed a nice shooting position on the American's tail. But Erickson had been carefully closing in on Lemmon's bandit. At the right moment he fired an AIM-9M Sidewinder that went right up the guy's ass. The explosion was spectacular.

When the two Americans turned to dust off the survivor, he was nowhere to be seen. "Well!" Lemmons said, looking around for the North Korean. "That was rude."

"The guy's a candyass," Erickson complained. "Whoops! There's a couple more of 'em. It looks like they're trying to flee the scene."

The two-man team burst into a split turn, both rolling to their outside. The two bandits were flying a course that ran perpendicular to them. "I'll take the guy on the left," Erickson said.

"Roger, High Roller," Lemmons said, turning his concentration to the other.

It was obvious the two North Koreans were in more than a simple break-contact mode. They were heading full-bore for home, obviously ordered to get back. Both Erickson and Lemmons hit their afterburners for a quick push, to move in close. A couple of minutes passed, and they were able to select their respective targets. The North Koreans began spewing flares but no chaff. High Roller Erickson and Lemmons each selected AIM-120 radar-guided missiles. When the SHOOT cue came up on their HUDs, they fired. The MiG-29s tried a breaking maneuver, but it did them no good.

The radar screens in Erickson's and Lemmons's aircraft were clean and stayed that way as they made a complete turn. The battle was over. Lemmons sank into thought for a moment. "Hey, High Roller, are you an ace?"

"Let me think," Erickson said, as he tried to remember the past twelve minutes. "Nope. I got a total of four. I'm one short."

"Well, I got three," Lemmons said. "Together we knocked down seven of the bastards. That's nothing to snort at."

"I just hope ol' Tight Lips got picked up," Erickson said.

Suddenly he exclaimed, "Hey! We must be at war with North Korea."

"Yeah," Lemmons said. "It would seem that way."

"And it's going to be a fighter war," High Roller Erickson opined. "That's even more exciting than hitting the Pick-Six at the Del Mar Racetrack!"

USS **Lincoln**
Combat Information Center
0800 local (GMT +9)

Commander Doug Hawkins, the CIC watch officer, took a deep breath and glanced over at the tactical operations officer Lieutenant Commander Stan Paulson. "Is it over?"

Paulson clicked his computer mouse to move in close on a certain portion of the electronic image that represented the outside world. "Contact is broken, sir. The North Koreans have beat a retreat."

"How many of our guys went down in that mess?" Hawkins asked.

"Three," Paulson replied. "One Hornet and two Tomcats. Our guys bagged nine of theirs. Patrol Prince Bravo scored seven."

"We won nine to three, huh?" Hawkins said. "That's a three-to-one kill ratio. Good in anybody's book." He suddenly felt lousy about mentioning the loss of three of their aviators like it was a ball game score.

"Sir!" a voice snapped behind Hawkins. When he turned he saw a young marine. "Admiral Collier requests your presence in the Flag Battle Center."

"Right," Hawkins said. He nudged Paulson. "Take over, Stan."

"Aye, aye, sir."

Hawkins followed the marine the short distance from the CIC to the FBC, stepping through the door that was held open for him. Admiral James Collier was studying his own monitors as Hawkins walked up beside him. The flag officer turned to the watch officer.

"That was unexpected," the admiral remarked. "It looks like we've got another war on our hands."

"Yes, sir," Hawkins replied. "They hit our patrols on the outer edges of their sweeps. I presume they've been monitoring our patterns."

"They also stayed away from our Redcrown," Collier said. "This was a calculated provocation. It didn't work out well for them though. What was the count?"

"We got nine of theirs, sir," Hawkins said. "We lost three. Prince Bravo brought down seven of them. That was Erickson, Fredericks, and Lemmons. Fredericks was one of our losses, but he ejected."

"Maybe we've got an ace," Collier said. "I wonder what brought all that on. I was under the impression that talks with North Korea were in the offing."

"I'd say they were testing the waters, sir," Hawkins said. "We've already sent out the word via DSCS."

DSCS—the Defense Satellite Communications System—was made up of a half dozen super high-frequency satellites over the Atlantic, Pacific, and Indian oceans. They connected commanders in the field or at sea with those headquarters and agencies that make the big decisions and issue the critical orders. Additionally, CVBGs also have FLTSATCOM, the Fleet Satellite Communications System that allowed naval vessels and shore facilities to talk with each other.

"I've already received orders," the admiral said. "I'm going to have a town meeting in the Flag Briefing Room in about fifteen minutes. Don't be bashful about interrupting with the latest breaking news, Commander." He took a deep breath. "Have you gotten any word on our three downed pilots?"

"Two have been picked up for sure," Hawkins reported. "We don't know the status on the other one yet. But all four Seahawks are out looking for him."

"Let's hope for the best," Collier said.

"You bet," Hawkins said. "Is that all, sir?"

•

"Yeah," Collier said. He knew that Hawkins was anxious to get back to the CIC. "Remember to keep me informed."

"Aye, aye, sir," Hawkins said. "That's my job."

As he went out the door, he met Commander Marianne DiLuca entering the compartment. They nodded to each other. DiLuca closed the door, then turned to the admiral. "Well, sir, it looks like those fuel requisitions will be filled now."

CHAPTER SIXTEEN

The Oval Office
Washington, D.C.
Saturday, 5 October
0700 local (GMT −5)

Jim Dawson, the White House Chief of Staff, looked over at his boss who sat glumly at his desk, taking small sips from a glass of skim milk. This thin beverage was about the only liquid his ulcers could tolerate. Dawson displayed a slight grin. "It looks like today's golf game is cancelled, huh, Mr. President?"

The President swung his gaze over to him and said nothing, but the expression on his face plainly showed a lack of amusement.

"Sorry, sir," Dawson said. "Poor attempt at humor."

The three others in the room, General L. C. Curtis, U.S. Army; Admiral Ted Hutchins, U.S. Navy; and General Bill Feldhaus, U.S. Air Force, all seemed to be in agreement. This was most certainly not the right occasion to attempt any joking. These representatives from the Joint Chiefs of Staff gave Dawson collective looks of censure that put him in a contrite mood.

Dawson took a deep breath, and nervously said, "Well! I wonder how much longer it will be before he gets here." He immediately regretted uttering the unnecessary statement since it was obvious the expected visitor would be there when he arrived.

General Curtis, sporting the master parachutist badge over which sat five rows of ribbons further enhanced by the combat infantryman badge above those service and campaign awards, scowled at Dawson. "You chatter a lot when you're nervous, don't you?"

Dawson shrugged.

"Have you ever served in the military?" the general asked.

"No," Dawson answered. "I've never been in the service."

"Then you should sign up for a hitch," the general suggested. "It would do you a world of good."

"Yes, sir," Dawson said. He was glad he wasn't in the military service at that particular moment. The three top men of the nation's armed forces would probably have ordered him taken out and shot for conduct unbecoming a soldier if he was a man in uniform. Another deep breath followed by a slow exhalation eased his nervousness.

The tension was lessened somewhat by the entrance of Johnny Kalos who wheeled in a serving cart with a wisely chosen assortment of liquid, sweet, and nutritious treats. He knew the group was stressed out and pretty close to showing some outright anger. He immediately topped off the President's glass of skim milk, then poured black coffee for the other four men. No one spoke as he next went to each individual to offer a tray of snacks. The jellied doughnuts proved to be the most popular.

The mood remained tense even during the consumption of the snacks. Not a single word was spoken among the somber quintet; the only human sounds being slurping and chewing.

Johnny, in his usual manner, stepped back out of the way as each individual ate and drank his fill. When it was obvious they desired no more, the valet gathered cups, saucers, and plates, then made his exit without uttering a word.

A moment later a light knock on the door sounded, followed by the appearance of the day's protocol secretary who stepped into the office. He was a thin, studious young man who spoke in soft, clear tones. "Mr. President, he's here."

"Show him in," the Chief Executive ordered.

The door closed. A couple of minutes passed, then once again the secretary's knock sounded. He stepped in, announcing, "Mr. President, I am pleased to announce the arrival of His Excellency Chong Jun, Ambassador from the Democratic People's Republic of Korea."

Everyone, with the exception of the President, stood up as the North Korean diplomat walked into the office. He was a short, somber man with his hair combed straight back. His eyes were sullen behind his glasses, and he did not smile. He carried a briefcase in his right hand as he walked to a position in front of the chair located six feet from the presidential desk. He bowed, and said, "Good morning, Mr. President."

"Good morning, Mr. Chong," the President said. "I have called you here for a very serious discussion."

"I am aware of the situation of which you speak," Chong said, his voice tinged with anger. He had received a full report on the air battle from Pyongyang the night before. The North Korean government made it absolutely clear that there had been no hostile moves ordered by Dear Leader against the United States carrier in the Sea of Japan. The entire episode was obviously instigated by the American government.

"I am outraged," the President said, "at the unprovoked attack by North Korean aircraft against United States Naval aircraft in international waters between the Korean Peninsula and Japan. I demand an explanation. Then an abject and public apology from your government."

Chong was so angry he almost trembled. He could not believe that such an outrageous, lying accusation would be spoken by the leader of the world's most powerful nation. This seemed more the conduct of a criminal gang leader. The ambassador gritted his teeth hard, then loosened his jaw to speak. "It is the government of the Democratic People's Republic of Korea who demand an explanation and apology, Mr. President.

Aircraft from the United States Carrier *Lincoln* made what was clearly a sneak attack on elements of the North Korean Air Force who were conducting a patrol exercise in conjunction with a training operation. This is permitted in international waters. No attempt was made to get close to the American vessel."

"We deny every word you have spoken," the President said. "I have the latest reports from the American admiral in that area. The incident was provoked by aircraft of the Democratic People's Republic of Korea."

"It makes me very angry that you said that, Mr. President," Chong said. "You have made it very clear through speeches and actions that the United States of America is hostile toward the people of North Korea. You have portrayed us as warmongers and part of a conspiracy to wage nuclear war not only against your nation, but our neighbors as well. You do this to justify your inexcusable conduct toward us. All this hostile, lying rhetoric on your part has convinced us you mean North Korea harm. The government in Pyongyang can only conclude that this latest criminal act is your prelude to attacking our sovereign territory and establishing a state of war between our two countries."

The President started to stand up and bellow across his desk, but he sat back down after rising just enough to get his buttocks off the chair. His eyes narrowed with rage, and his voice sank to a growl. "I am in no mood to have pointless and insidious statements directed my way. This act of aggression has gone too far. It was bad enough when you toyed with your nuclear threats, but the line has been crossed."

"We concentrate on developing our nuclear capabilities just because of this type of threatening posturing toward us," Chong said. "And do not threaten us, Mr. President. Our Dear Leader is capable of not only defending us from any American attack on our homeland, but of directing an all-out war against the United States of America that will bring it to its knees." He paused, his grip tightening on his briefcase before he resumed speaking. "I have nothing more to say, Mr. President. You are now fully aware of my country's attitude toward this unfortunate situation that you have caused. I am now awaiting further instructions from my government. I shall take my leave this very instant."

Chong walked out, leaving the Americans seething. Dawson was retrospective for several moments before he spoke aloud to no one in particular. "Y'know, he was *really* pissed off."

General Curtis of the Army snarled, "It was a fucking act, Dawson. What the hell did you think he was going to do? Just sit there and listen?"

"Wait a minute," Dawson said testily, now even happier he was not in the service. As a civilian he could stand up to any high-ranking general without fear of reprisal. He raised his voice. "I'm not kidding, godamnit! The guy was sincerely upset. That was righteous indignation we just saw here. It was like all this was completely new to him."

Curtis wasn't convinced. "It's probably a case of need-to-know. The North Koreans would prefer their diplomats overseas weren't in on the big picture of their misbehavior. Chong undoubtedly got the word that we had started the fight, and he's pissed off about it. But that sure as hell doesn't make him right."

The President leaned back in his chair. "I was staring him in the eye, and he did seem genuinely outraged."

"That's my point," Curtis said.

The President looked over at Admiral Hutchins. "You're absolutely positive that they started the fight?"

"Yes, Mr. President," Hutchins said. "No mistakes were made by our pilots. Copies of the tapes were flown back here and I personally reviewed the data. Our aircraft were obviously attacked. The North Koreans fired the first shots at both our F/A-18s and F-14s. Our guys were even ordered to leave the area when the bandits first appeared. But they couldn't withdraw once fired on. They went into a reactive self-defense mode."

"Would that assumption be taken by anyone else who perused the tapes?" the President asked. "Even neutrals?"

"Yes, sir, Mr. President," Hutchins said. "They would have to be experienced with the techniques of course, but you could get any qualified officer from any navy in the world and they would have to agree that the aviators off the *Lincoln* did not incite the aerial combat."

"Alright," the President said. "That's exactly what we're going to do then."

Hutchins shook his head. "No can do, sir. Both the methodology and technology are highly classified information. We'd give a lot of intel away if we showed outsiders the procedures we use."

"Godamnit!" the President said in angry disappointment. "There's a hell of a lot more to this situation than meets the eye."

General Feldhaus of the Air Force crossed his arms over his beribboned chest. "Bullshit, Mr. President. If this is the start of World War III—and I think it is—we better get an early advantage."

"And hold on to it," General Curtis added.

The President sighed sadly. "World War III. God save us all!"

ACN studios
1755 local (GMT −5)

Walt Harbaugh, news director of ACN, stood behind the camera as Pamela Drake made ready for the evening broadcast.

Drake was one hell of a journalist, no doubt about that, and he considered himself lucky to have her in his department. She had the looks to live the glamorous, easy life of an anchor news babe if that was what she wanted. She could sit on a set, looking sexy and beautiful, reading the news to adoring viewers every evening. There would be articles about her in *People* and other publications, appearances on talk shows, photo layouts in fashion magazines, and maybe a TV series would be made using a strong female lead based on her. But that wasn't Pamela Drake. If anyone had the audacity to use her as a contrived façade or paper doll, she would go after them like an

enraged lioness. The unfortunate coiffured, pretentious ac-
tress who had the temerity to portray Pamela Drake or a rea-
sonable facsimile thereof on television or in the movies,
would have her madeup, surgically altered features slammed
into the nearest brick wall. Harbaugh grinned at the mental
image he had just created in his mind.

Pamela Drake, for all her beauty, was a brainy, hard-as-
nails, gutsy journalist who went after stories with the tenacity
of a psychotic NFL linebacker. No situation was too dangerous, no person too threatening, and no circumstances too
sensitive to keep her from probing into any story long enough
and hard enough to dig out all the facts. Political correctness?
Drake didn't know the meaning of the phrase. She couldn't
care less about offending racial, religious, national, or philo-
sophical individuals or groups if they had done something
bad. The lady wanted the truth. And if it brought somebody
down, she dismissed it with her favorite expression: "Tough
shit!"

Now Harbaugh watched her stand off to the side of the set,
her delivery in her head and her tapes already cued up to
present yet another revelation that was going to do a hell of a
lot of shaking up within governmental institutions. Tonight's
Pamela Drake report would not only reveal current misconduct by federal law enforcement, but open old wounds that
would bleed like sliced arteries. And tonight's broadcast was
just the start. He studied her calm demeanor and casual manner, thinking that must be what a cold-blooded assassin looks
like before firing a bullet into some stranger's head on a job
assignment.

The technicians worked the lights, and the studio went dim
for an instant before the illumination on the set came up. Steve
Bowman, the weekend anchorman, looked up the instant the
camera light in front of him turned red.

"Good evening," he greeted his unseen audience. "And
welcome to ACN's *Weekend Video Journal.* We have several
reports to air tonight. The situation in Baghdad remains at
a critical level with one U.S. serviceman killed and two

wounded; layoffs in several auto plants in Michigan and Indiana have brought on threats of strikes that could begin as early as Monday morning; a twenty-two car pileup in dense fog occurred in California on Interstate 5; and Sheila Thompson has the weather for the rest of the weekend. But first, we have a breaking news report from Pamela Drake who has been investigating an explosion at a militia headquarters in Idaho." He looked to his left where Drake now sat at another news desk. "Pamela?"

"Thank you, Steve," Drake said. "The explosion in Deer Crossing, Idaho, that took the lives of at least sixteen persons was reported to have been an accidental event that occurred within the confines of a reputed militia safe house on a mountainside above the small town. I visited the site of the tragedy the day before yesterday for an update on the situation."

They cut to the tape she and Dewey had made, but they did not use her original report. Instead the viewers saw scenes of the devastation as Drake's voice-over described the former locations of the safe house, the homes, and the small business area of the filling station, café, and bait shop. As soon as the tape ended, Drake was back live on camera.

"As I stated at the start of this report, law enforcement authorities revealed that members of the militia within the safe house caused the explosion while engaged in bomb-making activities in the basement. The latest information released late yesterday afternoon announced that it had now been determined that five badly burned and mangled bodies were found in the rubble. However, my investigation has produced solid evidence that the actual source of the explosion was not as originally reported to the press. The detonations—and there were more than one—actually occurred *outside* the building. This was substantiated by Sheriff D. W. Doss of Joseph County, Idaho, during an interview I taped with him at the scene."

Now the interview with the sheriff came on the monitor, showing Sheriff Doss, a bit awkward but obviously enjoying himself, being interviewed. After he revealed that the FBI had discovered there were four explosions set outside the house, Drake asked who had been the agent in charge of the investigation. The last words uttered on the edited tape by the sheriff were "Charles Greenfield and A. J. Bratton." Once more Pamela Drake's image played across the television screen.

"A. J. Bratton is an unknown name to the average American," Drake said. "But Agent Charles Greenfield has been in the public eye before. He was the agent in charge of another unusual situation involving the militia in Idaho. This was the tragedy at Bull Run where an innocent farm couple by the names of Kyle and Betsy Smart and their children died in a mismanaged, erroneous raid on their isolated rural residence. Now this new situation at Deer Crossing has arisen and it has Charles Greenfield's name written all over it. Why the cover-up? What is it about four rather than just one explosion that has Agent Greenfield and his superiors so worried? And why the lie about an *inside* rather than an *outside* detonation? Or I should say *detonations* plural. Is this a cover-up of another FBI operation gone awry? Or was this a deliberate assassination where everything went wrong again? Innocent citizens were killed in addition to the five militiamen. These so-called collateral casualties number eleven; including three children."

At this point a quick cut back to the view of the wreckage of Deer Crossing was shown. Then the scene returned to Pamela Drake.

"The FBI and Charles Greenfield have some explaining to do to the nation. And another disturbing question pops up. Is Retired Admiral Thomas Magruder involved in this crime? He was assigned to the militia problem after Bull Run. Has he fallen into the cover-up syndrome along with the Feds? This reporter is demanding answers, ladies and gentleman, and I am going to get them."

There was a fade-out from Drake and a fade-in on Steve Bowman. She got up and walked from the desk toward her office. Walt Harbaugh fell into step with her. He put an arm around her shoulder. "You've done it again, Pamela."

She glanced up at him. "Walt, I'm only starting. This time some heads are really going to roll."

"You're going to get some very influential folks extremely angry with you, Pamela."

"Tough shit."

CHAPTER SEVENTEEN

General Headquarters, People's Air Force
Pyongyang, North Korea
Sunday, 6 October
1210 local (GMT +9)

It was a crisp day, giving solid promise of the cold winter soon to descend on North Korea. Lieutenant General Dai Yong of the People's Air Force, wearing his woolen uniform because of the chilly weather, ascended the steps leading to the entrance of his service's general headquarters.

The outward appearance of the building was immaculate and almost classical in the ancient Greek tradition. The exterior was diligently maintained by a crew of workmen who pressure-washed the structure on a regular basis. The Great Socialist Square to the front was surrounded by other government edifices, all as grand and impressive as Air Force headquarters. Visiting foreign dignitaries were frequently driven across the square to impress them with the magnificence and classical beauty of the neighborhood.

This was also where ranks of elite military units goose-stepped in tightly orchestrated parades across this immense open area on special holidays. T-72 tanks buffed to shiny brilliance with Russian *dospyekhi* wax, were always included in the exhibitions. The tank commanders would stand in the turrets to render salutes as they passed in review before Dear Leader and his entourage of old veterans. But behind the doors of the government buildings, the appearance of grandeur declined into outright tackiness.

This paradoxical façade would have shocked those foreign visitors, but General Dai thought nothing of it. A lifetime in North Korea had inured him to the hypocritical aspects of such conditions. The barracks of the parade-ground soldiers were also showplaces, constructed to impress guests from overseas. The uniforms of these specially picked ceremonial troops were the finest produced in the Soviet Union and later China. The garments, all individually tailored to each officer and soldier, were made of the choicest materials. In contrast, the troops out in the garrisons in the countryside were clothed in cheap khaki in the summer and quilted cotton in the winter. Their uniforms were recycled over and over again until literally coming apart at the seams. In addition, their billets were crude buildings with leaky roofs and poor heating systems. As far as the average North Korean was concerned, these conditions were the same worldwide. The governments had everything and the populace nothing.

Now, stepping from the grandiose exterior into the tacky interior of the headquarters building, General Dai entered the foyer. The electric power was down, and the twilight dimness was only slightly relieved by light coming in through the narrow windows. This condition occurred almost daily, sometimes lasting up to twelve hours in the harsh winter months.

Dai presented his ID to the guard at the desk next to the door. This soldier was one of the ceremonial troops who acted as security when not parading and showing off for Dear Leader. He handed the card back to Dai in silent permission for him to continue farther into the building for whatever purpose he might have.

Dai went down a long hall, his shoes making a scuffing noise on the worn wooden floor made uneven by warped boards damaged from plumbing leaks. He reached a set of rather rickety

stairs at the same time the lights came back on. Then the illumination flickered, and the building was dark again. Dai could see
well enough to hurry up to the second floor and turn down the
hall until he reached another door. A plastic plaque identified
the room behind it as the office of Vice Marshal Yen Nal Ui,
Chief of Air Force Operations.

Dai stepped inside where he was confronted by another
enlisted man at a desk. A candle burned on a nearby table to
provide light. The soldier wore the single stripe of a junior
corporal on his epaulettes, but appeared much too old to have
such a low rank; and his demeanor was one of outright arrogance. He stared up at the general without rising from his
chair. All this gave Dai pause, and he did not reprimand the
man's obvious disrespect. The government placed many people from the secret police in various positions as spies. The
ranks they displayed in these cover roles were much lower
than their actual commissions in the dreaded police organization. And they were dangerous to trifle with. They took offense to any slight; and one word of denouncement could lead
to the offender being hauled out of bed in the middle of the
night and taken to one of the infamous and much feared re-
educational camps. These installations were up in the far
north along the Manchurian border where starving prisoners
rarely survived their first winter of confinement. Dai could remember during the days when he was a young officer that a
maid had denounced the colonel in the home where she
worked. The entire family—husband, wife, and three children—disappeared from the face of the earth. The maid's own
departure had been quick and mysterious. Although no one
dared utter it; there was no doubt she had been an agent of the
secret police, and had been reassigned to another location to
ferret out more disloyalty.

Dai smiled politely at the old soldier, saying, "Good morn-
ing, Comrade Junior Corporal. I have been summoned to visit
Comrade Vice Marshal Yen Nal Ui. I am Lieutenant General
Dai Yong."

The junior corporal leisurely pulled a clipboard from his
desk drawer. Suddenly the lights came back on. The junior

corporal blew out the candle, then turned his attention back to the appointment list. He took his time perusing it, though it was obvious only three names were written on the page. He slowly replaced it and looked up into Dai's face for several moments. Finally he said. "The comrade vice marshal is expecting you. Go in."

"Thank you, Comrade Junior Corporal," Dai said.

Vice Marshal Yen Nal Ui was seated at his desk dozing. He was an old comrade who had been the commander of a MiG-15 squadron in 1950 at the start of the war against Imperialism when North Korea invaded South Korea. He was now eighty-five years old and no longer had any official functions other than checking out what was going on in the Air Force when particular information was needed. His main duty was to appear on the reviewing stand with Dear Leader during holidays. At those times he wore a uniform especially prepared for him; cleaned and pressed, with all his medals pinned on. He sat with other oldsters, some who suffered from senility to the point they were not quite sure of where they were. That was a bit of a shame since being in the presence of Dear Leader was considered a place of honor.

Now Marshal Yen wore a plain tunic as he napped with his head hanging down, spittle running from his mouth down onto his chin. Dai cleared his throat softly. He repeated the action, this time louder, and the old marshal's eyes opened slightly. After a moment he became aware of his visitor's presence. *"Ne?"*

"Anyeonghaseyo, Comrade Vice Marshal. I am Lieutenant General Dai Yong. I received word you wished to speak to me."

"You did? I do?"

"Yes, Comrade Vice Marshal."

"Just a moment, Comrade," the old marshal said. He opened a drawer, then looked back at Dai. "Didn't we serve together in the old 23rd Fighter Regiment in 1952?"

"No, Comrade Vice Marshal," Dai answered. "I was not born until 1954."

"Oh," the oldster said. He turned his attention back to his desk drawer, finally retrieving a document. He unfolded it and blinked at it with his watery eyes before remembering to put on his glasses. The lenses magnified the size of his eyes, and Dai wondered just how strong the spectacles had to be to en-large the words enough for the comrade vice marshal to read them. The junior corporal suddenly appeared with pad and pencil, sitting down in a chair next to the wall.

Ten minutes passed, before the old man sat the paper down, removed his glasses and looked up into Dai's face. "I wish to inquire about the attack of the Imperialist aircraft against our people on 4 October."

"It occurred during a training mission, Comrade Vice Marshal," Dai said, noting that the junior corporal was taking down every word of the conversation in shorthand. "Are you familiar with *Wonsukapda Yong*—Operation Avenging Dragon?"

"Yes, Comrade," the vice marshal replied. Then he blinked and asked, "What is it?"

Dai answered, "It is a joint army-navy-air force training exercise." He paused to make sure the oldster understood. "It was during a phase of Operation Avenging Dragon that a for-mation of our aircraft was pounced on by American war-planes without warning."

"Those damn Saber Jets!" the vice marshal exclaimed, re-ferring to the American F-86s of the Korean War.

"These were F/A-18s and F-14s," Dai said. "The Ameri-cans don't fly F-86s anymore."

"I see," the vice marshal said. "Did they shoot down any of our aircraft?"

"We lost nine comrades," Dai said. He was unable to lie about the figures, since the results of the battle were monitored by several agencies. "The Yankees, unfortunately, only lost three."

"I'm not too surprised," the vice marshal said. "A sneak at-tack against our boys had them at an outright disadvantage."

The junior corporal interrupted. "If the aircraft were on a training mission, how was it that they were fully armed and able to defend themselves and shoot down three of the Americans?"

Dai was ready for that one, and he was not surprised the

junior corporal was audacious enough to intrude in a conversation between two high-ranking officers. "They were fully armed because of procedures I had put into place for our training exercise. Our aircraft ordnance crews need practice in loading missiles onto the aircraft. They are graded on the amount of time it takes them to place the weaponry on the proper stations. This includes switching the ordnance for another type when the missions are altered at the last minute."

"That is a very good procedure, Comrade Lieutenant General," the vice marshal remarked.

"Thank you, Comrade Vice Marshal. The configuration also aids our pilots in becoming accustomed to flying aircraft under different loads."

The old man turned his attention back to the remainder of the document in front of him. It took a quarter of an hour for him to wade through it, while Dai stood at the front of the desk with the arrogant junior corporal lounging in the chair. The vice marshal looked up at Dai. "I have all the information I need, Comrade Lieutenant General. Thank you for coming. *Anyeonghi kaseyo.*"

"*Anyeonghi kyeseyo,* Comrade Vice Marshal," Dai said. He avoided the junior corporal's eyes as he turned to leave the office.

White House Press Room
Washington, D.C.
1300 Local (GMT −5)

Ron Avisstad, the President's press secretary, walked up to the podium with grave misgivings. He hid his anxiety and smiled at the assembled press corps waiting to jump on him. He was not pleased to note that Pamela Drake was seated among the journalists.

"Good afternoon, ladies and gentlemen," he said in his usual cordial manner. "It's nice to see you all respond to a Sunday conference. Let me assure you, we aren't holding it today to be sneaky. There are some important items on the President's plate, and we won't have a regularly scheduled get-together until week after next. Today was the only time we could meet with you without a long delay. First, I have some announcements to make, then we'll turn to our favorite game of give-and-take, i.e., questions and answers. Or, as I personally like to refer to it, verbal dodgeball."

The media people chuckled slightly, most taking side glances at Drake. The bombshell she dropped the night before on ACN's *Weekend Video Journal* was on everyone's mind.

"Alright," Avisstad said. "The threatened strike at the auto part manufacturers in the Midwest has been given a cooling-off period per the President's order. He feels this is the best way to deal with a situation that has the potential of causing a great deal of hardship to so many people." The press secretary was famous for never using notes, and he quickly continued. "There is also the matter of the attack by North Korea on aircraft from the U.S. Carrier *Lincoln* in the Sea of Japan. The president has called in the North Korean ambassador to lodge a vigorous protest regarding this incident. The reaction from Pyongyang has been as expected. They denied being the instigators, accusing the United States of making the initial attack. There will be a showdown on this matter at the United Nations."

Pamela Drake, calm and composed, sat in her seat as if she had nothing in particular on her mind. She glanced over at Dewey Turnbull with the rest of the camerapeople. Dewey had been given strict instructions to betray no emotion or anticipation prior to Pamela speaking. He stood at his camera and tripod, monitoring the image of Ron Avisstad in the viewer.

"The final announcement I have is in regard to the Educational Finance Bill that will be sent to the White House for the President's signature at the end of this week. The President will veto it, and send it back to Congress for reconsideration. I believe he has previously expressed his reasons for his opposition to the measure." He took a deep breath, still avoiding eye contact with Pamela Drake. "I'd be happy to take your questions." He glanced around, glad to see Pete Cianno of a Chicago newspaper raise his hand. "Yeah, Pete?"

"Why is the President ordering a cooling-off period in the problem at the auto part manufacturing plants?"

"As I said," Avisstad answered, "he wishes to avoid a situation that could cause great hardship to a good number of people."

"What people?" Cianno asked. "The CEOs?"

"The President is concerned about everyone," Avisstad said. His eyes swept the room on the opposite side of Drake where another hand was raised. He pointed, "Yes, sir?"

"Does the President consider the current trouble with North Korea bad enough to bring about the possibility of a nuclear war?"

"The situation is indeed serious, and if not handled properly, could well lead to a nuclear conflict in Asia," Avisstad said, hoping the potential gravity of nuclear warheads flying between North Korea, China, and Japan would overshadow Pamela Drake's FBI story. "However, the President and his cabinet are even now in contact with other nations to deal effectively with this problem. This is not going to be a unilateral undertaking on our part."

Another reporter was picked, this time a young woman from a national news syndicate. She asked, "Why is the President going to veto the Education Finance Bill? His previous explanations were very ambiguous as far as many people are concerned."

"He is in complete disagreement with the concept of putting all monies for schools into one federal fund to be divided among the states. He feels very strongly that this would seriously undermine local control of schools in our very diverse nation."

Drake still held back as the questions kept coming. The losses in the attack of North Korea were discussed, more explanation was demanded of the coming veto, and some domestic issues were covered lightly.

Drake gave a subtle nod in Dewey Turnbull's direction. He kept his big camera running, but picked up a smaller one and aimed it at her. When she was sure Dewey was taping her, Drake raised her hand.

Ron Avisstad sighed silently and everyone in the room grinned. The press secretary cleared his throat. "Yes, Pamela?"

"It has been discovered that the FBI is conducting another cover-up regarding antimilitia operations in Idaho," Drake said. "This concerns the explosion at a militia headquarters in the town of Deer Crossing. The preliminary report was that it was an accidental detonation inside the building, but I have learned that the explosion was not only outside the premises, but came from four separate places. Innocent lives were also lost as happened at the tragedy in Bull Run where the entire Smart family—husband, wife, and children—were killed by the FBI. Does the President have any statements in regard to this latest incident?"

"Our first knowledge came from your broadcast last night, Pamela," Avisstad said. "So far we've not had the time to substantiate the facts as you claimed they occurred. I can assure you that an aggressive investigation will be launched, and a full disclosure will be made to the American public."

"FBI agent Charles Greenfield who was in charge at the Bull Run incident was also the investigator at Deer Crossing," Drake said. "He is the one who made the announcement that the explosion was an accident that happened inside the house. He also failed to mention the four sources of the blasts. Do you have any comments on that?"

"That would be part of our investigation," Avisstad said.

"There is also Admiral Thomas Magruder to consider," Drake pointed out. "Is he a suspect in this cover-up?"

"We are not sure of any cover-up, Pamela," Avisstad said, his voice calm. "When a complete investigation has been completed, we will release the information to the public." He quickly added, "Through you people, of course."

"Are you saying that you think Agent Greenfield simply forgot the explosion was from the inside?" Drake asked. "And that it merely slipped his mind that four sets of explosives went off?"

"As I said," Avisstad insisted, "we have no answers to questions until an investigation has been made."

"Do you suspect a rival militia group attacked the cabin at Deer Crossing?" Drake went on.

"I can answer no questions until we've made that investigation," Avisstad said testily. "I have no information to pass on to you." He glanced around the room. "There'll be no more questions today. Thank you for coming, ladies and gentlemen."

Avisstad quickly turned from the podium and walked to the egress door. He stepped through where White House Chief of Staff Jim Dawson stood. Dawson held out his hand. "You did a great job on that Idaho story, Ron."

"It wasn't so hard actually," Avisstad said. "I didn't know anything, so I couldn't slip up."

"I'm surprised Pamela Drake isn't concentrating on A. J. Bratton," Dawson remarked, as the two continued down the short hallway leading to the interior of the White House.

"Do me a favor, Jim," Avisstad begged. "Please don't tell me anything about the CIA being involved in this."

"I've got a feeling you'll be discussing the Agency before this thing is over and done with."

"Jesus! We've got a probability of World War III on the horizon, the problems in Iraq, and now illegal activities of the CIA that went on with the President's knowledge."

Dawson gave him a look of both empathy and sympathy. "I have a bottle of scotch in my desk."

"Lead me to it!"

CHAPTER EIGHTEEN

USS Lincoln
Hangar bay
2300 local (GMT +9)

The trio from the Super Hornet gang—Lieutenant Commander "High Roller" Erickson, Lieutenant "Peanut" Lemmons, and Lieutenant "Tight Lips" Fredericks—walked into the hangar bay and paused to gaze around at the area that was literally booming with activity. Dozens of aircraft were being crawled over, under, and into by a myriad of hyperactive technicians who shouted instructions, advice, questions, and the grossest of expletives in a bedlam of loud voices.

Power tools whirred and buzzed while machinists, electronics technicians, and others labored on avionics, structures, and engines in what appeared to be a semiorganized riot of maintenance and repair gone mad. There was also a line of impatient workers lined up at the various storekeepers' cages, waiting to draw needed tools and materials. All fidgeted with impatience and irritation. These were obviously people who had a lot of work to do in a very short time.

Fredericks let out a low whistle. "That's a hell of a big night shift, isn't it?"

Erickson, glancing around for his own F/A-18E, shook his head. "There's only one shift aboard this aircraft carrier, Tight Lips. A *continual* shift. They don't let up until somebody has been worked to the point that he's walking around in a daze, muttering to himself."

"Right," Lemmons agreed. "Then he's quickly replaced by somebody else who's been allowed the unspeakable luxury of lounging around in his rack for at least two whole hours."

"I wonder about the status of our birds," Fredericks said. He looked around, then spotted one of the supervisory staff. "Let's go check with the chief over there."

Erickson violently shook his head. "Hell, no! It's times like this that chief petty officers are at their crankiest. I think it'd be better if we strolled over to the squadron area and checked in with our plane captains."

"Hell! They're cranky, too," Lemmons pointed out.

"We gotta ask *somebody*!" Erickson said. "And they're the easiest to deal with." Then he added, "Not that that's saying a hell of a lot."

"You're making a choice between roaring lions and growling bears," Fredericks observed. "Either species bites. And bites hard!"

The three aviators walked through the bay, dodging around busy people who crisscrossed the area on a myriad of errands. Some pushed carts with various parts destined to be placed in an aircraft or on a workbench for repair or overhaul; others wheeled tool chests as they went from one aircraft they had finished to begin work on another; and of course there were the bearers of clipboards, who were mostly aviation maintenance administration specialists who were charged with coordinating and scheduling all the activity. These latter airmen were just about as cranky as the chief petty officers and plane captains. The material on the clipboards was not to remind them of things that had to be done; instead the documents were used to back them up in arguments that mostly dealt with priorities and schedules.

When Erickson and company located their aircraft in the mishmash, they were glad to see the Super Hornets were all together. Erickson's plane captain, Monger, was working with two others on a supernumerary F/A-18E that belonged to Erickson's cabin bunky who had gone home on emergency leave.

"Hey, Airman Monger," Erickson called up in a cheerful voice. "How's it going?"

Monger, who was sitting in the cockpit, glanced over the side of the aircraft. He didn't seem pleased to note the presence of three pilots who had obviously come to visit him. The plane captain did not reply to Erickson's salutation. He preferred to wait for the pilot to have his say.

"Don't want to bother you," Erickson said.

Then what the fuck are you doing here? Monger's mind silently asked.

Erickson continued, "We're just checking on the status of our aircraft."

"You and Mr. Lemmons is in good shape," Monger said. "This here's Mr. Babbits's bird. Since he went home to see his hurt kid, it has now been turned over to Mr. Fredericks—" He swung his gaze and glared at Tight Lips. "—who got hisself shot down."

Tight Lips Fredericks glared back. "I'm sorry I had the audacity to get my ass blown out of the sky, Airman. It might surprise you to learn I didn't do it just to inconvenience you."

Monger's expression remained impassive. "Glad you wasn't killed or hurt, Mr. Fredericks. But you're one hell of an inconvenience whether you want to be or not."

"I appreciate your concern," Fredericks said sardonically.

Now Monger looked back at Erickson. "Anything else, sir? I'm pretty busy right now."

"Nope," Erickson said. "Just checking, Airman Monger. Thanks a lot. Have a nice day."

"My day's been going on for eighteen hours now and it ain't been nice yet," Monger said. "And I don't expect it to get better." He turned his attention back to his chores in the cockpit.

The three Super Hornet pilots turned away to retrace their steps back through the frantic activity. Lemmons pointed over to the starboard side of the bay. "Hey, there's a couple of the Tomcat boys."

"Let's go have a chat," Erickson suggested. "I haven't had a chance to talk to any of 'em since that little encounter we all had."

They made their way over to where Ski Waleski and Loopy Johnson stood on the edge of the F-14 parking area. They waved as the F/A-18 aviators walked up to them. Ski showed a lopsided grin. "It looks like you guys are the top guns around here. Congrats on your kills."

"We got a couple of breaks," Erickson said modestly. "I'm glad to hear the two Tomcat guys got picked up."

"I was one of them," Waleski said. He winked at Fredericks. "We ought to form a club."

"Yeah," Fredericks said without enthusiasm. "We could call it the Sea of Japan Society of Swimming Aviators."

"So!" Erickson said. "How do things look in Tomcatville?"

"We're ready to go," Johnson said. "How are the Hornets?"

"*Super* Hornets, thank you," Erickson said with a wink. "It seems we're ready to go, too. The maintenance guys are tuning up a bird for Tight Lips, so we'll be back a hundred percent."

"We've ended up one airplane short," Johnson said. "So somebody's going to be left behind when we jump back into Flight Quarters."

"And, since I lost my bird, I'm elected," Waleski said sadly. He indicated the people swarming over a nearby aircraft. "These are some super folks. Maybe they'll solve my problem for me by banging one together out of spare parts."

"Between them and the flight deck crew, we aviators look like we have it made," Lemmons said. "I'm almost ashamed of us."

"Me, too," Erickson said. "That is, until the exact moment that a catapult throws my ass off the carrier. I really feel like I'm doing my part when my eyeballs are slammed into the back of my skull."

Fredericks glanced at his watch. "That's exactly what we'll be doing in a few more hours."

"C'mon, you guys, let's get out of the way," Erickson suggested.

The quintet of combat flyers turned to egress the frenzied hangar.

North Korean submarine Sango
Sea of Japan
Monday, 7 October
0500 local (GMT +9)

The boat was the best in the People's Navy, and its officers and crew were handpicked for assignment aboard after careful scrutiny by the top brass. All had proven they were loyal followers of Dear Leader; that they had been at the top of their classes in the various submarine training programs taught by Soviet submariners; and their professional conduct and efficiency had earned them the highest marks in their respective classes.

The *Sango* was one of twenty-two *Romeo* class boats in the DPRK submarine service. These undersea vessels had a displacement of 1,700 tons submerged. All were 251 feet long with twenty-two-foot beams. The difference between the *Sango* and her sisters was the upgrade in equipment. The propulsion was a pair of Soviet Peremashina diesel-electric engines that generated 3,000 shaft horsepower, driving the boat at 15 knots on the surface and 10 knots underwater. The *Sango* also boasted the latest in active and passive sonar. Additionally, she had six forward torpedo tubes and two aft that accommodated the fourteen twenty-one-inch Soviet Bystriugor torpedoes. This ordnance was a special development for diesel boats belonging to Warsaw Pact nations and those behind the Bamboo Curtain. They were manufactured before the Soviet Union turned its full attention to the construction of large nuclear submarines.

The commanding officer of the *Sango* was Senior Captain Horangi Hwan. Normally the highest rank of a submarine skipper was commander, but because of Horangi's special qualifications and boat, he performed his duties two grades higher with all the extra benefits in pay and privileges. His second-in-command Captain Topda Jung also enjoyed a higher rank. The officer cadre was backed up by the chief petty officers who ran the groups of some forty ratings with an iron-fisted discipline that bordered on cruelty. If the fear of kicks and punches weren't enough to inspire them to spectacular performance, there were portraits of Dear Leader in every compartment of the boat.

Now under way on a carefully planned and coordinated attack patrol, the *Sango* eased toward the position occupied by the American carrier USS *Lincoln*. Two squadrons of three subs each accompanied the *Sango,* moving back and forth in groups and as well as individuals. Captain Horangi and his crew maintained a steady course among them, electronically hidden from the preying sonar of hunting ASW aircraft.

USS **Lincoln**
Viking S-3B
Number 3 catapult

Lieutenant Carl Dawkins sat at the controls of aircraft, tensed up like the other three people with him. COTAC Lieutenant J. G. Elaine Drew, TACCO Lieutenant Harry Marx, and SENSO Petty Officer Third Class Dan Benson made up his crew. They were part of the ASW patrols put on an Alert 5 earlier that morning. That meant the *Lincoln*'s half dozen submarine hunters would be launching five minutes apart until all were airborne and operational. The Seahawk helicopters were being held back as a reserve force.

The *Lincoln* was turned into the wind, its speed up to 30 knots and Flight Deck Control had already sent out the word to get all those airplanes into the air.

Thus, Dawkins and crew, with the plane's nosewheel lowered into the catapult shuttle, waited to begin the day's work. A green shirt held up a board that showed the projected weight of the Viking. They were loaded for bear that day, toting along four Mk-50 Advanced Lightweight Torpedoes. Drew gave the signal to indicate the weight written on the board was correct. This was an important factor as it informed the launch crew how much steam pressure to apply in relationship to the aircraft's weight. Too much would rip the nose gear off; and too little would result in the airplane being thrown off the bow into the ocean. This would be extremely inconvenient since the bow of the carrier would be bearing down on them.

Dawkins glanced into his rearview mirror and saw the jet-blast deflector raised into position in his direct rear. "Get ready, folks!" he called out in his usual manner.

Drew showed a forced grin. "Here comes the fun part."

"Right," Dawkins said. "Get ready to positively giggle with delight."

The engines were revved to full power, but the aircraft itself was anchored to the holdback the green shirts had attached to the nose gear strut. Less than a half minute passed before the catapult officer signaled while kneeling and pointing toward the bow.

The holdback snapped and the Viking was fired down the catapult to come under Dawkins's control as it went airborne. He made a turn to port to go up to the desired altitude, then he eased onto the vector given him in the ready room. He spoke into the intercom: "We're on patrol so let's get to work."

North Korean submarine Kal Mulkogi

The captain was nervous, but he did a good job hiding his apprehension from his crew. A check of his watch showed he was to make the first of three periscope views in the vicinity of the American carrier. After a quick glance, the periscope would come down and he would note the big vessel's position. It wasn't much time, but the prying eyes of an ASW aircraft might pick it up.

His mouth was dry and the palms of his hands were damp with sweat. He took a deep breath. "Periscope depth!"

"Periscope depth!" repeated the plane control petty officer.

The submarine tilted upward toward the bow as it began to rise the necessary twenty meters to a spot where the extended periscope would go above the surface of the water. The petty officer watched the depth gauge, noting the needle's progress. The words on the instrument were in the Cyrillic alphabet of the Russian language that he could not read, but the Arabic numbers were something he learned in the submarine petty-officer academy. The seamen in the service were not taught to read numerals on gauges or instruments since this knowledge would aid any potential defectors. For this same reason, enlisted men in the People's Army were not instructed in the art of map reading.

"Level off!" the petty officer ordered the plane operator. As soon as the bubbles in the old Soviet leveling instrument were in the center, the climbing stopped. "Periscope depth, Captain!"

"Up scope!" the captain ordered. He waited until the instrument was extended, then he put his eyes up to the viewer. The horizon was clear as he made a complete 360-degree turn. "Down scope! Set new depth of fifty meters!"

"Fifty meters!" the petty officer responded.

The captain checked his watch. He would repeat the procedure in another half hour. He glanced over at the bulkhead just above the navigator's station. The photograph of Dear Leader gave him courage.

Viking S-3B
0530 hours

SENSO Dan Benson had become one with the high-resolution radar system as they scanned their assigned sector. When not on hunt-and-kill duty, Benson showed every symptom of suffering from a very acute case of attention deficit syndrome. It was as if all his intense studying to earn his rate had sapped whatever abilities he had to concentrate outside of ASW activities. He came out of A-School well-trained and prepared for duty in the fleet, but he had become the quintessential absent-minded professor but without a college degree. The petty officer continually lost things, forgot appointments, and paid no attention to other people when they spoke to him on subjects in which he had no particular interest.

But he monitored his instruments with a passion and concentration that bordered on fanaticism. Casual observers sometimes thought he *knew* something was out there and it was only a matter of time before an enemy submarine would reveal itself to the young zealot. When Benson did find something, he was casual but quick in his reactions. When he didn't find anything, he would return from the patrol just as laidback, showing no signs of disappointment.

"I've picked up something," he said suddenly but softly. "It's gotta be a freaking periscope."

"No shit?" Harry Marx, the TACCO, remarked, turning his attention to the situation. "I don't see anything."

"Neither did I," Drew joined in.

"It's gone, but it was there," Benson insisted.

"That's good enough for me," Marx said. He got on the horn. "Carl, let's drop a half dozen sonobuoys in this area."

"Roger," Dawkins said, beginning a slow turn.

North Korean submarine Kal Mulkogi

"Periscope down!" the captain ordered. He took a deep breath, relieved that this second exposure of his boat was over. "Take it down to fifty meters."

The chief petty officer responded by having the plane operator whirl his wheel into a dive position. He watched the depth gauge, mentally counting off the slow crawl downward; *thirty meters, thirty-five, forty*—" Moments later he called out, "Fifty meters."

"Hard turn to port!" the captain ordered.

"Hard turn to port!" the helmsman replied, and used his steering apparatus to swing the rudder to accomplish the correct maneuver.

The captain, watching his electronic compass, waited until they had swung ninety degrees. "Hard turn to starboard!"

"Hard turn to starboard!" the helmsman echoed.

The submarine made a half dozen more erratic movements before settling on a course of 270 degrees. The captain was pleased. They had performed a dangerous task, and were now heading out of harm's way.

A good day's work for Dear Leader!

Viking S-3B

Dan Benson now had the approximate location of the submarine. He and Harry Marx had worked close together, using the Viking's MAD equipment to put a precise location on the target.

"We got it!" Benson said. "Attack criteria!"

Dawkins wasted no time in cutting loose an Mk-50 torpedo. The aircraft shook slightly in its sudden unsymmetrical mode, but the pilot ended the disturbance with some instant trimming. The fish hit the water and disappeared as the Viking made a sharp turn.

"It's live!" Benson gleefully reported. A moment passed before he spoke again, this time in a louder voice. "Acquired!"

"Homing!" Drew called out. "It's homing!"

North Korean submarine Kal Mulkogi

"Torpedo approaching!" the senior sonar man yelled out. "Coming fast."

The captain bellowed, "Dive! Dive!"

The plane operator quickly whirled the wheel all the way as the executive officer punched the large button to blow the remaining air out of the tanks. Everyone braced against the abrupt, steep tilting of the deck beneath their feet. The sudden change in pressure made the crew's eardrums pop in protest to the rude treatment.

The captain, his eyes wide with acute apprehension, looked to the port side of the boat where he knew the torpedo was rapidly approaching. Suddenly, for the briefest millisecond, he perceived an orange flash and the strange sensation of both dry and wet heat.

Most of the crew died in that instant; the last three men in the aft torpedo tubes succumbed three seconds later as the *Kal Mulkogi* broke in two.

Viking S-3B

"Explosion!" Benson yelled. A spontaneous collective cheer sounded dully in the roar of the engines. "We oughta see something out along the line of 283."

Dawkins eased onto the course, setting on the autopilot so he could scan the ocean's expanse with the others. Elaine Drew was also anxiously gazing at the wide expanse of the Sea of Japan. Less than a minute later a slight movement on the water caught her eye. It was a thick spread of oil, growing rapidly wider.

"Uh oh!" Drew said. "I hope we don't get in trouble with the EPA."

"We'll get in trouble with the U.S. Navy if there's another sub out here and it slams a torpedo into the *Lincoln,*" Dawkins said. "Let's get back to work."

Harry Marx looked over at Benson already back at his instruments. "We're way ahead of you."

"Man!" Benson exclaimed. "That's a clean, undeniable kill. My eyeballs tell me that, and my equipment confirms it." He laughed. "We are some bad dudes." He glanced forward to Drew. "I say again; three bad dudes and one bad dudette."

North Korean submarine Sango

The sonar man had reported the explosion and the sounds of a submarine breaking up. Senior Captain Horangi stepped the short distance across the control room to the navigator's table. "Have you located the exact position of the lost submarine?"

Senior Lieutenant Sanyang looked up from his plotting chart. "It was the *Kal Mulkogi,* Comrade Senior Captain."

"A shame, but he died avenging the Imperialists' crime

against Dear Leader," Horangi said, referring to what the North Koreans conceived to be a sneak aerial attack.

"When will we get a chance to strike the American carrier, Comrade Senior Captain?"

"It's up to me, Comrade Senior Lieutenant," Horangi said. "As soon as I am convinced we can sneak through our squadrons and align properly, I shall fire a salvo. If we can get off three or four torpedoes, we can sink the enemy vessel even if their anti-submarine aircraft locate us."

"Dear Leader will be proud of us, Comrade Senior Captain."

"*Chamuro!*" Horangi agreed. "Let us hope that our other comrades can continue to create enough confusion for us to get into a proper attack position."

Viking S-3B

"Carl," Marx said. "We've got another reading. Swing over to 273."

"Jesus Christ!" Dawkins said. "The place must be crawling with North Korean submarines."

"I wonder if anyone else is getting any action," Drew said. "If we're the only one, CDC will move some aircraft over to join us."

Benson interrupted. "I'm getting a good reading on buoy four. Something's woke it up."

Drew checked her instruments. "Make a quick 180."

"Roger that," Dawkins responded. "Just what the hell are we dealing with here? Can you guys figure it out?"

"They're diesel-electric," Marx reported. "Frankly we don't know a hell of a lot about the North Korean Navy, so I can't tell what type. From what I've gathered during past intel briefings, they use a lot of old Soviet stuff in their submarine fleet."

"Man!" Benson exclaimed. "There must be a pod of 'em!"

"A pod?" the other three asked in unison.

"Like whales, godamn it!" Benson snapped. "God! It means a herd or flock. Don't you fucking officers know nothing?"

"I know a fucking petty officer that's going to know what

the inside of a brig looks like for disrespect to officers," Marx retorted.

Dawkins laughed. "When I turn in my after-action report, I'll put in it that we killed two or three pods of submarines."

"Two contacts!" Benson said. "Can't get both, but we can get at least one. Attack!"

Dawkins kicked off another Mk-50, glad to feel the aircraft leveling. He could take off some of the trim he'd been using.

"It's homing," Drew informed the others.

"Explosion!" Marx yelled.

Down below, forty-five meters beneath the surface, one of the *Romeo* class North Korean subs took a hit just abaft of the control tower. The detonation of torpedo and submarine ripped the boat apart, sending concussion waves through the water that rocked another of the underwater vessels a kilometer away.

"I got another boat down there buzzing the buoys," Benson said, as matter-of-factly as if knocking out submarine after submarine was a daily occurrence. "You'll have to make another 180."

"You call, I haul," Dawkins said, making a sharp turn that almost put the Viking on its side.

"Contact!" Marx said. "A good one! Attack!"

Dawkins loosed the third of the four Mk-50s, and swung out wide before going back over the area. He had no sooner leveled out then the sea boiled beneath them. This time the bow of the sub broke out of the waves, hesitated, then slid back.

"Hat trick," Benson crowed. "Just like in hockey. We scored three goals."

North Korean submarine Sango

The boat rocked violently, and Senior Captain Horangi looked inquisitively over to his sonar chief petty officer. The man's face was strained with a combination of fear and alarm. "Two of our comrades have been hit! Both are breaking up and going to the bottom!"

"Where away?" Horangi asked, thinking the latest enemy strikes added up to a total of three losses.

"280, Comrade Senior Captain," the chief petty officer replied.

"Comrade Helmsman!" Horangi barked. "Set a course for 280. Flank speed."

The sub creaked from the rapid maneuver and the crew held on to escape the centrifugal force the movement generated. When they were on course, Horangi went over to the navigator for a final check of their position.

"Prepare four forward tubes for firing!" Horangi ordered.

The torpedomen in the bow had everything prepared for the expected order. In fifteen minutes the underwater missiles were in their tubes and prepared for firing. The chief got on the intercom. "Tubes one, two, three, and four ready, Comrade Senior Captain."

"Periscope depth!" Horangi ordered.

The instant they had reached ten meters, he ordered the cylindrical instrument raised. He peered through the lens and found an excellent three-quarters view off the port quarter of the USS *Lincoln*. The range was a bit more than five thousand meters. Horangi wanted to get closer, and fought the temptation to send out a quick spread of torpedoes, then dive and run. He knew it was only a matter of short minutes before discovery. He forced himself to count slowly; *yol, ahop, yodol, ilgop, yosot, tasot, net, set, tul, hana*—

"Fire one!" he screamed so loud the sonarman could hear him over the loud pinging in his earphones. "Fire two! Fire three! Fire four!" Then he turned from the periscope. "Periscope down! Dive! Dive! Dive!"

USS Lincoln
Bridge

Captain Ted Manners received the word of four incoming torpedoes in a calm manner. Some on the bridge were to say later that he acted with the same calmness he showed during normal maneuvering. He watched the radar repeater for the exact direction of the attack. In one instant he considered what would happen with a sharp turn to starboard or a sharp turn to port.

"Hard left rudder," he ordered in a calm voice. "Port engine all back. Starboard engine ahead full."

It took the *Lincoln* a bit of time to organize herself, but when she began the maneuver, she did it in a slow but sure manner, gaining speed with each passing second. The torpedoes continued their course, closing in rapidly. The number one, the farthest to port of the spread, streaked through the waves. If the ordnance had been a generation younger, they might have honed in on the ship's hull, but these weren't the best in the old Soviet arsenal. The Russians always had a sense of acute uneasiness about their North Korean comrades, and their military aid program was not as complete as it could have been. The most reliable ordnance was not issued to the volatile Communist nation out of fear it would be used in some reckless adventure.

The number one torpedo struck the *Lincoln* just below the waterline, failed to explode, bounced off and turned outward to run off into empty ocean space. The other three missed completely.

Viking S-3B

"Well! We have one torpedo left over," Dawkins said. They had received the word to return to the carrier a few minutes before.

"Yeah but we sure as hell batted a thousand with the three we used," Benson said, happier than he had been since the day he joined the United States Navy. "Maybe we'll get a medal, hey, guys?"

"I thought we were just a bunch of fucking officers," Lieutenant J. G. Elaine Drew said. "Why would you want to share medals with the likes of us?"

"I get a little irritable sometimes," Benson said defensively.

"If you want to make a court-martial offense out of it, go ahead. Drag my enlisted ass to a captain's mast."

"Yeah," Marx said. "That'd be a great idea, right? We bring charges against a SENSO for calling us *fucking officers* during a time he was instrumental in sinking three enemy submarines."

"Especially when the term he used has been instinctively uttered by ratings since the Peloponnesian Navy first set sail a few thousand years before the birth of Christ," Dawkins said.

"That's right!" Benson said. "It's tradition, by God." Both Marx and Drew gave him dirty looks. He treated them to a crooked half grin. "But I'll never use it again. I promise."

"Rig for landing," Dawkins said. "We're going into the race-track to run a few laps before they call us in."

CHAPTER NINETEEN

United States Capitol building
Washington, D.C.
0900 local (GMT −5)

Rear Admiral Thomas Magruder, U.S.N., Retired, ascended the Capitol steps in quick, determined strides. His appointed counsel William Kappellmann, although fifteen years younger, had trouble keeping up with the old sailor. The Justice Department lawyer grimly held on to his briefcase and forced himself to keep up with the demanding pace.

The representatives of the press had shown up at the entrance of the famous building earlier that morning. They quickly caught sight of the pair and turned camera lenses and microphones their way. Magruder, hatless and wearing a conservative gray suit, showed a positive smile as the mob descended on them. Kappellmann assumed the look of the confident attorney with a client innocent of all crimes and sins.

An eager young journalist called out, "What about the cover-up, Admiral? Why did you do it?"

Magruder started to reply, but Kappellmann interrupted him. "We have absolutely no comments to make at this time, ladies and gentlemen, other than to inform you that Admiral

Magruder will answer *all* questions put to him by the House Committee on Public Safety and Security. He has done no wrong and has nothing to hide. Thank you."

"What about *our* questions?" an irritated representative from a tabloid demanded to know.

"Are you gonna plead the Fifth?" a reporter from a New York newspaper inquired.

Kappellmann said, "We have no comments. Thank you." As a government lawyer he had dealt with persistent reporters on numerous occasions. He learned long ago not to be confrontational with them.

A young lady shrilled, "Admiral Magruder, is there a conspiracy between you and the FBI?"

"No comment!" Kappellmann insisted as they pushed their way through the prying throng. "The admiral is going to have his day in court as guaranteed by the United States Constitution."

When they reached the landing, Magruder saw Pamela Drake standing just inside the door. He looked at her as if slightly amused as he came to an abrupt halt in front of her. "Why aren't you with your colleagues outside shouting questions, Pamela? Surely you don't expect a private interview with me. Or do you?"

Drake smiled. "I have a subpoena, too, Admiral. You and I are both going to face the House Committee on Public Safety and Security to answer questions."

"Well, Pamela, I'm honored," Magruder said. "You and I are among the first witnesses called by that new committee. They really didn't have much to do until your broadcast. I'm sure the congressmen are grateful to you for focusing attention them."

"That's the result of good, informative journalism," she said. "I'm honored as well. It'll just be you and me today."

"Nope," Magruder said. "There's another one."

Drake frowned. "Who?"

Kappellmann took the admiral's arm and quickly led him past her. They walked down the hall and met another barrage of questions from more waiting journalists. Once more the

admiral and attorney ignored the shouted inquiries, going
straight into the hearing chamber. An officer of the Capitol Police opened the door for them, keeping the preying members of
the media at bay.

The select audience turned as the pair entered, eyeing the admiral who had been featured on every TV news show aired over
that previous weekend. Additionally, commentators, pundits,
and talk-show hosts had quickly responded to Pamela Drake's
broadcast, enjoying hours of speculation and opining about the
news story she had broken over ACN's weekend show.

Another policeman stood at the double doors of the bar
that impeded entrance to the witness table just beyond. He
motioned to Magruder and Kappellmann to take seats in the
front row on the right side. The pair sat down, and the lawyer
turned his attention to his briefcase, opening it to peer at the
documents inside to make a last-minute check.

A couple of minutes later Pamela Drake came into the chamber. The officer motioned to her and pointed to the front row on
the opposite side of Magruder and Kappellmann. She walked to
an open seat and sat down. When she glanced to the left, she
almost jumped to her feet. Sheriff D. W. Doss of Joseph County,
Idaho, grinned at her and waved. Suddenly Drake wished she
had taken advantage of her boss's offer of an attorney. She nodded to Doss, then quickly turned away. If she'd had no problem
manipulating statements from him, then government officials
wouldn't, either. A cold feeling ran through her as she sensed
trouble.

"Come to order, please!" a police officer ordered politely,
interrupting the conversations going on in the crowd. "All
those having business with the House Committee on Public
Safety and Security come forward to be heard."

A door at the right rear of the room opened and three congressmen paraded in. Representative Karl Olson, Democrat
of Minnesota, chairman of the House Committee on Public
Safety and Security, led the way, followed by the two members Representative Billy Tall Elk, Republican of Oklahoma
and Representative Peter Scagnelli, Democrat of New Jersey.

Their entourages of secretaries, interns, and assistants trailed behind them. As soon as the congressmen took their seats, the underlings grabbed chairs along the wall to the rear.

Representative Olson banged his gavel. "This special hearing of the House Committee on Public Safety and Security is hereby called to order." He turned to Scagnelli. "Who is our first witness, Congressman?"

"That would be Admiral Thomas Magruder, United States Navy," Scagnelli replied. "He is represented by counsel from the Justice Department." He nodded to Magruder and Kappellmann. They took the hint and walked through the bar gate to take seats at the witness table.

Olson nodded to the hearing clerk. "You may swear in the Admiral."

Magruder stood up, and the clerk handed him a Bible, saying, "Do you swear to tell the truth, the whole truth, and nothing but the truth, so help you God?"

"I do."

"Sit down, Admiral," Olson said. "How are you today?"

"Fine, thank you, Congressman," Magruder replied.

Olson acknowledged Kappellmann. "Hello, Bill. I see you're all set for the proceedings."

"That I am," Kappellmann replied in cheerful confidence.

"As you've both been previously informed, this gathering today concerns an explosion that occurred at a place called Deer Crossing, Idaho," Representative Olson said. "I understand that you were involved in that unfortunate detonation, were you not, Admiral?"

"I was *not* involved in the detonation," Magruder said. "I came along after the fact, as did the members of my organization."

"Of course," Representative Olson said, irritated. "I didn't wish to imply that you set off the explosives."

"We understand, Congressman," Kappellmann remarked, not wanting the chairman to get upset. "No offense taken."

Olson's full attention was on Magruder. "Does this organization of yours have a name?"

"Not officially," Magruder answered. "We are a task force ordered to deal with illegal activities of various national militia organizations. Our group was formed on a temporary basis by presidential order. I was asked to head up the effort."

Olson referred to some papers in front of him. "Were the members of this task force drawn from government sources, Admiral?"

"Yes, Congressman."

"What government agencies were involved?" Olson asked.

Kappellmann replied, "That is classified information, Congressman."

"Is this classified information covered by the Home Defense Act?" Olson asked.

"This is a question that hasn't been dealt with," Kappellmann said. "But since Admiral Magruder and his people were dealing with a terrorist threat, it may well be."

Olson scowled. "The Home Defense Act was put on the books for the specific purpose of giving law enforcement a certain amount of leeway in monitoring, arresting, and detaining individuals and groups who wish to harm this country by acts of terrorism. Cover-ups of misdeeds by government officials are not protected under that particular umbrella, Counsel."

"I am well aware of the contents of the Home Defense Act," Kappellmann said testily. "And I assure you that I do not take them lightly."

"Is there an FBI agent in your organization by the name of Charles Greenfield?" Olson asked.

"The information is classified, Congressman," Kappellmann repeated.

"I heard his name mentioned in particular as an investigator at the explosion site on ACN during a report given by Pamela Drake," Olson said.

"It is still classified information whether Pamela Drake reported his presence or not," Kappellmann insisted.

"Very well," Olson said. "Admiral Magruder held a news conference in Idaho in which he announced that the explosion of the militia headquarters in Deer Creek, Idaho, was an accident that occurred in the interior of the building. Is that correct, Admiral?"

"Yes," Magruder said. "I did make that announcement."

"I believe that along with some militia members, some innocent people in the town were also killed," Olson said.

"That was also covered in my statement," Magruder said. "Eleven innocent people died, unfortunately, and that included an entire family. At that time we weren't exactly sure of how many people were in the militia house at the time of the explosion."

"That sounds horribly like what happened at Bull Run," Olson said.

"My organization was not present at the Bull Run tragedy," Magruder said. "We had not been appointed yet. And I might add that we were not present at the Deer Crossing tragedy, either."

"Was that an accurate statement you made on television about the source of the explosion?" Olson inquired.

"No," Magruder admitted. "The event occurred from outside the structure."

"Was there one explosion at the site?"

"No, Congressman," Magruder said. "In point of fact, there were four. One on each side of the building."

"When did you learn that fact?" Olson asked.

"At the beginning of the investigation," Magruder said. "My case team figured that out very quickly."

"I see," Olson said. He looked at Scagnelli. "Congressman Scagnelli, do you wish to examine Admiral Magruder?"

"I do," Scagnelli said. He paused a moment to organize his own papers as if they contained very sharp, probing questions that would bring out new, startling information. When he finished, he gave Magruder a steady gaze. "Why did you misrepresent the facts about the number of explosions?"

Magruder grinned inwardly. It was obvious Scagnelli was a lawyer. Only an attorney would use the phrase *misrepresent the facts* rather than the one word *lie*. "We had hoped that by speaking only of one explosion, the culprit or culprits would get the impression that our investigation had been careless or hasty. Then we could continue the scrutiny without alarming our quarry. As a matter of fact, I had planned to announce the case was closed to reinforce this façade, but there's not much point in doing that now."

"Do you have any suspects?" Scagnelli asked.

"No, we do not."

"Is this another ploy to keep from panicking the perpetrators?"

"No it is not. We have no suspects."

"What incident compromised your investigation into the Deer Crossing Explosion, Admiral?" Scagnelli asked, already knowing the answer. "I'm referring to the fact your investigative strategy was undone."

"The broadcast of ACN's *Weekend Video Journal* that included a special report by Pamela Drake revealed our surreptitious tactics," Magruder said.

"So noted," Scagnelli said. He looked at Chairman Olson. "I have no more questions of Admiral Magruder."

"Nor I," Congressman Tall Elk interjected.

"Very well," Olson said, satisfied that Magruder's falsehoods had been brought out into the open. "You are excused, Admiral." He motioned to the Capitol policeman. "We're ready to view the tape of Pamela Drake interviewing Sheriff D. W. Doss."

The room was darkened and the tape played on a large display monitor. The exact presentation given on ACN news was shown three times. When the lights came back up, Olson said, "Call the witness Sheriff D. W. Doss."

Doss, wearing a Western-style suit complete with cowboy hat and boots, left his seat and waited at the bar gate for Magruder and Kappellmann to pass through. Then he walked up to stand behind the chair formerly occupied by the admiral. He was dully sworn in, then he sat down. At this point the questioning was turned over to Congressman Billy Tall Elk.

"Sheriff Doss," Tall Elk said. "What is the jurisdiction of your office?"

"Joseph County, Idaho, sir."

"You are the sheriff of that county?" Tall Elk asked.

"Yes, sir."

"And that jurisdiction includes the town of Deer Crossing?"

"Yes, sir."

"Were you involved in the investigation of the explosion at Deer Crossing on the second of October of this year?"

"I didn't actually investigate it, Congressman," Doss replied. "I was the first local law enforcement officer on the scene after the State Police. I went looking for survivors, but I didn't find none. I could only get into the ruins of the house nearest the highway and there was no way I could dig away the rubble with only my hands. The Idaho State Police had arrived about a half hour earlier, but they hadn't searched for victims."

"Did they instigate an investigation?"

"No, sir. They said that new regulations required they inform the FBI office in Coeur D'Alene about any incident that might have been did by terrorists. And that sure looked exactly like that."

"I imagine it did," Tall Elk said. "Did you stay at the scene long, Sheriff Doss?"

"I stayed the rest o' the day," Doss answered. "I knew all the folks that lived in Deer Crossing, and I was really hoping we'd find 'em alive. But we didn't."

"Do you know when the federal investigators arrived on the scene?"

"Yes, sir. They showed up in the late afternoon. I was still there. And I came back the next day when they started digging around."

"Was one of them named Charles Greenfield?"

Doss nodded. "Yes, sir. I met him there and another one whose name I can't recall right now. But I have it in my notes. Anyhow, I hung around while Agent Greenfield and his crew sifted through ever'thing."

"Was he the one who told you there was actually more than one explosion and that they were all outside the house?" Tall Elk asked.

"Now he didn't really *tell* me personal-like," Doss said. "Actually, I overheard him saying it to another FBI agent."

"And you repeated this during an interview you gave Pamela Drake of ACN, correct?"

"Yes, sir," Doss said. "Nobody informed me to keep things to myself. When Miss Drake asked me about the explosion, I just pointed out there was four instead of one and the stuff had been set around the house."

"And you mentioned Agent Charles Greenfield?"

"Sure I did," Doss said. "I didn't know the federal authorities wanted their names kept secret." He frowned. "They should have told us. Hell! There's a half dozen Idaho State Policemen who know about him, too."

"Then the FBI did not tell any of you local law enforcement officers about maintaining silence about the investigation?"

"Not a one of 'em said a thing," Doss said. "I suppose they thought we was just hanging around and wasn't picking up on anything. We may not be big-city detectives, Congressman, but we sure as hell ain't a bunch of dumb hicks, either. We keep our eyes and ears open. We listen and we take notes. We're just as professional as New York, Los Angeles or any other large law enforcement organization."

"I'm certain you are," Tall Elk said. "I'm from a small town in Oklahoma, and our law enforcement folks serve us well." He looked to Congressman Olson. "I'm finished with the sheriff."

"Alright, Congressman," Olson said. He nodded to Scagnelli. "Do you have any further questions for Sheriff Doss? No?" He nodded to the Idaho lawman. "You're dismissed, Sheriff. We thank you for you testimony."

"Glad to be of service, Congressman," Doss said, standing up.

"Call Pamela Drake!"

Drake smiled her best on-camera smile as she came forward to be sworn in and seated. When she settled in behind the microphone, she was the picture of calm self-assurance.

"Miss Drake," Olson began, "we wish to ask you several

questions regarding your presentation on television Saturday night."

"Of course, Congressman," Drake said. "I'd be most happy to cooperate."

Congressman Tall Elk of Oklahoma once again took over the proceedings. "When you interviewed the sheriff, did you realize you had stumbled on to classified material involving the investigation?"

"Why of course not, Congressman Tall Elk," Drake said. "I was under the impression that if there were any restrictions about revealing information, that the sheriff would be fully cognizant of them."

"Did you *think* there might be some problems with security in that interview?"

"Certainly not," Drake said. "Why should I have?"

"Did you make any early inquiries to the FBI or Admiral Magruder about the story you were planning on airing?" Tall Elk asked.

"I'm afraid that Admiral Magruder has not always been cooperative with me," Drake said. "It is my firm belief that whether the interview contained classified material or not, he would squelch it."

"Then you considered the possibility?" Tall Elk persisted.

"As I stated before, I was certain that Sheriff Doss would not compromise any secrets about the explosion."

"Why did you feel it necessary to get the name of the FBI agent who let slip the information about the true source of the explosions?"

"That's good journalism," Drake said almost serenely. "One gets all the information available in order to present a more complete story."

"But was it necessary to air that agent's name?"

"Of course," Drake said. "He is well-known as the man in charge of the tragedy that occurred at Bull Run in Idaho. An innocent farmer and his family were killed. The public has a right to have the full information on an incident that was connected with another similar occurrence." Drake also remembered the name of A. J. Bratton, but her initial inquiries had failed to find any information on him. She thought it best not to bring him up at the hearing.

Tall Elk scowled. "You don't seem to regret having caused harm to an official investigation, Ms. Drake."

"I obtained the information legally and aboveboard, Congressman," Drake said. "Of course, I'm sorry if my broadcast put a damper on things." But her mind said, *tough shit*!

Tall Elk leaned back in his chair. "I have no more questions of this witness."

Olson gestured to Scagnelli. "Any questions, Congressman?" When he shook his head, Olson dismissed Drake, announcing, "This session of the House Committee on Public Safety and Security is closed."

CHAPTER TWENTY

Park Beach residence
Chongjin, North Korea
1900 local (GMT +9)

The wind off the Sea of Japan was damp and chilly, penetrating the heavy civilian clothing worn by the trio of high-ranking officers. They stood close together, looking seaward from the beach. The trio was dressed in a manner that would have been ludicrous outside of North Korea. Out of style overcoats from Czechoslovakia, running shoes, expensive slacks from France, and a combination of headgear made up of a Russian fur cap, a hunting cap complete with bill and earflaps, and an American Stetson with the brim pulled down made up the attire.

Up above the garishly dressed men, was the sprawling home of Admiral Park Sung of the DPNK Submarine Service. His companions Colonel General Kim Sung Chien and Lieutenant General Dai Yong were his guests for the evening. The dinner, that had been preceded by a long cocktail hour, had been finished a half hour before. Another protracted period of drinking followed before they decided to go outside. They were not in need of fresh air; instead they wished to avoid the recording devices in the house. Now on the cold beach, each sipped from an individual fifth of scotch whiskey as they stared out at the nothingness of the night seascape. Their shivering was as much from fear as it was from the frigid weather.

Park broke the silence with a low-toned but sharp critical remark directed toward Dai, the Air Force general. "The air above my boats swarmed with American antisubmarine aircraft." This, out of the sound of those damning recording devices, launched the meeting that was behind the evening's activities. "My brave crews fought valiantly, but half of them are at the bottom of this very ocean we now look out upon."

"You yourself stated the casualty rate would be high," Dai retorted.

"But I expected to have some protection!" Park snapped. "As it was, there was not one of your airplanes attacking the Imperialists as they leisurely homed in on our submarines and dropped their torpedoes."

"Speaking of torpedoes," Dai said, "it would have been of great benefit to us if your vaunted submarine captains had fired a few at the American carrier. That rather large problem would have been taken care of quite handily."

"My best submarine did exactly that," Park said. "Senior Captain Horangi, the premier commander in our fleet, loosed a spread that evidently missed. Unfortunately, because of pressure from the Americans, he had no time or opportunity to launch another attack. He had to dive deep and, even after taking that precaution, he barely avoided being discovered."

"I lost nine aircraft on Friday last," Dai protested. "We were forced to reconsider our tactics."

Kim who had been glumly listening to the exchange, turned to his coconspirators. "*Noknok!* This is not the time to throw accusations about. We must coordinate our efforts, and that can only be done by maintaining open communication between us."

"What do you mean?" Dai asked. "We are communicating right now, *anio*?"

Kim scowled at the Air Force general. "You should have told Comrade Park that you would be unable to fly on Monday."

"Yes!" Park agreed.

"How could I?" Dai argued. "We cannot openly discuss tactical problems! Such conduct would betray our plans to government spies. You must keep in mind that at this time Dear Leader in Pyongyang thinks the Americans attacked *us*! Not the other way around. That is why we must be victorious when the truth comes out."

"If this fails," Park said, "we will be lucky if we are only sent to a labor camp."

"Forget labor camps," Kim said. "If our noble plan is discovered before a satisfactory completion, we will be shot."

"Think of what will happen to our families," Park said.

A picture floated through Dai's mind. It was his homely, dull-witted wife in a labor camp rice paddy, spreading human feces for fertilization as she waded through the fetid, muddy water. He almost smiled. Then another mental image suddenly replaced the first. It was a mass grave in which his bullet-pocked corpse was rotting with those of Park and Kim.

Kim took a big swallow of scotch. "Let us not dwell on negative thoughts of the future, Comrades. There is an immediacy that must be employed in this situation. Comrade Park has lost a lot of submarines, and he will not be able to redeploy the survivors unless he is given a firm assurance of aerial protection. It would be a useless effort unless the American planes are destroyed."

"That is absolutely correct!" Park proclaimed.

Kim continued, "Additionally, I have many troops on the DMZ waiting for the opportunity to launch an attack that will carry them down our beloved peninsula to the southern end. The situation in that area is growing more difficult with every passing day. There are motorized infantry, tanks, artillery, and support troops crammed into an area that can barely support them. They will not be able to tolerate this condition longer than three more days before the situation in the bunkers and tunnels becomes insufferable. But I dare not order them into action until I can be certain that carrier-based American Navy aircraft will not be able to strike them from the rear." He turned and faced

Dai. "You must get your airplanes back into the air. Now, Comrade! *Ije!*"

Dai was slightly drunk. "What do you think I have been doing, Comrade Colonel General? I have reorganized my regiments to launch a full-scale attack on the carrier *Lincoln* with enough MiG-21s and MiG-29s to blanket that part of the Sea of Japan."

Kim was skeptical and worried. "If you fail, Comrade Dai, it will be the end of us as Comrade Park has already pointed out. We will get no second chance."

"I know this well!" Dai said. "Do you think I wish to be dragged out and shot?"

"But what if you fail?" Park asked, frightened.

"I will not fail! Damn it all!"

Park reached out and grasped Kim by the sleeve. "What if he fails, Comrade Kim? Can we cover ourselves? Is it possible to cast the blame away from us? What about the Chinese *sochuldul*? Could we not put the culpability on them?"

Dai glared at him. "I would have thought a submariner braver than that! You are a reactionary, Comrade Park! Do you wish to crawl back to our previous status with the Chinese humiliating us?"

"They were not humiliating *me*!" Park protested. "Dear Leader sent none of them to the People's Navy." Now he was angry. "And I will not stand for you to insult the Submarine Service!"

"I was not insulting the *Chamsuham Him*," Dai said in slurred words. "I was insulting *you*!"

Park, staggering a bit, dropped his bottle and assumed a karate fighting pose. "You filthy *sochul*! Let's see just how brave an airplane pilot is when it comes to hand-to-hand fighting with a submariner!"

"*Kidarida!* Wait!" Kim yelled in a tone of supplication and anger. "We are all upset and drunk. Very drunk. Let us pause and take deep breaths."

Dai, who was also ready to launch a karate attack, dropped his arms to his sides. Park did the same, and they began breathing exercises as Kim asked of them. They inhaled deeply, but

Park sucked in air so rapidly, he almost hyperventilated. He staggered backward and fell down. Kim walked over and helped him to his feet.

"Now!" he said. "Listen, Comrades. We must very carefully plan the next few days." He put a hand on Dai's shoulder in a fatherly way. "When will you be able to launch this overwhelming attack you have spoken of?"

"Orders have already been issued, Comrade Colonel General Kim Sung Chien," he said in a tone of determination. "I have not just been sitting around on my hands. Tomorrow morning, just before dawn, all the fighters under my command will begin the new operation. Waves of fighter regiments and squadrons will come at the USS *Lincoln* from four sides. These sorties will begin at fifteen minute intervals to confuse the Imperialists. Every comrade pilot is fully briefed, and all have sworn to fight to the death."

Kim was impressed. "Did they swear this oath on photographs of Dear Leader?"

"That is exactly what they did," Dai said. He sneered at Park. "We have not been sitting around crying because we took a drubbing. The People's Air Force is made of sterner stuff! We quickly re-formed and took on a new strategy for knocking the Yankee airplanes from the sky."

Now Park was angry again. "Are you implying that the submariners of the Democratic Peoples Republic of Korea have been cringing and weeping with fear?"

"No!" Dai said. "Just *you*!"

Now Park was back in the fighting position, ready to settle the matter with hands and feet. Kim grabbed the admiral and shook him until he relaxed and stood up straight. Then Kim glared at Dai. "You must be more polite, Comrade Dai! We cannot win with petty bickering!"

Dai, wavering on his feet, nodded his head and bowed. "I apologize, Comrade Park. Forgive me."

"Ah!" Park said in disgust.

"Give him your pardon, Comrade Park!" Kim snapped.

Park bowed, saying, "I accept your apology, Comrade Dai."

"Hullyung ham!" Kim said. "Now, Comrade Dai, how soon

do you think the situation in the sky will be secure enough
so that Comrade Park can command his submarines to go out
again and attack the carrier?"

"Within an hour of our launching the attack," Dai said.

"Very well," Kim said. "When that hour is reached, or if
you feel the opportunity has arisen earlier, you will broadcast
the code words Lion Heart—*Saja Simjang*—three times to
Comrade Park."

"I understand," Dai assured him.

"Now, Comrade Park," Kim said, "upon receiving the two
words, you will send your submarines out to attack the carrier.
The sooner you can neutralize the vessel the better. If the
American naval aircraft have no carrier to return to, they will
have to fly to Japan or South Korea. Either way, they will not
be able to attack my soldiers from the rear when they cross
the DMZ."

"I also understand what is wanted of me," Park said.

Dai added, "Another advantage to us if the *Lincoln* is sunk
is that the naval aircraft will have to withdraw from the fight
because they will not be able to return there for rearming and
refueling because there will not be enough fuel or ammunition for them at the U.S. Air Force bases."

"And when that happens," Kim continued, "you must broadcast the code words *Saja Simjang* to me. When I have received
the message, I will order an immediate attack across the DMZ
and victory will be ours within seventy-two hours."

Dai, now in a better mood, laughed aloud. "I cannot wait for
the glorious moment when the three of us go to the National
Palace in Pyongyang to present the entire Korean Peninsula to
Dear Leader. Then we will inform him of our clever plan that
brought about such a glorious victory."

"Dear Leader will embrace us!" Kim cried out.

Park picked up the bottle of scotch he had thrown down.
He raised it high, shouting, "I propose a toast."

Kim and Dai lifted their own fifths of liquor.

Park yelled out, "To the new and mightier People's Democratic Republic of Korea!"

"Sungni!" Kim bellowed. "Victory!"

Magruder's headquarters
Lands End, Idaho

FBI Agent Charlie Greenfield was contrite and apologetic. "I feel like such a fucking idiot."

Admiral Thomas Magruder looked across the kitchen table where he sat with Greenfield and A. J. Bratton in the former militia fortification. The old Navy man, who had regretted a few rash and careless actions of his own in the past, was genuinely sympathetic. "Stop kicking yourself, Charlie. It's all over and done with."

Greenfield could not be comforted. "It was like those words 'loose lips sink ships' on those old World War II posters. I was talking my head off while local law enforcement people were within hearing. Especially that Sheriff Doss. I remember the guy. He wasn't doing much except wandering around the site. I stopped paying attention to him when I realized that he was being careful and not contaminating the area."

Bratton smirked. "You had your head up your ass, Greenfield."

"Shut your fucking mouth, Bratton!" Greenfield snapped.

"You watch the way you talk to me, you arrogant son of a bitch!"

"I've just starting talking to you," Greenfield said. "And I'm not going to mince words during the conversation." He paused, then deliberately asked, "How did you get it done?"

"Get what done?" Bratton asked.

"The explosions," Greenfield said. "Those four fucking explosions at the militia safe house."

"Jesus!" Bratton exclaimed angrily. "You just shoved your head back up your ass again, FBI guy. That was obviously pulled off by a rival militia group."

"There are no effective militia groups, either rivals or confederates of the Deer Crossing bunch," Greenfield said. "They've been reduced to little splinter groups trying to figure out how to stay out of sight and out of mind."

"Hang on now, both of you," Magruder said. "Charlie, have you conducted an investigation on your own?"

"Yes, sir," Greenfield replied. "We've determined that the explosion was caused by MS Tetrytol blocks. This little goodie comes sixteen to a box. This is not the sort of explosive employed by terrorists. In fact, it is not considered all that useful by the U.S. Army Corps of Engineers. It is only rated as fair as a cratering charge, and gives off concentrated, dangerous fumes following detonation."

Bratton shrugged. "So what?"

"We were able to gather up enough wooden splinters and bits from the boxes to figure out a partial serial number," Greenfield said. "M.S.T. 120 dash something, something 04. But that was enough for us to find out it was manufactured in 1962 by Du-Bose Chemicals in their Ralston, South Carolina plant."

"I doubt if stuff that old would be stable," Bratton said.

"It would take experts to handle it," Greenfield admitted. "At any rate, it went from the factory to the United States Army's Special Warfare Center at Fort Bragg, North Carolina. From there it was shipped to Vietnam in 1965 where it was subsequently transferred to Air America for operations in Laos. It was to be used for the construction of airstrips in jungle areas."

"Okay," Bratton said. "And Air America was part of the CIA. Big deal. But if the stuff wasn't the best for cratering, why send it for the construction of airstrips? In fact, why use the stuff at all?"

"Probably because the best explosives were needed in Vietnam," Greenfield suggested. "I don't know. But the fact is that it was in Laos and in the hands of the CIA, and was never heard of again. At least there was no paper trail. Then we discovered it at Deer Crossing, Idaho."

Magruder turned a suspicious look straight into Bratton's face. "What about it, A. J.? Did the CIA decide to take action to wrap up our militia adventure on its own?"

"Of course not," Bratton said. "This is speculation pure and simple."

"It sounds pretty damned logical to me," Magruder said. "How else could an explosive owned by the CIA in Southeast Asia end up in Deer Crossing, Idaho?"

"I'm telling you we didn't have anything to do with the explosions at Deer Crossing," Bratton insisted.

Magruder stood up. "This is most definitely not the end of this episode. I'm reporting back to the President, and if you or any of your pals are behind these detonations that killed eleven innocent people along with our star witness, there is going to be one hell of a price to pay." He walked from the door toward his office, then turned around for a final word. "This is worse than Ruby Ridge or Bull Run."

Again, Bratton shrugged.

CHAPTER TWENTY-ONE

USS Lincoln
Sea of Japan
Tuesday, 8 October

The replenishment crews of the combat support ship USS *Wichita* and the USS *Lincoln* had spent several muscle-cramping hours replenishing the carrier's badly depleted fuel and ammunition inventories. These specially assigned sailors, distinguished by their green jerseys and white cranials, did not work in an environment as dangerous as the flight-deck crews, but there were risks just the same. A snapped cable could whip around and take off somebody's head, cargo could fall with a crushing weight on an unwary seaman, or a net might swing around and knock some unfortunate crewman overboard.

This operation was an unscheduled, additional replenishment that was welcomed by the entire carrier complement. That day's replenishment was the result of multiechelon coordination. It all began when the President of the United States issued vocal orders via a telecom to the Chief of Naval Operations. The CNO immediately contacted the Commander of the Naval Supply Systems Command. This lady wasted no time in passing the word to her subordinate organization that served the area encompassing the Sea of Japan. It took only these three calls to get some very important administrative wheels running at full speed in an operation in which no delays or mismanagement would be tolerated. The amount of goods brought in was well above and beyond that of normal resupply since for all intents and purposes the USS *Lincoln* was in a newly declared war zone.

The ideal condition for this restocking activity would be within a sheltered body of water such as a bay or harbor out of the potential disturbance of wind and waves. Unfortunately, the *Lincoln* could not be taken off station since heading for a friendly port would leave the Sea of Japan unprotected and open to the return of unfriendly vessels. The Japanese prime minister was contacted with a request to provide ships from his country's Maritime Self-Defense Force to cover the Sea of Japan. However, the Japanese government was not completely convinced the United States was in the right regarding this latest conflict with North Korea. They politely declined to provide any aide. "*Sumi-masen*—so sorry!" Thus, the replenishment operation had to be done while under way.

The *Wichita* came up alongside the carrier, matching its heading and speed exactly. When the time was right, a rig transfer was set up by shooting a line from one vessel to the other. A one-inch jackstay was attached to the line and a pulley arrangement called a travel block was hooked on. This travel block held a cargo net in which the goods being transferred from the *Wichita* to the *Lincoln* would be carried. In this case a winch was used to pull the net along the line. As much as 1.5 tons of cargo could be brought aboard at one time. But the first items transported were not supplies. The fuel lines needed to pump JP-5 aviation fuel and oil were the priority one order of business, thus were passed over first. Not until that most important task was completed, would the workcrews concentrate on getting food, stores, and other items transferred.

While all this was going on, the bridges in both ships were filled with busy people keeping tabs on the sea and weather conditions, to make sure nothing untoward happened. An unexpected, sudden shift in wind or current would cause a calamitous collision between the vessels. Further precautions of another nature were also taken. Rather than chance being electronically tracked or monitored by any prowling North Korean aerial patrols, all communication between the carrier and the replenishment ship was done with flag signals.

The resupply was beneficial for much more than the *Lincoln*'s ability to fight. The collective morale of the crew soared to heights that seemed unimaginable in previous days. Although their heavy workload went on unabated, the sailors and airmen really felt that someone out there cared about them. That former sensation of isolation was swept away by the traveling cargo nets that brought work material and a few comfort items as well.

With the aircraft fuel topped off to an abundant wartime-footing level, Lieutenant Commander Gene "High Roller" Erickson was able to organize his experimental flight per Admiral Collier's personal orders. He also took them out on several training sorties where they could hone their coordination and methodology. His squadron leader raised hell about having four pilots and two RIOs pulled from his operations, but the admiral would hear no arguments.

Erickson's Alpha Team consisted of him in his F/A-18E, and Lieutenant Charlie "Tight Lips" Fredericks with RIO Lieutenant J.G. Merlin "Magic" Donovan as his wing backup in the F/A-18F that had been formerly flown by Erickson's absent roommate.

Lieutenant Benny "Peanut" Lemmons led Bravo Team with Lieutenant Stan "Scat Man" Tailor and Lieutenant J.G. RIO Pete "Dodger" Callahan flying on his wing in their two-seater. Because the RIOs were Donovan and Callahan, they were called the Irishmen, and the name became a sobriquet for the backseat men.

In actuality, the group's training flights were also serious patrols in case of another attack by the North Koreans. They had to use a simulated enemy because no other aircraft could be spared to act as their adversaries. The only thing Erickson could do was form and re-form into different formations as they dove, climbed, and turned to develop the flying procedures they would need in meeting various enemy combat formations. Unfortunately they would have to work up to their maximum abilities and teamwork during actual combat. In that case, things could get hairy while they were trying to get the kinks out of their procedures. Bad decisions and worse luck would mean lost aircraft and crews.

As the flight training continued with launches, sorties, and landings, the entire crew of the *Lincoln,* from bridge to engine room, referred to this experimental unit as the High Roller Flight after Erickson's call sign.

High Roller Flight
Wednesday, 9 October
0645 local (GMT +9)

The flight was on a fighter sweep operation a bit more than twenty miles to the north-northeast of the *Lincoln.* Their mission that day was typical for a sweep; they were to engage any enemy targets of opportunity that came their way. They were doing what fighter crews do best, i.e., looking out for trouble.

Both teams were in one of Erickson's favorite formations. This was the German *Schwarm* in a Finger Four designation. Fredericks and Donovan flew to his immediate left rear in the Alpha Team portion of the formation. Bravo Team's Lemmons was to Erickson's right rear, flying parallel with Fredericks, while Tailor and Callahan were to Lemmons's right rear as Tail-End Charlies. They flew in a tight, orderly formation for nearly a half hour before the day's work really began.

"We've got bogies at eleven o'clock ahead," Donovan announced, breaking in to the radio silence.

"Right," Erickson came back. "I got 'em."

Callahan chimed in with, "I count nine—ten—there's twelve!"

"Maintain formation," Erickson ordered, "and let's turn straight at 'em."

The flight swung slightly until they were dead-on to the rapidly approaching enemy aircraft. The bogies were in an unorganized cluster, and from their actions they had also spotted the Super Hornets.

"Okay," Erickson said. "My IFF isn't making any squawks. Volley from formation. 120s. Lock and fire."

This was one of his unique combat orders that meant for each pilot to select a target to his direct front, lock on it, and fire as quickly as possible. He wanted to use the longer-reaching AIM-120s. Their maximum 45-mile range far outclassed the ten miles of the AIM-9M Sidewinders.

Four of the missiles streaked outward, wobbling a bit like snakes trying to zero in on prey. Within short seconds all were locked solidly on four North Korean aircraft. After another couple of beats, distant explosions gave evidence of quick death as did the abrupt disappearance of the victims' blips on radar.

"Divide and conquer!" Erickson said tersely. "To the right!"

These words indicated they were going to get the enemy to split off in two directions, then they would concentrate on one of the groups. In this instance, it would be the one on the right.

"Execute—now!" Erickson ordered.

He and Fredericks broke to the left while Lemmons and Tailor went right. The North Koreans, obviously not well coordinated, broke into two groups. Five went after the Alpha Team while three headed for the Bravos.

"Alpha break!" Erickson said.

He and Fredericks reversed their direction and headed after the three chasing the Bravos. Lemmons and Tailor turned outward to bring their pursuers in closer to the Alphas. Now the hapless North Koreans were between the two groups of High Rollers. In less than a minute both Erickson and Fredericks had loosed AIM-9s. They each got one, then Fredericks had time to kick out another to get the third.

Donovan, monitoring his radar in the backseat, announced, "Five bandits have turned and are coming our way from three o'clock."

"We're locked on!" Callahan said. "My RWR is blinking!" His pilot, Tailor, immediately went into evasive action, kicking out chaff and flares.

The other three Super Hornets continued after the attackers, loosing three AIM-120s. A trio of the North Koreans turned into fiery balls while the two survivors suddenly broke and fled the scene.

"We're back!" Tailor announced.

Erickson and Lemmons were already on the nervous Nellies trying to break contact, and blew them out of the sky within sixty seconds. Magic Donovan announced, "The radar screen is empty."

"Concur," Dodger Callahan chimed in.

"Form up and let's get back on the sweep vector," Erickson said. "Where away, Magic?"

"Turn to zero-four-eight," Donovan replied.

As Erickson began the turn to the correct azimuth, he quickly ran the dogfight through his mind. "Hey," he said. "Those were all MiG-21s, right?"

"Affirmative," Dodger Callahan replied.

"Those bastards must be holding back on the 29s," Erickson remarked thoughtfully. "They'll be using them for the big punch."

"Prob'ly," Lemmons said unconcerned. He didn't give a damn whether he faced MiGs or Sukhois. The aviator wanted action.

Erickson sank back into the random access memory of his brain and mentally stacked the MiG-21 against the MiG-29. The 21 had a maximum speed of 1,385 miles per hour, a range of 721 miles, a service ceiling of 57,000 feet and could tote some 3,000 pounds of munitions. And the MiG-29's top speed was 1,430 miles per hour, its range 932 miles, with a service ceiling of 55,774 feet, and an ability to carry over 9,000 pounds of weaponry in addition to a larger cannon. Thus, the MiG-29 could go farther and faster, but not quite as high. But it evidently had three times the punch of the MiG-21 when it came to ordnance delivery on target.

"I'm going to tell you something, guys," Erickson said.

"When the 29s come out, things are going to get real rough up here."

Tomcat fighter sweep

"My God!" Lieutenant Glenda Simmons, RIO in Lieutenant Commander Loopy Johnson's aircraft, said over the earphones in her boss's helmet.

Johnson's eyes immediately went to his radar. "We do have bogies out there don't we, Simmons?" He raised his wingman. "You guys see what we see?"

"Affirmative," Lieutenant Skank Healey replied.

His RIO Steve Montana interjected, "There's ten blips dancing out there in front of us."

"Hey, Loopy," Healey said, "here's a chance to catch up on the Hornets' score."

"You're right," Johnson agreed.

"We're ready to cover your ass anytime you want to move in," Healy said.

"Well, as our cousins in the RAF say, 'Talley ho, chaps!' " Johnson said.

The two-aircraft formation of F-14s cut to the left, giving the impression they were vacating that particular part of the Asian sky. The RIOs monitored their screens, giving a running account of the North Korean reactions to their pilots' maneuverings.

"Four of 'em have split off," Simmons reported.

At that point, Johnson made a further turn that led them away from the MiGs. Healey stuck with him, not losing an inch when Johnson whipped into a classic Immelmann with a half-loop followed by an immediate half-roll. Both aircraft got their locks and kicked loose an AIM-120 each. They locked on the two survivors and again fired. The remainder of the MiG-21s broke contact.

"The sky is clear," Lieutenant Glenda Simmons reported.

USS Lincoln
Combat Direction Center

Rear Admiral James Collier studied the radar displays to his direct front. He had taken over the direction of the escalating air battle, and the lower-ranking denizens of the CDC did their best to stay out of his way.

Things actually looked good at that point. So far the carrier's airwing had lost no planes while destroying sixteen of the enemy's. The general mood within the center was one of stunned elation. MiGs seemed to be falling from the sky like raindrops. But Admiral Collier had no feelings of optimism. He felt the North Koreans had made a probe, sacrificed some expendable aviators, then withdrawn to decide what they were going to do. The *Lincoln* had a total of forty-eight aircraft—36 F/A-18s and 12 F-14s. A squadron of the Super Hornets were out there along with four F-14s. That left thirty-two aircraft on board. Collier didn't like the number of North Koreans who had shown up for the day's fiery activities. He gestured to Commander Doug Hawkins.

"Get PriFly on the horn and tell them to scramble the rest of the F-14s," the admiral ordered.

"Aye, aye, sir!"

High Roller Flight

High Roller Erickson got a call from Checkers. This was a special call sign that informed all aircraft that they were now under the direct control of Admiral Collier. Erickson gave an immediate response. "This is High Roller."

"Your status looks good on my screen," Colliers said. "What about your contact with the enemy?"

"We've knocked down twelve," Erickson said. "We're still fueled and armed enough for some more action. The bandits seem skittish today."

"Stay on your original sweep," Collier ordered. "Wait!

You've got a bunch of bogies out to your two o'clock. Check 'em out."

"Wilco," Erickson said.

The High Roller Flight turned onto the proper vector. In less than sixty seconds they made contact. FFI indicated they were ten enemy aircraft. "Free-for-all," Erickson announced. "Wingmen, mind your buddy's tail."

With these few words, Erickson had ordered independent action, but wanted the flight to maintain team integrity. He was less than a thousand feet above the enemy formation, and he dived to the left to cut out an aircraft or two for some loving attention. Three MiGs split out then zoomed back to engage. Erickson was glad that Fredericks was hanging back there to keep a watch on his six. He toasted the lead MiG and the second vomited flares and chaff as it made a violent maneuver to escape. The third North Korean was good. He faked following his buddy, then rolled over on his back, dove, and came up behind the two Hornets.

"He's locked on me!" Fredericks shouted.

"Break and dive deep," Erickson ordered.

Fredericks complied, getting out of harm's way. The MiG didn't care since he wanted the lead pilot. He had his sights— and radar—on Erickson. High Roller made a half-roll, continuing straight ahead inverted. After five seconds he went into a half-loop, going straight back at the bogey. He was close enough that an AIM-6 did the trick.

"Good kill!" came Magic Donovan's voice.

"Join up," Erickson said. "Peanut! Where the hell are you?"

"I'm—having—trouble—" His strained voice indicated he was pulling Gs.

"Scat Man!" Erickson said.

"I'm—with—him—" Then his voice came easier. "Okay, High Roller, we've pulled out of it."

"I can see your fucking flares," Erickson said. "It looks like Christmas over there."

"C'mon and join us," Lemmons invited. "The bandits are turning around for another go. There's a half dozen of 'em."

"Tight Lips," Erickson said. "Break off and we'll go on our own. Shoot whatever looks the best to you."

"Roger!"

Within short seconds Erickson could see that the MiGs had been frustrated by Lemmons and Tailor. The North Koreans were coming back in for another try on the Hornets' fours. He kicked the afterburner a bit to pick up some speed, then made a slightly skidding turn that brought him into position. An AIM-6 was sent out. It was joined by another from Fredericks. Luckily, both had fired at different aircraft, and their efforts reduced the six attackers to four. This quartet was now well closed in on Lemmons and Tailor.

"Break turn to your right, Scat Man," Lemmons ordered.

Tailor made the move, and Lemmons went to the left, pushing the stick all the way in that direction before yanking it back. They caught the North Koreans flatfooted, and the Reds now noted the other two Hornets coming after them. They wisely broke off contact, that fifth, last, and sometimes most important phase of air combat.

The High Roller Flight re-formed. Everyone was soaked in sweat and panting with the physical efforts of the dogfight. Erickson took a few moments to catch his breath. "Checkers, this is High Roller," he said into his mike. "We're gonna have to come back for more bullets and gas."

"We'll be waiting for you, High Roller," came back the admiral's reply.

USS **Lincoln**
Combat Direction Center

Admiral James Collier took a noisy slurp of coffee, stepping to the side to allow the regular crew of the CDC to catch up on the work they'd missed while he was in their way.

Commander Doug Hawkins went from station to station to make sure everyone was still settled in and functioning. They had been at their consoles and position boards for many hours and all were stretching arms and rubbing their stiff necks. When he was satisfied everything was squared away, he walked over to join the admiral.

Collier said, "Your people are doing a fine job, Doug."

"Yes, sir," Hawkins said. He poured himself a cup of coffee. "It's pretty obvious our guys are heavily outnumbered up there."

"The screens don't lie," Colliers acknowledged. "They've done phenomenally well, but my gut instincts tell me the North Koreans haven't sent in their best yet. We're outnumbered bad, and if the bastards go kamikaze on us, we could lose all aircraft and the carrier, too."

"What are the chances of getting the Air Force in South Korea to jump in and lend a hand?" Hawkins asked.

Collier showed a humorless smile. "Been there, done that. They can't spare a single aircraft. The whole damned DMZ looks like it's ready to explode. They have their own preset missions to fly if and when that happens."

"I take it you've been talking with Big Dog Robinson," Hawkins surmised.

"Yeah," Collier said. "When I suggested we get a little help from the Air Force he told me he'd already looked into that. Robinson always played to the worst-case scenarios. I'd hoped he could get General Hamm to put a little weight behind the request. But—" The admiral shrugged.

A young ensign, her face determined and businesslike, walked up to the pair of officers. "PriFly reports that all the F-14s are up now, and the first Hornets that went out are now coming back for refueling and rearming. They expect the first Tomcats to follow shortly."

"Thank you," Hawkins said. He looked at the admiral. "That would be High Roller Erickson and his flight coming in with those other Hornets. They've been up to their asses in MiGs."

"They'll be going right back into the fray as soon as they're taken care of," Collier said.

"Yeah," Hawkins said. "I sure wish we could get some help from the Air Force."

F-14 Tomcats

Lieutenant Ski Waleski and his companions were more than happy when the other eight aircraft joined them. The North Koreans had appeared in their sector in heavy strength and made aggressive moves from several different directions. There was only poor coordination between the various enemy flights and squadrons, but that was enough to harass the hell out of the Tomcats. The best that could be done was pure defense.

The MiG-21s loosed R-77 missiles for long-distance work and R-60MKs for closer encounters. Unfortunately, Wee Willy Frederickson and his RIO Ned Peters were blown out of the sky by one of the latter. They had been evading a radar launch from one MiG, but inadvertently caught a heatseeking R-60MK from another. Their aircraft went up in a violent explosion that spewed chunks of debris outward to flutter down to the Sea of Japan far below.

The Tomcat squadron leader Commander Tony "Dawg" Boudreaux made an immediate and accurate judgment of the situation as he led his people into the combat area. Each leadman and wingman would have to work independently from the others. There were just too damn many enemy aircraft to do anything else.

The contest turned into a disorganized melee as the F-14s went to the attack. The small Tomcat force flew in the swarm of North Koreans as a fiery maneuver-and-exchange developed between the opposing forces.

Kim Il Sung Air Base, North Korea

The Chinese Air Force teacher-pilot Colonel Tchang Won may have thought all his instruction fell on deaf ears, but there were a number of fliers in the elite *Pokpungu* (Storm) MiG-29 Brigade who had listened carefully to him and learned to apply the valuable lessons he taught. These quiet, efficient aviators had gone unnoticed by Tchang in the midst of countless mistakes, poor judgment, and unabated arrogance demonstrated by the majority of the class.

Major Yong Do and his close friends Captain Chun Sung and Captain Jung Hwan flew together in the Pokpungu Brigade. All three were special government agents classified as *tukpyolui taeriindul.* Unlike the secret police, they had no power of arrests but could send information straight up to higher authority bypassing normal administrative channels. They had made clandestine notes on those pilots who showed the most aptitude after partaking in Tchang's excellent classes, sending the names to the highest echelons of the People's Air Force. Thus it was easy to gather the best young aviators into a single regiment of the brigade during the initial organization phase.

That meant that the first regiment's thirty-six aircraft were flown by the most dedicated and skilled pilots of the entire People's Air Force. Even the least of these were better than all the others in the second regiment. But the MiG-29s flown by that inferior unit could still deliver a lethal punch through the excellence of their aircraft, which was considered the best fighter in the world in many aviation circles.

Now, with all seventy-two of the Pokpungu Brigade's MiG-29s armed and fueled for action, the pilots stood in six ranks of twelve men each. They had been given their mission orders the night before, and the senior officers had spent most of that day listening to the exchanges of the MiG-21 pilots over their radios during the earlier dogfighting. It was obvious they suffered extremely heavy casualties, but now it was time for the elite Pokpungu to show their stuff.

The brigade commander, an old comrade who no longer flew operationally, had the veteran's ability to appreciate fighting talent when he saw it. He had quickly sized up Major Yong and his squadron as the best of the best. He gave them the honor of leading the attack.

When the order was given, Yong assembled his squadron and they rushed for the dozen aircraft allotted them. Within ten minutes of being scrambled, they were airborne, and heading for the battle out over the sea.

The battle

The North Korean attack formations maintained positions some fifty miles from the Carrier Battle Group. They were not about to fly into a section of the sea where the U.S. Naval Surface Force was located. Even though the Americans were understrength, their guided-missile destroyers and frigates were armed with a very impressive array of ordnance. The only time attacks occurred within that danger zone was when the rolling, swirling air battle stretched into the area. When the North Koreans noted how far into harm's way they had wandered, the flight leaders ordered immediate withdrawals. The PDRK aircraft got back to where they were far enough away that the U.S. Navy's heat- and radar-seeking missiles could not easily sort them out from American planes. The ships had as much chance of hitting their own Super Hornets and Tomcats as the MiGs in the whirling, twisting up-and-down of aerial combat.

When the High Roller Flight rejoined the fray, Commander Ski Waleski and his group—minus Frederickson who had gone down in flames—came back to the carrier to replenish the weaponry loosed at the MiGs. After some cold drinks were delivered to them in the cockpits during rearming and refueling, they went directly to the catapults to be hurled skyward into the man-made hell so high above the sea's surface.

The seamen and airmen who had harbored deep resentment toward the aviators during the numerous alerts and General Quarters, now turned a complete 180 in their assessment of the pilots. Now they were the ones working their asses off, and it appeared as if a hell of a lot of them were going to be killed in the process.

Major Yong Do led his squadron toward the fighting where the MiG-21s were obviously taking a serious beating. The mood of excitement grew in each cockpit as they went through a quintessential, by-the-book process of the phases of air combat as they eased into the battle. First they detected the enemy in the airborne fighting that was no less than an aerial riot. Yong remembered much of Colonel Tchang's teachings as he maneuvered his squadron through the closing phase, going higher to gain the most advantageous position. Then came the attack itself along with further maneuvering to close in and shoot down the other side's airplanes. The final phase of disengagement would not come for another hour.

The MiG-29 regiment swept down in waves of echelons, picking out targets via their radar and IFFs. Within short minutes, they were engaged in dogfights with Tomcats and Super Hornets. The by-the-book formations of leader and wingman disintegrated on both sides as the aerial combat heated up to maximum levels.

High Roller Erickson kicked his F/A-18E into a violent break-turn as he followed a blip on his radar. The target designation circle showed around the signal, and Erickson knew the guy's alarm must be buzzing like a swarm of killer bees gone mad to let him know he was locked on tight. When the pilot took a clumsy turn into the opposite direction, the American took advantage of the sloppy flying to cut inside. An AIM-9 Sidewinder air-to-air missile blew off its station on Erickson's right wing, zipping across the space to collide with the North Korean's tailpipe.

Five miles away, Major Yong Do was having a hell of a time. These American naval aviators were a damn sight better than he had been told. His superiors had informed him they were morally corrupt, drunken reprobates who spent their off-duty hours in government brothels ravishing nonwhite women who had been forced into prostitution. He had never heard of the Top Gun School or the hard-ass simulated dogfights at Naval Air Station Fallon, Nevada, where air wings were put through a rigorous training routine during work-ups prior to going out to fleet operations. Yong was beginning to seriously think that he and his comrades were not superior to or even the equals of the Yankee Imperialists.

But at least he was flying a MiG-29.

Suddenly Yong's radar warning system indicated he had an

aircraft on his six. His rearview mirrors showed fleeting glimpses of what he perceived to be an F-14 Tomcat. The North Korean major went into a split "S", making a half-roll, then pulling back on his stick to half loop into the opposite direction. Unfortunately for him, the Tomcat pilot kept right up with him like they were flying in an airshow formation. Yong slammed into a half-loop again, this time flying inverted back into his original course. The American stayed right with him. The North Korean knew his opponent would be in an excellent firing position within seconds. The Yankee wouldn't even have to use a missile. He could hammer Yong's aircraft with his M61A1 Vulcan Gatling gun. Now the MiG pilot was sweating with stark fear. He was desperate enough to take the only chance left to him.

Yong suddenly reduced his engines and hit the air brakes. At the same time he pulled back on the stick. His aircraft slipped into the Cobra maneuver made famous by Russian pilots in aerial displays. This caught the American aviator unaware and just as he passed over Yong, the North Korean fired a short-range R-60MK heat-guided missile. The Tomcat blew apart just as Yong slipped back into normal forward flight.

The maneuvering had carried him to the fringes of the battle, and he was able to take stock of the situation. As a *tukpyolui taeriin,* he had the authority to make tactical decisions even if they went against his superior officer's order. Yong also had an extra task in addition to flying and fighting. He was to radio the code *Saja Simjang*—Lion Heart—to let it be known the situation had stabilized enough for the North Korean Navy to dispatch its submarines to torpedo the American carrier *Lincoln.* But all his gut instincts told him the situation was not well in hand. In fact, the whole concept and employment of Operation Avenging Dragon now seemed like a blundering misjudgment.

Yong radioed a check-in call for his squadron. Only three out of the eleven pilots he had brought with him responded. He now estimated that the Americans were enjoying a kill ratio of five- or six-to-one against both the MiG-21s and 29s. Something indeed was incredibly wrong and out of the ordinary. The submarines would stand no chance now. Yong switched to the regimental-wide channel.

"Pusojidyo do situldyo!" he radioed. "Break and withdraw!"
The battle was over.

CHAPTER TWENTY-TWO

Pamela Drake had come up empty-handed when it came to getting information on the mysterious and elusive A. J. Bratton. The conventional route of inquiries into the FBI failed to turn up even a minute trace of the guy. The only solid thing she knew about him was that he had been a part of Magruder's organization in the antimilitia campaign. That wasn't much to go on, and would have stymied most people, but to a journalist like Drake the situation was only a minor inconvenience. She shrugged it off and began her usual round of phone calls to round up a few favors owed her—some that had saved more than one misbehaving government official's career by not revealing certain sins and indiscretions—confident that she would have the lowdown on the elusive Mr. Bratton before she went to lunch that day.

What she got was absolutely nothing. Nil. *Nada.* None of those reliable informants could give her an iota of information. It was like A. J. Bratton was either a cover name or he didn't

really exist. The latter consideration was beyond both probability and possibility. Someone somewhere had to know of
him.

Drake was forced to turn to her last resort; and this would
involve personal contact with a weird little guy employed
deep in the musty bowels of ACN's basement archive department.

Marvin Schmedlapp was a short, stoop-shouldered little man
with skinny arms and legs and a potbelly. At the age of fifty-
five he had grown bald, letting the hair around the fringes of
his head grow so long that he looked like a miniature, rumpled
Benjamin Franklin. A bushy moustache grew under his pug
nose, and his watery eyes held a perpetual expression of acute
myopia. People who spoke to him weren't really sure if he
could see them or not.

Marvin was a bachelor living with his aged mother in a
small Georgetown condo. He had worked in ACN's archive
department since his 1969 graduation from Columbia University with a degree in Library Science. His poor physique
and health precluded any worry about the draft or service in
Vietnam, and he immediately launched his career in ACN's
New York office where he established himself as a quiet little
eccentric with an amazing talent for gathering, storing, and
recalling facts. Many times when he was consulted, he could
recall an amazing amount of details about people and incidents that had crossed his desk years before. When the broadcast network began changing over to computers, tapes, and
disks for storage of the knowledge gathered daily by its army
of reporters, Marvin quickly adapted to the new processes.
His computer literacy increased rapidly as did his value to the
network. He was soon transferred down to the Washington
bureau where his dedication to archiving would be invalu-
able. He was placed down in the second basement of the
ACN building with a brand-new computer system installed
especially for him. Part of Marvin's job was entering old
news items into the new system. Some of this intelligence

went all the way back to the first days of broadcast radio in the 1920s. Because he was trained the old-fashioned way in library techniques and filing, the little man felt it was sacrilege to put this historic material into an electronic medium. He fell back on his library training, and set up numerous card files somewhat like the Dewey system used in libraries for decades. Marvin had his own codes and cross-references that only he could decipher. Eventually his various bosses discovered he could access this self-designed system more accurately and fully than the computerized version which suffered badly from the GIGO—Garbage In, Garbage Out—syndrome due to careless journalistic practices by a good number of the staff. Anyone who needed information on past personages or activities was given accurate and complete details from the thousands of cards in Marvin's personal system. All this, bolstered by the little fellow's fantastic photographic memory, made for a fail-safe system of complete information.

The problem was that over the years Marvin had grown so weird that people avoided all contact with him unless it was absolutely necessary. This included the intrepid Pamela Drake. Her relationship with Marvin Schmedlapp was particularly unpleasant for her personally after she discovered that he was madly in love with her.

Drake stood in front of the elevators in the ACN Building foyer. She had pressed the DOWN button, but ignored the elevator when it arrived. The thought of speaking personally to Marvin Schmedlapp was more than she could endure. Drake started to go back to her office, but knew she was putting off the inevitable, so she pressed it again. When the elevator arrived, she reluctantly stepped inside. After a deep breath, she reached over and pushed her finger against the button that would take her down to the second basement.

It was dark and musty when she stepped into the Archive Department. A door to her left offered ingress into the bowels of what she knew was the bailiwick of Mr. Marvin Schmedlapp.

Drake walked slowly to the door, pushed it open, and stepped through.

The desk where Marvin usually sat was unoccupied, and once more she was tempted to turn and flee. But after a moment's hesitation, she tapped the call bell to summon service.

"A moment!" came a thin vibration from parts unknown. "A moment, if you please!"

Drake actually shuddered, but closed her eyes and took another steadying breath. She opened them just in time to see Marvin Schmedlapp step into view from the row of cabinets. He gave her a toothy grin.

"Why, Miss Drake!" he said in that reedy voice. "I haven't seen you in ever so long! Well, not in person, of course. I watch your broadcasts faithfully. Yes! Faithfully and reverently, too, I might add. Mother and I never miss you."

"That's flattering, Marvin," Drake said. "I need some—"

"I've written you notes, Miss Drake," Marvin said. "Memos, if you will. I send them to you through the company mail." He paused and licked his lips. "You never answer them, Miss Drake."

"I'm awfully busy," Drake said. "And I'm in a hurry right now. I need—"

"Information," he interrupted, leering at her with those seemingly unfocused eyes. "Everybody that comes down here wants *information*!" He widened his grin. "And I have it."

"Yes," Drake said. She cleared her throat and spoke in a louder tone. "A. J. Bratton."

"Mmm," Marvin mused. "A. J. Bratton. Bratton—comma— A. J." He closed his eyes for a moment, then walked back into the rows of cabinets without uttering another word.

Pamela waited, feeling very uneasy in the eerie permanent twilight of Marvin Schmedlapp's world. When he suddenly appeared from a different direction, she jumped. "Oh!"

"I have returned to you," he announced.

"Thank you, Marvin," she said. "A. J. Bratton?"

"CIA."

Pamela turned and hurried away.

USS **Jefferson**
The Persian Gulf
1400 local (GMT +3)

The orders had come in over the DSCS system. The words were few, short, and to the point. The first person to make an official reaction was Rear Admiral William Grant; the second, who had been verbally alerted by the admiral, was Captain Jackie Bethlehem. She turned to her own chain of command to pass the word down to officers, petty officers, and ratings. The third to receive information from the flag officer was Captain Jason Coggins the air-wing commander. All these stalwarts immediately saw to it that every human being under their personal control and command was made aware of the new situation.

The USS *Jefferson* and Carrier Battle Group 14 were being transferred from the Persian Gulf to the Sea of Japan. It seems there was a war going on over there.

FBI Headquarters
Washington, D.C.
1300 local (GMT −5)

Carl Chassen, the Bureau's Director of Operations, picked up the black phone on his desk, punching the interior line button. "Yes?"

His secretary's voice was tinged with a warning tone. "Pamela Drake is here, sir."

"Send her in, Hedda."

"Are you sure, Mr. Chassen? She's still waiting in the outer office," the secretary said. "It would be easy to have her turned away. She has no appointment."

"I have no problem with seeing Ms. Drake," Chassen assured her.

"You should insist she call first and make arrangements."

"I can think of no reason to delay speaking with her,"

Chassen said calmly. "I have the time today, and there's that golf game tomorrow with the Attorney General. She's already broadcast her big news revelation about Deer Crossing, and they've had a congressional hearing in which Admiral Magruder testified in the presence of a lawyer from the Justice Department. What possible trouble could she make?"

"Mr. Chassen," the secretary said seriously, "she would not be here unless she could make trouble."

"Send her in, Hedda," Chassen said calmly in a tone of condescension. "There's a good girl."

When Pamela Drake stepped into Chassen's office she was the picture of competent feminine assurance. Her hair was styled in a way that gave an impression of a serious professional woman dedicated to business. Her makeup was also tasteful, giving her attractive features a quality of pleasant competence. Chassen stood up and indicated a chair at the side of the desk facing him.

"Please sit down, Pamela," he said. "It's so good to see you."

"Thank you, Carl," she said, demurely settling on the chair. "How have you been?"

"Pretty busy," he said. "But that's the way it always is around here. Busy. Busy."

"I can well imagine," she said. "And I do appreciate you seeing me without an appointment."

"I was pleased to accommodate you," he said, sitting down. "Well! And what can I do for you?"

"I have a couple of points to cover about the Deer Crossing episode," she said.

"Really? You mean you haven't come across any other little items other than that tired incident?" he asked. "I'd have thought the hearing in front of the House Committee on Public Safety and Security would have cleared up any hidden agendas."

"Oh, dear, Carl!" Drake said. "I hate to sneak up on you. But there is one little-bitty item that hasn't been properly explained."

"Alright," he said magnanimously. "Fire away."

"Why was there a CIA operative present at not only Deer

Crossing, but also at Lands End?" Drake asked cheerfully. "In fact, the aforementioned gentleman has been a member of Magruder's team from the get-go."

A quick twitching of one eyebrow was the only indication of Chassen being caught unawares. He smiled. "There are no CIA operatives involved in our antimilitia efforts, Pamela."

"A. J. Bratton," Drake said. "That's his name. A. J. Bratton. He's CIA as sure as the Pope's Catholic, and he's been in on that operation all along."

"That would be against the law, Pamela," Chassen said. "Where in the world did you get that information?"

"From various witnesses who have made casual statements," Drake said. "The guy evidently didn't even use a cover name. Either that or the nom de guerre A. J. Bratton has been used so much it's become common knowledge."

"You're barking up the wrong tree there, Pamela," Chassen said.

"He's been with the CIA for quite a few years, Carl," Drake said. "He was quite active in Southeast Asia with the Air America operations."

"It would be illegal for the CIA to conduct or participate in operations within the United States," Chassen said.

"But those four detonations outside the militia safe house are going to make people think that the episode was an assassination," Drake said. "And that's a specialty of the CIA, isn't it?"

"If that's what it is, it was handled very sloppily," Chassen said.

"That's wouldn't be the first time, would it?" Drake remarked. "Do you want to talk about Ruby Ridge or Bull Run?"

"Aw, Christ!" Chassen said. "This is a waste of time, Pamela. If you're going to sit there and nag about the CIA, you might as well go."

"You realize I'll be quoting your denials," Drake threatened.

"You realize I don't give a shit."

Drake smiled and stood up. "Thank you, Carl. Toodle-oo!"

"Have a nice day, Pamela."

The Oval Office
1900 local (GMT −5)

White House Chief of Staff Jim Dawson felt he was seeing a rerun on television. The same group of people who had been in the office on October 5th, was back. Each had taken the same seat, and each was as edgy as they had been the last time. Of course three of them were dressed exactly the same, too, but that was no surprise. All were military men and wore the uniforms of their respective services.

General L. C. Curtis of the U.S. Army unconsciously ground his teeth; Admiral Ted Hutchins of the Navy nervously tapped his left foot; and General Bill Feldhaus of the United States Air Force nibbled at his right index fingernail. The President sat at his desk, outwardly calm but inwardly seething.

"The son of a bitch!" Curtis suddenly blurted.

"Which son of a bitch, Larry?" the President asked.

Feldhaus answered for him. "The North Korean ambassador."

"We're going to have to sit here and listen to the little bastard recite," Hutchins said, crossing his legs. "It'll be another demand for aid or—or—" He stopped speaking out of frustration for a moment. "Well, shit! Who knows what those sons of bitches have up their sleeves?"

Dawson looked at his watch. "He should be here within the next quarter of an hour."

The ever-faithful and dependable Johnny Kalos entered the office with his serving cart. But this time there were no jelly doughnuts or other treats. Johnny had only a pot of coffee and cups. The gentleman's gentleman had known the men would not be in the mood for nibbling. What they needed was hot, strong coffee to tingle their nerves to alertness. After serving his offering, Johnny left without speaking one word during his presence. The five men sipped the hot brew in silence as their desire for further discussion faded in the somber mood of the occasion.

The day's protocol secretary, this time a plump young man of the intern staff, stepped into the office after rapping lightly and respectfully on the door. He stood taller, drew his shoulders back, and pompously proclaimed, "Mr. President, I am pleased to announce the arrival of His Excellency Chong Jun, Ambassador of the Democratic People's Republic of Korea."

"Let him in," the President said sullenly.

Everyone, with the exception of the Chief Executive, got to their feet as the short, somber man entered the room. His demeanor surprised them. The usually arrogant Oriental gentleman seemed positively humble. Even contrite. He bowed to the President.

"I bring you greetings from the government of my nation, Mr. President."

"So noted, Ambassador Chong," the President said. "What is the business of this visit to my office?"

"I have a letter to deliver to you that comes personally from the foreign minister of North Korea," Chong replied. He reached into the briefcase he carried and pulled out an envelope. He stepped forward, placed it in front of the President, then bowed deeply before stepping back.

The President broke the seal and pulled the missive out. He read silently for a few moments, his eyes opening wider with each line he perused.

The President of the United States
The White House
Washington, D.C., U.S.A.

Dear Mr. President:

It is with great humility and sadness that I send this letter to you. My government takes full responsibility for and deeply regrets the unfortunate clash between the Air Force of the Democratic People's Republic of Korea and that of the naval aircraft of the United States of America. This feeling of deep regret extends to the incident on October

7, when a submarine of the Navy of the Democratic People's Republic of Korea loosed torpedoes against the American Carrier USS *Lincoln* in the Sea of Japan on October 9.

Allow me to assure you that the government of the Democratic People's Republic of Korea had absolutely nothing to do with these outrages. These crimes were carried out by rogue members of our military establishment without the command, knowledge, cooperation, or permission of our central government in Pyongyang.

The Democratic People's Republic of Korea offers its deepest and sincerest apologies for these actions to the government and people of the United States of America. Our Dear Leader Kim Jong Il wishes to assure the President of the United States of America that the perpetrators of these crimes will be punished to the maximum severity of the laws of the Democratic People's Republic of Korea.

Our ambassador will be prepared to discuss reparations at a time that is convenient to you.

> Jung Hwan
> Foreign Minister

The President sat the letter down and looked up at the North Korean. "Thank you, Ambassador Chong. A suitable reply will be drawn up and presented to you at the earliest possible moment."

Chong bowed. "Thank you, Mr. President. Do you require anything else of me?"

"Not at this time, Mr. Ambassador."

Chong made an abrupt exit from the office. The President passed the letter over to General Feldhaus who quickly read it. "My God!"

General Curtis was the next to examine the missive. He shook his head in wonder as he handed it to Admiral Hutchins. The flag officer laughed aloud. "By God above! I don't give a damn if I go blind this very minute. Because now I've seen *everything*!"

Dawson looked at the President. "What sort of message did the North Korean deliver to you?"

"They have issued an apology and taken the rap for the fighting on the Sea of Japan," the President said.

Dawson took the letter from the admiral and quickly scanned the lines. "What in the hell is going on?"

The President leaned back in his chair and put his feet up on his desk. "That, my boy," he said grinning, "is something we've yet to find out."

CHAPTER TWENTY-THREE

United Nations
New York, New York
Friday, 11 October
0945 local (GMT −5)

America's UN Ambassador Sarah Wexler could hardly keep a straight face as she sat at her desk in the General Assembly. Directly behind her, fighting down a grin that threatened to split his face, her aide Brad Heaton waited for the Iranian ambassador Mohammed Sayyad to begin his speech after being recognized by the General Secretary. The entire American delegation knew what the content of the spiel would be. The murderous clash of American and North Korean aircraft over the Sea of Japan had dominated the world news media for the past two days.

The Iranian, confident and gloating, went through an act as if he were a thespian appearing in a highly dramatic scene. He hoped to expand the theatrical aspects of his speech by a short, staged delay. First, he deliberately took his time cleaning his glasses; then he took several slow sips of water before arranging his speech in front of him. Last, he looked up toward the

Secretary General with a determined expression of self-righteousness before clearing his throat to speak.

"Several weeks ago," Sayyad began, "on September 19th I was required to make a protest in front of this august body. This unpleasant task was forced upon me because of criminal actions directed against the sovereign territory and people of the Islamic Republic of Iran by armed forces of the United States of America. Sadly, and to the deep regret and bitter disappointment of the Iranian people, this organization did not take any action in denouncing the American government for its uncivilized behavior. As we feared, this lack of censure encouraged the Americans to commit yet more acts of violence against innocent and peaceful people. This time their victims were the peaceable citizens of the Democratic People's Republic of Korea. Once again, American aircraft off one of their many intrusive carrier ships were unleashed to wreak havoc and murder. This time the outrages occurred on the Sea of Japan when training flights and normal coastal patrol flights of the People's Air Force of North Korea were made victims of unprovoked and dastardly sneak attacks by the Americans. The government of the Islamic Republic of Iran now demands that in the least—the *very* least—the Security Council of the United Nations condemn and censure the government of the United States of America for this gross misconduct." He paused, removed his glasses, and took another drink of water. "Thank you."

The Secretary General nodded his acknowledgment. "Thank you, Mr. Ambassador." He looked to Wexler whom he expected to make a reply. But the American lady sat immobile, seemingly slightly bemused. The North Korean Ambassador Toon Sung, however, had raised his hand. This was to be expected. The Secretary General said, "I now recognize the representative from the Democratic People's Republic of Korea."

The DPRK representative began speaking rapidly, as if in a hurry to get his presentation over and done with. "I wish to make a statement in regards to the incident which the gentleman from Iran has referred to. The clash between the armed forces of the Democratic People's Republic of Korea and the

United States of America occurred through the actions of certain high-ranking members of the DPRK's Army, Air Force, and Navy. My government has issued apologies and tendered offers of reimbursement to the government of the United States. As this issue is being diplomatically and properly settled between those two governments, there is no reason to involve the United Nations in the proceedings. Thank you."

The Iranian ambassador's eyes opened wide in surprise. He almost got to his feet, but fell back to his seat after only half rising. He turned a perplexed look to the ambassador from Syria, gesturing in a questioning manner. The Syrian, also obviously shocked, could only shrug in return.

Now Sarah Wexler raised her own hand and was called on by the Secretary General. "It is obvious that the gentleman from Iran knew absolutely nothing about the subject on which he has just addressed this international association. I would suggest that the next time he deigns to speak to the General Assembly, Security Council, or whomever, that he makes sure he knows what the hell he is talking about. Thank you."

General Headquarters, People's Army
Pyongyang, North Korea
0630 local (GMT +9)

Colonel General Kim Sung Chien was frightened witless. Operation *Wonsukapda Yong*—Avenging Dragon—had come apart at the seams. The fighter planes of that *kopjaengi* General Dai Yong had been roundly defeated at a rate of some ten-to-one by the American naval fliers off the USS *Lincoln*. Sudden unexpected orders had been personally issued by Dear Leader ordering an immediate cessation to Avenging Dragon. No doubt the secret police must be moving in to find out who was behind this supposed training operation that had turned out to be a catastrophic out-and-out attack on the American vessel.

Kim had issued direct immediate orders to the DMZ a bit before midnight the night before. All extra units along with soldiers, tanks, weaponry, and other material were to be withdrawn immediately and returned en masse to their home garrisons. Delays would not be tolerated. This caused a big disturbance in the tunnels and dugouts at the DMZ as troops were awakened and screamed at to hurry them along. The sleepy soldiers stumbled through a packing routine for the unexpected journey. Kim wanted everything back to normal by the time any investigations reached that part of the line.

The next thing he'd done was make a personal phone call to Rear Admiral Park Sung, the submarine force commander. When Park's sleepy voice came through the receiver, Kim spoke two very meaningful code words: *"Momchuda ije—* Stop now!" That was the signal to say everything had gone to hell; cover our asses; the Secret Police are nigh! Park would put his boats back on a normal standing, with half the crews sent on liberty while the other half would be sent out on routine patrols. But the only thing Park said in return was, "I did not receive the signal *Saja Simjang.* The submarines remained in port."

Kim hung up, thinking that was a small blessing. However, there was no doubt that Dear Leader would be furious when he was informed of the complete unvarnished truth of what had happened. Many valuable aircraft had been destroyed along with the loss of some of the best pilots of the nation. It was also an intense loss of face to be so badly mauled by a numerically inferior enemy.

The three conspirators would have to throw up some very blinding smoke screens to cloud the facts. Somehow they would have to convince the powers-that-be that subordinates had taken the training operation, and through misguided zeal and poor judgment had turned it into a shooting match with the United States Navy. The problem was with Lieutenant General Dai Yong of the Air Force. He had not answered his phone. Kim could only hope that he was out doing his best to confuse the issue where his aviation command was concerned. That large loss of valuable aircraft, including brand-new MiG-29s, was going to make it a particularly sticky situation.

Kim, sitting at his desk, opened the bottom drawer. He looked inside at the 7.62 millimeter Chinese automatic pistol sitting on top of the organization and staff manuals he used for reference. The colonel general desperately hoped the weapon would not be his final escape from responsibility for the plans that failed.

The Oval Office
Washington, D.C.
1130 local (GMT −5)

The place had not been so crowded since the President took office. He looked out across the room and mentally counted eight people gathered in chairs arranged in a semicircle in front of his desk.

The White House Chief of Staff Jim Dawson was there of course. Also in attendance were Admiral Thomas Magruder, FBI Agent Charles Greenfield, and CIA Operative A. J. Bratton representing the flag officer's antimilitia organization. Directors of Operations Carl Chassen of the FBI and Kerwood Forestor of the CIA were next to each other. Jeremiah Horton who headed up the Homeland Security Administration sat with Senator Ben Hamilton of Idaho.

The President was upset. "I knew things were too good. The situation with North Korea suddenly and unexpectedly got wrapped up nice and pretty like a Christmas present. I had just congratulated myself when this shit was dropped in my lap."

"I'm sorry, Mr. President," Chassen said. "But I was caught flat-footed when Pamela Drake called on me and brought up the CIA question." He turned to Magruder. "Your outfit was careless as hell, Admiral!" Next his eyes shifted to Greenfield. "And you should have kept him advised on security matters."

Magruder was angry, too. As an admiral, he didn't like being dragged out on the carpet like an Annapolis middie. Especially by a civilian. "Back off, Chassen! Things were whirling in confusion out there. It's easy to waltz out from behind a desk and start displaying your amazing hindsight after the facts."

Greenfield snarled. "Bratton should have kept his head down!"

"I was put there for a reason!" Bratton shot back.

"Enough!" the President roared. "There's enough blame to go double or triple around this room. I have my fair share coming, too. But doling out reproofs is not going to solve the problem we're here to discuss. That Idaho sheriff picked up A. J. Bratton's name somewhere out there in Deer Crossing. He's the one that dropped it on Pamela Drake."

Senator Hamilton spoke confidently, "I have taken care of Sheriff D. W. Doss. After a long talk I had with him, he's ended up in a high-paying position on the governor's security staff. And he suddenly cannot recall hearing about anybody called Bratton."

"Godamn it!" Chassen snapped. "It's on fucking tape!"

"Now he thinks the name he heard was Brandon," Hamilton said. "There was a state police detective there by the name of Agent Brandon. He must have confused it with A. J. Bratton."

"Sure," Forester said with a grin. "It's just a coincidence that there is a CIA operative with a similar name."

"Whatever," Hamilton said.

"Knock it off!" the President commanded. He glared at Bratton. "Did you blow up that militia house?"

"Yes, Mr. President."

"By whose orders?"

"It was a tactical decision on my part," Bratton said.

"I knew it, godamn it!" Greenfield said. "You godamn cowboy! You weren't running around in the wilds of Cambodia, you were in fucking Idaho, U.S.A."

Chassen smirked. "That's why it's against the law for the spooks to operate within the boundaries of the United States. They're time bombs with defective fuses."

Magruder turned a cold look on Bratton. "You killed Darrel Kent, you stupid, unthinking bastard!"

Bratton shrugged. "Collateral casualty."

"Just like those innocent people who died in town, right?" Greenfield snapped.

"Yeah," Bratton said. "Just like those innocent people who died in town."

"Alright! Alright!" the President said. "What we've got

going here is an undeniable need to establish a cover-up. If this gets out, there'll be more than an impeachment. Criminal charges will be flying at us from all directions. Now let's figure out where we start."

Jim Dawson, who had been sitting quietly through the series of recriminations, finally spoke. "We'll have to go straight to Duncan Brandon to squelch the story."

Everyone looked at him confused. Senator Hamilton asked, "Who the hell is Duncan Brandon?"

"Pamela Drake's boss's boss," Dawson replied. "He's the CEO and majority stockholder in ACN, and unknown to the general public."

"And there's some more action that must be taken," the President said. "I've given this a lot of thought after previous consultations with Admiral Magruder. The admiral and I spent most of last evening in each other's company."

Dawson sat down, knowing what was coming.

The President continued, "A. J. Bratton will retire immediately—*immediately*—from the CIA. Understood?"

"Yes, sir," Bratton said, stunned.

Next the President turned to Carl Chassen. "The Federal Bureau of Investigation will issue a statement that absolves Agent Charles Greenfield from all culpability regarding the disaster at Bull Run."

Chassen frowned. "Let's give this some thought. There are serious implications here."

"I have been given a good deal of inside information, Carl," the President said. "I've learned from unimpeachable sources that he was given intelligence that was both erroneous and outdated. I don't think you will want to delve further into this."

"But, Mr. President—"

"And *you* will also be retiring immediately." The President stood up and glanced at Dawson. "Take care of contacting Duncan Brandon."

"Right away, Mr. President," Dawson acknowledged.

"That is all," the President said, walking around his desk toward the door. "This meeting is adjourned."

United Nations
New York, New York
Monday, 14 October
1400 local (GMT −5)

Mr. Mohammad Sayyad, the Iranian ambassador to the United Nations, had spent an emotionally uncomfortable weekend. His embarrassment over the speech he made in regards to the fighting between North Korea and America stuck in his ego as deep as a knife thrust. The chiding of Madame Ambassador Sarah Wexler about not knowing what he was talking about had twisted the blade. It was more than a proud male Persian could endure. He had actually come to the defense of a culpable atheistic nation in his blind eagerness to slam the United States. The mess had boiled over to the point he had insulted his fellow Islamics, making him look bad in the Middle-Eastern press.

Now he was ready to make his payback gesture.

He had begun working on his presentation Saturday evening, laboring on it until late Sunday afternoon. Now, after sitting through a morning of impatiently waiting for earlier scheduled items on the agenda to be addressed, he had enjoyed a leisurely lunch and was ready to launch his attack. At the first opportunity he raised his hand.

The Secretary General, not surprised by the gesture from the pompous Iranian, nodded in his direction. "The chair recognizes the Ambassador from the Islamic Republic of Iran."

"Thank you, Mr. Secretary General," Sayyad said. "I wish to put forth a motion before this body." He glanced sideways at the Syrian ambassador who had already been clued in to provide a second to the suggestion. "Once again, ugly events in which innocent people died have occurred in the United States of America. This time a dozen people were killed by no less than four bombs set off under the most suspicious circumstances. This occurred in Idaho at a place called Deer Crossing. This is the very same state in which other loss of life occurred to a farm family at Bull Run. The United States government lied initially about the circumstances of the tragedy, but was soon forced to admit a cover-up. I must emphasize that this is not what I alone am saying. These facts were brought out by no less a person than the American journalist Pamela Drake over the ACN television news network. Just last evening during her newscast, she stated she was investigating strong allegations that the CIA was deeply involved in the Deer Crossing tragedy." He took a quick glance at Sarah Wexler. "It is now time to reconsider the proposal of inserting a multilateral peacekeeping force into the sovereign area of the United States of America."

A very angry Sarah Wexler turned to her aide Brad Heaton. "That godamn bitch Drake!" she hissed between her teeth. "If there was ever a reason to get rid of the First Amendment—" She didn't bother to finish the sentence.

Heaton nodded his head as the Iranian droned on.

CHAPTER TWENTY-FOUR

Democratic People's Republic of Korea
15 through 17 October

In the DPRK exists an organization so clandestine and under wraps that its official name is known only to those of Dear Leader Kim Jong Il's inner circle. Even the group's mundane administration such as payrolls, timekeeping, and vacation schedules are locked deep within the National Palace.

Its existence has become somewhat known over the decades, and the common people call it by the incorrect but accurately descriptive name of *Pimilui Kwonwi*—the Secret Authority. Many use the shortened acronym *Pimkwon*. But no matter what it is called, it means trouble for those citizens it seeks out for special attention and treatment. Naughty children are warned to behave or Dear Leader will send the *Pimkwon* to take them far away to some dark, cold place.

It was at the exact stroke of midnight on 15 October that the *Pimkwon* launched what their operational orders defined as Operation *Wonsunge Sanyang,* i.e., Operation Monkey Hunt.

Estate of Colonel General Kim Sung Chien
15 October
0100 local (GMT +9)

Kim lay in bed beside his sleeping wife, staring fearfully into
the darkness of the bedroom. He could barely perceive the
sound of slowly approaching automobiles rounding their way
through the hills that made up the Glorious People's Estates.
This was where he and other high-ranking members of the
government and armed forces had their sprawling, luxuri-
ously appointed residences.

Kim had done absolutely no work the day before. He informed his adjutant he was not to be disturbed as he withdrew
to his office and locked himself in. He knew there was no
point in holding on to wild hope that his quick dispersal of the
troops he had mustered along the DMZ would cover his plot
to launch an attack on the south. It was only a matter of time
before the *Pimkwon* agents would arrive to pick him up. At
least a dozen times he'd gone to that desk drawer where he
kept the automatic pistol, taking it out with the intention of
blowing his brains out. And a dozen times he'd replaced the
weapon. The colonel general couldn't muster the courage to
kill himself, even if it would save him from the consequences
of his failed plans.

Kim decided he would not attempt any lies or cover-ups
when he was taken to the Interrogation Center. He would con-
fess all, answer any questions they had, and implicate all the
people they wished to arrest in connection with the investigation. This was common practice of the *Pimkwon* when Dear
Leader would use any incident as an excuse to persecute those
persons he felt were no longer reliable, but had no solid proof
any wrongdoing on their part existed. It was easy to lump
them in with other wrongdoers.

Kim thought that perhaps his cooperation would net him a
touch of mercy. Not that he expected to survive the ordeal.
Mercy in the case of arrest in the Democratic People's Republic of Korea was being summarily executed by firing squad as

quickly as possible. The alternative was to be starved and worked to death in a labor camp.

Kim got out of bed and went into his dressing room to put on the full-dress uniform he had prepared before retiring just before midnight. He dressed carefully, making sure he didn't mess up the arrangement of his medals. After being formally attired, he walked down the hall to his fifteen-year-old daughter Hong's bedroom. He looked in on her, able to make out her sleeping face in the illumination of the Mickey Mouse night-light. Her comfortable, predictable existence would soon turn into hell-on-earth in a labor camp.

"Chonum huhoe haeyo," he whispered softly. "I am sorry."

He turned away and had just placed the braided cap on his head when he heard the cars driving up outside. The colonel general hurried to the door to open it so his wife and children would not be awakened by loud knocking. Just as he opened the portal and stepped through it, three *Pimkwon* agents stepped from the autos. He nodded to them.

"Annyong haseyo, comrades," he said with forced cheerfulness. "I have been waiting for you."

One of the agents wordlessly pointed to an open car door. Kim walked to it and got into the vehicle, taking a vicious punch to the back of his head. No arrests or detainments were made in North Korea without blows, kicks, and pummeling.

Not even for a colonel general.

Dai official residence
Kim Il Sung Air Base
0115 local, (GMT +9)

The *Pimkwon* agents not only knew that Lieutenant General Dai Yong and his homely wife slept in separate bedrooms, but which particular ones they occupied. The largest policeman, winner of the previous year's armed forces karate tournament, kicked open the front door and charged up the stairs, turned left, then rushed into Dai's bedroom, followed by his pals. They leaped on the general and began beating him.

Dai awakening to naked terror, screamed in pain as he tried to squirm away. The agents maintained their hold on him, pulling him to the floor. He crawled on his hands and knees toward the door as they repeatedly kicked his pudgy buttocks. When he got out into the hall he could see his wife standing by the door to her bedroom. Her face, bloated from sleep, looked particularly unattractive.

"Yong!" she screamed in fear. "What is happening? *Cho-nun musowoyo!*"

Before he could answer, the lieutenant general was picked up and hurled down the stairs. He bounced and rolled until he hit the first floor as limp as a rag doll. Two of the arresting officers rushed down after him. The third turned to Mrs. Dai, grinning arrogantly. "Any questions, *kwibuin*?"

She gathered up her courage and announced sharply, "My father is Chief of the Bureau of Mining."

"*Orisogun amso!*" he said, snarling. "Stupid cow! Your father is in handcuffs on his way to a camp in the north. They say he'll not last half the winter." He regarded her ugliness with a sneer. "You will be there soon."

Mrs. Lieutenant General Dai watched him hurry down to join the others who were now dragging her husband out of the house by his feet.

Park residence
Near Chongjun Submarine Base
0315 local (GMT +9)

Vice Admiral Park Sung met the arresting officers with defiance when they charged into his bedroom. He leaped from the covers and assumed his best quarterdeck posture used for dressing down a badly disciplined crew.

"*Kidarida!*" he bellowed. "Hold up there! How dare you charge in here! I am Vice Admiral Park Sung the commanding officer of the North Korean Submarine Force!"

His wife, still quite attractive though close to middle age, sat up with the covers pulled to her chin. She didn't like the way the three men who had awakened them so rudely, were regarding her. When one of them turned from her to punch her husband she screamed in terror.

Park knew if he continued his bravado, he would be given a thorough and painful beating that would be repeated at the Interrogation Center. He wisely shut up as he rolled with the kicks. After a moment or so of the punishment, he was hauled to his feet and frog-marched from the room. The senior *Pimkwon* agent followed, then turned back to Mrs. Park. He pulled the cover from her, reaching down to rip off her nightgown. He seemed strangely amused by her nakedness.

"Arumdaun yoja!" he exclaimed with admiration. "You are a beautiful woman. Take my advice. When you arrive at the camp make yourself available to the highest ranking member of the guard staff you can find. That way you can get an inside job during the winter. You will last a little longer."

Emotional shock set in quickly, and the confused woman began shaking violently as her mind sank into blessed unconsciousness.

Residence of Vice Marshal Yen Nal Ui
Pyongyang
0500 local (GMT +9)

When the three *Pimkwon* arrived at the old marshal's house, they were admitted inside by his aide. Although the man wore the uniform of a junior corporal, it was only his undercover investigatory role while working in the marshal's office. He had been on duty the day that Lieutenant General Dai Yong had been called in to explain about the shooting down of a North Korean aircraft during a training mission. In reality, the junior corporal held the rank of major in the Secret Police.

The officers who arrived saluted the major. One explained, "Orders have come down that the old veteran is to die peacefully in his sleep."

"I understand," the major said, knowing it had something to do with accepting General Dai's explanation. "Do you know if he will have a state funeral?"

"Yes, sir," the officer-in-charge said. "It will even be on television."

"I will take care of it myself," the major said. "Wait here for my return."

The major went up the stairs to the main bedroom where the marshal slept. The old man lay on his back, snoring softly through his open mouth. The major took a pillow and pressed it down on his face. The struggle was pitifully weak, ending after only a couple of minutes. After feeling for a heartbeat, the major left the room and descended the stairs to the foyer where the trio of *Pimkwon* agents waited.

"It saddens me to report that Vice Marshal Yen Nal Ui has succumbed to a heart attack."

"Excellent!" the ranking agent said, pulling an official document from his pocket. "That is exactly what it says on this death certificate. What a coincidence!"

The four men laughed at the joke.

Estate of Colonel General Kim Sung Chien
17 October
1030 local (GMT +9)

Kim Hong was the fifteen-year-old daughter of Colonel General Kim. Hong had known the best life that the Democratic People's Republic of Korea had to offer. A luxurious home, fabulous fun-filled vacations, shopping in the special government department store where the latest fashions were available for purchase, the best of food and treats, and countless other perks. Now, for the first time in her life, a dark cloud loomed over her family. Two days before, sometime between the hours that she had gone to bed and awakened, her father had walked off the face of the Earth. Disappeared. Vanished. Her mother wept in fear and grief, unable to speak coherently. Hong's efforts to find what had happened went unanswered.

Now the young girl sat on her four-poster bed in her room. All her perkiness and haughtiness had evaporated. Every instinct told her that danger lurked nearby; that something mysterious and terrible had obviously happened. But she couldn't quite figure out what it was.

Suddenly the door burst open and her personal maid walked boldly into the room. This was the young, pretty one her father admired so openly. Hong glared at her. "How dare you walk in here like that! Get out of my room!"

The maid stuck out her tongue, then walked over to the closet and opened it. She began pulling Hong's clothes out, throwing them into a pile on the floor. Hong, infuriated, leapt from her bed and walked over. She slapped the maid across the face.

"I ordered you to get out of here!"

The maid hit her back. Once! Twice! Thrice! Hong staggered backward and fell against her dresser. The maid kicked her. "You are finished, you stuck-up little bitch. Your lecherous father has been arrested and they will be here for you and your mother and your brothers and sisters, too! All of you will be worked to death in the camps. We servants are being allowed to take what we want and sell it."

"You are lying!" Hong said, now weeping openly.

"I can use the money to buy food at the market," the maid said, stooping to gather up the garments. "I will send it to my family in the country. Last month my sister's baby died. The child starved to death while you grew fat feeding your selfish face. At least my family will last a bit longer now."

Hong, rubbing the welts on her face, collapsed to the floor as the maid walked from the room.

CHAPTER TWENTY-FIVE

First Presbyterian Church
Summerfield, Idaho
Friday, 18 October
0955 local (GMT −7)

Admiral Thomas Magruder and FBI Agent Charles Greenfield walked up the steps of the church, trailing the townspeo-
ple who had also come to the memorial service for the late
Darrell Kent. An usher at the door handed a printed program
to each attendee as they entered.

The vestibule held a memorial display dedicated to Kent. It
was mostly photographs taken of him during different phases
of his life. The pictures, all enlarged for the occasion, showed
him during his various school years of the 1940s and 1950s.
The best one—occupying the center of the exhibit—was taken
during his days in the 82nd Airborne Division. It was a formal
studio portrait in his Class A olive-drab uniform. A parachutist
badge on a regimental background was pinned to breast of his
"Ike jacket" just above the left pocket. His unit crests were on
each epaulet attached to the green tab that identified him as a
leader of a combat unit. The blue shoulder cord of the infantry
and his sergeant chevrons topped off the uniform. Darrell Kent

looked amazingly young as he sat for that portrait at the onset of his adulthood.

Magruder's eyes wandered over to the side of the exhibit. "What's that?"

He and Greenfield walked up to a small table. It held Kent's old typesetting tools; including a pica pole, makeup rule, and typesetting stick that were laid out on the blue ink-stained apron he had used for many years.

"Interesting," Greenfield remarked.

"He was very proud of having been a journeyman compositor," Magruder remarked. He thought a moment. "Y'know! Benjamin Franklin was a printer."

A voice spoke behind them, interrupting their conversation. "Excuse me."

Magruder and Greenfield turned to see a young man. "Yes?"

"I take it you were friends of my father," the young man said. "My name is Tom Kent."

"We only knew him for a very short while," Magruder said, offering his hand.

"You're not from his militia group, are you?" Tom asked.

Magruder shook his head. "No."

"None of them showed up today," Tom said. "I suppose most of them are in hiding somewhere. I was never sure what to think about my dad's involvement in the movement. I don't think he was pleased when they turned so political."

"Well, your father impressed us in a most positive way," Magruder said.

"Thank God for DNA," Tom said. "Without it he'd never have been identified. All they found was a small hunk of his left arm."

"We're sorry for your loss," Magruder said.

"I appreciate your condolences," Tom Kent said. "And thank you for coming."

As he walked away, Greenfield leaned close to Magruder and whispered, "It's a shame we can't tell him how Darrell died in the service of his country."

"Maybe someday we can," Magruder said. "I hope so."

"We'd better go in for the services," Greenfield suggested. "It sounds like they're starting up."

The pair left the vestibule and entered the church.

Department of International Relations
Beijing, China
1400 local (GMT −8)

The room chosen for the meeting was the best appointed in the building. A giant painting of Mao Tse-tung had been hung on the side wall. Mao's influence in Red China had waned considerably over the years following his death, but there was still a reverent mystique about the man. This was particularly true with North Koreans. Two representatives of that country— Jung Hwan, the Foreign Minister of the Democratic People's Republic of Korea, and Toon Sung, the nation's ambassador to the UN—sat on one side of the table.

The two Chinese gentlemen sitting opposite their guests were Wang Cho the senior diplomat and Tung Kai the junior. They both displayed paternalistic expressions toward the North Koreans, and when Wang spoke his voice had the tone of a disapproving father toward sons who wished to atone for a wrongdoing.

"The Government of the Chinese People is pleased with the punctuality in which you carried out the delivery of the letter to the President of the United States," Wang said.

Jung, his teeth clenched in shameful anger, only nodded.

"We trust you will maintain tighter control over your higher-ranking military and naval cadre," Wang continued, "so that further embarrassments will be avoided. This was most disconcerting."

Again Jung only nodded.

"For the time being," Wang said, "the Government of the Chinese People does not wish for your leader Kim Jong Il to proclaim any more nuclear threats. It would be counterproductive at this time due to the disgraceful fiasco of having much of your Air Force destroyed by American carrier aircraft. The action taken also showed a marked amount of unreliability and untrustworthiness. Therefore, you will instruct Kim Jong Il to wait for explicit instructions of when to threaten the stability of this region and when to pressure the American government for more aid. All this must remain as in the past, completely under the direction of the Communist Chinese Government."

Jung sucked in a breath of vexation before speaking. "We understand Comrade."

"We Red Chinese are moving into the Space Age," Tung said. "One of our comrades has been sent into orbit around the Earth. We hope to catch up with the Americans and Russians within a decade. Naturally, we no longer have patience with barbaric, backward behavior that is inappropriate in these modern times."

Wang asked, "You can see our point, can you not?"

"Yes," Jung said hesitantly.

"Excellent," Wang said. "I believe we have finished with you. You may leave."

The two North Koreans stood up and bowed, then turned and walked from the room. When they were out in the hall, Jung exclaimed, "What arrogance! *Oman!*"

Toon, his face now paled visibly with anger, spat, "*Chung-gukui sochuldul!* Chinese bastards!"

USS **Lincoln**
The Admiral's cabin
Sea of Japan
1730 local (GMT +9)

Rear Admiral James Collier poured himself a snifter of brandy. This was a special treat he allowed himself only on the most special of occasions. His strong willpower enabled him to follow this self-imposed rule to the letter. Sometimes the admiral would be tempted to have a brandy for no other purpose than to enjoy the pleasure provided by the drink; but his stubbornness would kick in to remind him that if he got into the habit of enjoying the treat on a regular basis, the pleasure would slowly diminish over time. Thus, on those rare times when he felt he deserved it, James Collier relished in the slow sipping of the very expensive imported *Monastero San Francesco* brandy that he savored above all. It was distilled in limited quantities in a monastery high in the Italian Alps.

Now, swishing the snifter of the drink in his hands, he sat in the cabin recliner with his feet up. The occasion for this rare treat was not to celebrate the overwhelming air victory won by the aviators of the USS *Lincoln*; rather it was to mark the finish of all reports, documents, inventories, communiqués, and other paperwork pertaining to the battle. That bothersome and sometimes nonsensical hubbub had finally died off. Other echelons of staff and command were now perusing the mighty paper storm unleashed by the USS *Lincoln* because of those administrative requirements. Everybody would now leave Admiral James Collier the hell alone. A knock on the door interrupted his reverie.

"Come in!"

Lieutenant Commander Gene Erickson stepped into the cabin. He came to a severe position of attention and rendered a sharp salute. "Sir! Lieutenant Commander Erickson reporting to the admiral as ordered."

Collier returned the salute. "Ah, yes! I've a few questions to ask you, Erickson. But first, would you care for a brandy?"

"Thank you, sir."

"Get a snifter out of the cabinet over there," Collier said.

Erickson fetched the snifter and walked over to the recliner. Collier poured him a generous helping of the expensive liquor, then motioned him to take a seat in the chair opposite.

"How many aircraft have you shot down since we came on station here?" Collier asked.

"Fifteen, sir," Erickson answered, taking a loud slurp of the brandy. "The last ones were like a turkey shoot though."

"Well, the little bastards shouldn't have picked a fight with us, eh?"

"I understand North Korea apologized for the attack, sir," Erickson said, slurping at the brandy again.

Collier frowned at the rude treatment Erickson was giving his precious liquor. "That brandy is quite expensive, Erickson."

"I'm not surprised, sir," Erickson remarked. He tipped the snifter back and swallowed the remainder. "It's pretty good."

"Yes," Collier said, deciding not to give him any more. "I called you in here to find out how your High Roller Flight worked out."

"I was satisfied with the arrangement, sir," Erickson reported. "The dogfights were unconventional, what with the dozens of aircraft buzzing around, but my teams managed to stick together. We knocked down a total of twenty-eight."

"God!" Collier exclaimed. "You people massacred them, Erickson. You *massacred* them!"

"Frankly I was surprised at the extent of our success," Erickson remarked. "They performed a hell of a lot better back in the Korean War of '50 through '53."

"True," Collier agreed. "But in those days they had plenty of Soviet fuel to put in a lot of flying hours. Nowadays their training time in the air is woefully inadequate."

"Yes, sir."

"I called you in here because the *Jefferson* has been ordered over here to the Sea of Japan," Collier said. "The original intent of the transfer was to lend us a hand in dealing with the North Korean Air Force. But that won't be necessary now. So, the upper echelons have decided to let them relieve us. They will take over the responsibilities for monitoring activity in the Sea of Japan."

"Are we heading back to the States, sir?" Erickson asked eagerly, thinking of going on furlough to Las Vegas.

"We are indeed," Collier said. "But *you* are not. I've been on the horn with the CNO himself, and it's been decided that the High Roller Flight is going to transfer to the air wing on the *Jefferson* to continue your experiment." He took a sip of brandy, savoring the taste on his tongue before swallowing it. "So get your folks together. Your F/A-18s are being transferred with you. There is even some thought of adding some other aircraft to your High Roller Flight. How would you like to be in command of a VFAX?"

"An experimental fighter-attack squadron?"

"Exactly," Collier said. "If it turns permanent you could get a promotion out of it."

"That'd be great, sir."

"Fine, Erickson," Collier said. "That's all I had to tell you. Why don't you get together with your aviators and have a few beers?"

"Maybe we'll order some brandy instead, sir."

"Why don't you just have some beer?" the admiral asked. "You and your guys will appreciate it more." He reached in his pocket and pulled out a twenty-dollar bill. "Here. The suds are on me."

"Thank you, sir!" Erickson stood up, saluted, and marched from the cabin.

Pyongyang, North Korea
State television
Saturday, 19 October
2000 local (GMT +9)

A day of mourning was officially declared by Dear Leader to mark the funeral of Vice Marshal Yen Nair Ui of the People's Air Force. It was the only show on that Saturday night's schedule. The old comrade's corpse lay in state, wearing the full-dress uniform of his branch of service that had been festooned with all the thirty-two medals he had won in service to the Democratic People's Republic. A well-turned out honor guard stood rigidly at attention around the coffin as the specially chosen "grief-stricken" crowd filed past to pay their final respects. They all wept openly and a couple of the women seemed close to swooning. The announcer would come on periodically to extol the old man, pointing out the honors he had won a half century earlier in the war with the Americans.

His former orderly—the phony junior corporal—was now

back to his rank of major, serving as an assistant commander at a prison in Haeju. This was one of the main interrogation centers of the *Pimkwon*. At that moment the three prisoners Kim Sung Chien, Dai Yong, and Park Sung were going through the brutal hell of questioning. Between the three of them, they coughed up the names of two dozen innocents to share the blame for their failed scheme.

Dear Leader would be happy to get rid of a few more people he didn't trust very much.

CHAPTER TWENTY-SIX

ACN offices
Washington, D.C.
Monday, 22 October
0930 local (GMT −5)

It was unusual for Walt Harbaugh to be in his private office. He sat at his desk, restless and edgy, wishing he were out on the studio floor. The news director of ACN did ninety-nine percent of his work in the building's studios at several worktables he used as administrative stations. His secretary would find him there when it was necessary to take care of paperwork. But this morning's business could only be conducted in the confidential confines of this little-used compartment set off on the fifth floor of the building. And Harbaugh definitely was not looking forward to it.

His secretary rapped on the door, then stepped inside to inform him that Pamela Drake had arrived. Harbaugh could see his star journalist standing outside. "Come in, Pamela," he called out.

Drake stepped past the other woman who immediately left and closed the door. Drake noticed that Harbaugh sat straight and tense in his chair.

"Good morning, Walt," Drake said. She looked around the room. "I don't think I've been in this office more than three or four times in all the years I've worked here."

"I don't spend much time in the place myself," Walt said. "I'd offer you a cup of coffee, but there's no pot nearby."

"That's okay," Drake said, sitting down. She smiled at him. "So what's up?"

"We're going to kill the CIA story," Walt said, hurrying to the point.

"You don't mean the one about Deer Crossing, right?"

"That's the one," Harbaugh said. He rushed into an explanation. "I had a call from Duncan Brandon at home last night. ACN is going to lay off the whole thing."

Drake leaned forward in anger. "Hey! That's one hell of a big story. I would think the network chief would appreciate the full meaning behind it. The CIA is breaking the law as an organization. This isn't a case of one of its agents independently turning out to be a traitor or going off the deep end as an individual. The organization itself is becoming involved in domestic issues where they don't lawfully belong. The public has a right to learn all about it."

"They won't be learning on ACN," Harbaugh said. "This is a very serious and sensitive issue, Pamela. The repercussions are far-reaching."

"You're damn right they are!"

"Listen very carefully to what I have to say, Pamela," Harbaugh said. "Magruder will not discuss this situation with anybody. That Idaho sheriff has now stated that he made no statement about the CIA—"

"It's on tape!" Drake yelled.

"He now says there was a mix-up of sorts between the name he gave you and a detective of the State Police. And one more very important thing I must mention. This comes under the new Homeland Security Regulations."

"We have the First Amendment working for us, Walt!"

He shook his head. "I don't wish to get into an unpleasant harangue about this. Duncan Brandon says kill it. So the story is dead. Period."

"It's a story I am definitely going to tell," Pamela insisted.

"You won't tell it over ACN."

"Then I'll godamn well quit!"

"Pamela, it's not worth it," Harbaugh said. "Let it go. This is big. Even bigger than you can handle." He watched as she sank back into her chair. "If you insist on going on with this, you could find your popularity with the viewers slipping badly. Mr. Brandon wanted you to be informed that your story caused a great deal of embarrassment for the U.S. in the United Nations. The Iranian ambassador used it to revive the insistence that a multilateral peacekeeping force be sent into American sovereign territory. The people who want that CIA thing forgotten have the power to put you under a very bright and unpleasant spotlight. You could even be made to appear as if you were following an un-American agenda." He paused to give her a moment to think before adding, "Rumors might be floated that you were in cahoots with certain movements that are hostile to the United States."

"What the hell do they think I am?" Pamela yelled. "A godamn Islamic? Do they picture me living in a harem with the other wives of some anachronistic Arab extremist and doing the bastard's bidding?"

Harbaugh was silent for a moment, then he spoke slowly and deliberately. "Pamela, your career as you know it could be swept away in a flash. Everything you've worked so hard for would be gone and unrecoverable."

There was something in his voice that chilled Pamela Drake to the bone. The truth was being trampled on; buried to be forgotten. She sat for a moment staring at the floor before speaking. "Alright, Walt. Tell Mr. Brandon that I've gotten the word."

Harbaugh watched her slowly rise from the chair and walk out the office door, leaving it open. His secretary appeared, an expression of confusion on her face. "Is everything all right, Mr. Harbaugh?"

"No, Betty," he said under his breath. "Everything is definitely *not* all right."

South Korea
The DMZ
0700 local (GMT +9)

Lieutenant General Donald Hamm had spent a solid twenty minutes peering across the DMZ through the same battery commander's scope he always used. Behind him, Colonel William Atkinson and Lieutenant Commander Harry Robinson, waited patiently. Finally, the general stepped back, smiling smugly.

"Things are back to normal," he said. He glanced at Robinson. "I hate to admit this, but it all came about because of those pilots off the *Lincoln*. Your people did a fantastic job."

"Oh, yeah!" Robinson agreed. "The kill ratio was fantastic. We ended up with several multi-aces. I wish I'd been in on it."

Hamm chuckled. "Poor fellow. Here you were stuck with us dogfaces while your friends were out there earning those laurel wreaths of a glorious victory."

Atkinson, the Chief of Intelligence in Hamm's headquarters, walked over to the scope. He spoke as he focused. "When I received the first reports of the mass withdrawals, I thought I'd lost my mind. It seemed like a cruel hallucination, but I pinched myself and I was wide awake. Then the satellite photos confirmed it. The sons of bitches were hauling ass to the rear."

"That's how I felt when the news of the apology came," Hamm said.

"How's that cliché go?" Robinson asked. "All's well that ends well, right?"

"Right!" Hamm said. "C'mon! Let's get out of here so the troopers around here can get back to their jobs."

The three officers left the trench, heading back to where the Humvee waited for them.

North Korea

The fallout from the great plot of Kim, Dai, and Park affected some two dozen persons of whom twenty-one were innocent of any connection with the scheme.

The three leading conspirators were executed at a labor camp near the Manchurian border. They were attired in dirty, ill-fitting prison overalls and were barefoot when the truck carrying them arrived at the execution site. The hours of interrogation and beatings showed on their battered features as they were kicked off the back of the vehicle. They were unable to get to their feet before being dragged to the firing line. Young soldiers roughly pulled them to their knees and faced them in the correct direction. Kim was the toughest of the trio, and he was aware of what was happening. Although his eyes were swollen so tightly shut that he couldn't see, and his battered testicles still emitted sharp pains from the many electric shocks given that part of his anatomy, he felt a sense of peace. It was now over. No more days of sleeplessness while enduring the unending brutal questioning. It was as if he'd had no life before his arrest, and his entire existence had been one of confinement and torture. It was a comfort of sort to realize whatever came next would be better than what had gone on before.

The executioners were the same soldiers who had pummeled them into position. They drew their pistols and stepped back to avoid having blood splattered on their uniforms. The officer-in-charge gave the commands dispassionately.

"Chunbi hada! Kyonuda! Soda!"

The practiced firing squad pulled their triggers simultaneously and the bullets hit the three skulls at the same time, knocking the victims forward to fall on their faces. Dai the fighter pilot still moaned and required a second shot.

Senior Captain Horangi commander of the submarine *Sango* met his fate the same way the day before. His superlative leadership and fighting abilities had caused several higher-ranking naval officers to regard him as a rival for promotion and medals. They denounced him as a coconspirator with Vice Admiral Park. After three days of interrogation by the *Pimkwon* he confessed to everything. His case was a simple one of denouncement, thus no establishment of facts was necessary.

The women of Colonel General Kim, Major General Dai, and Vice Admiral Park were sent to a dismal labor camp designed to work all prisoners to death within six months. Mrs. Park, the most attractive, remembered the advice of the secret policeman who had ripped her nightgown off on the night her husband was arrested. Her offer of her body to the camp officers was turned down since they all had younger women. But the kitchen staff—a dozen trustees arrested for criminal rather than political crimes—took her desperate proposition as a group. Between her scullery tasks, she entertained them in the back storeroom whenever it was demanded of her.

At least she would survive the first winter.

USS Jefferson

Carrier Battle Group 14 was on its way to the Sea of Japan to relieve Admiral John Collier's force. When the *Jefferson* and her sister ships arrived on station it would be a time for two changes of command, a new air wing, and various transfers of other personnel.

Captain Jackie Bethlehem was leaving her beloved ship to prepare for the first steps up to flag officer country. She had been selected for advance courses at the Naval War College in Newport, Rhode Island. Rear Admiral William "Coyote" Grant would find another star for his epaulets in his assignment to the Division of War Plans Coordination at the Pentagon.

When the C-2A Greyhound landed to pick them up to begin their trips to their new duty stations, it brought in their replacements. Rear Admiral John Miskoski and Captain Paul Tarkington stepped out onto the flight deck to take over. No change-of-command ceremonies had been planned because of the urgency of the battle group to get on station and be immediately ready for action. The new officers were accompanied by the replacement air wing commander Captain Randal

Jagger and newly promoted Commander Gene Erickson. The latter and his yet-to-be formed VFAX, would be in the vanguard of Jagger's aviators.

A new era was brewing.

GLOSSARY

0-3 LEVEL: The third deck above the main deck. Designations for decks above the main deck (also known as the damage-control deck) begin with zero. The zero is pronounced as "oh" in conversation. Decks below the main deck do not have the initial zero and are numbered down from the main deck, e.g., Deck 11 is below Deck 3; Deck 0-7 is above deck 0-3.

ABAFT: Toward the stern or rear of a vessel.

ACLS: Automatic Carrier Landing System. System used to guide the aircraft to the deck automatically.

AIR BOSS: A senior commander or captain assigned to the aircraft carrier, in charge of flight operations. The "boss" is assisted by the miniboss in PriFly, located in the tower on board the carrier. The air boss is always in the tower during flight operations, overseeing the launch and recover cycles, declaring a green deck, and monitoring the safe approach of aircraft to the carrier.

AIR WING: composed of the aircraft squadrons assigned to the battle group. The individual squadron commanding officers report to the air wing commander, who reports to the admiral.

AIRDALE: Slang for an officer or enlisted person in the aviation fields. Includes pilots, NFOs, aviation intelligence officers, maintenance officers, and the enlisted technicians who support aviation. The antithesis of an airdale is a "shoe".

AKULA: Late-model Russian-built nuclear attack submarine, an SSN. Fast, deadly, and deep-diving.

ALR-67: Detects, analyzes, and evaluates electromagnetic signals; emits a warning signal if the parameters are compatible with an immediate threat to the aircraft, e.g., seeker head on an antiair missile. Can detect enemy radar in either a search or a targeting mode.

AMRAAM: Advanced Medium-Range Antiair Missile.

ANGELS: Thousands of feet over ground. Angels twenty is twenty thousand feet.

APC: Speed-holding automatic throttle.

ASAP: As soon as possible.

ASW: Antisubmarine Warfare.

AVIONICS: Black boxes and systems that compose an aircraft's combat systems.

AW: Aviation antisubmarine warfare technician. The enlisted specialist flying in an S-3, P-3, or helo USW aircraft.

AWACS: Advanced Warning Aviation Control System. Long-range command-and-control and electronic-intercept aircraft.

AWG-9: The primary search and fire control radar on a Tomcat. Pronounced *awg nine*.

BACKSEATER: Also known as the GIB, the Guy In Back. Non-pilot aviator available in several flavors: BN (Bomber/Navigator), RIO (Radio Intercept Operator), and TACCO (Tactical Control Officer) among others. Usually wears glasses and is smart.

BALL: Optical landing aid to keep the pilot on the proper glide path.

BAT TURN: Pilot talk for a very sharp turn.

BB STACKER: Nickname for ordnance man, i.e., Red Shirt.

BEAR: Russian maritime patrol aircraft, the equivalent in rough terms of a U.S. P-3. Variants have primary missions in command and control, submarine hunting, and electronic intercepts. Big, slow, good targets.

BITCH BOX: One interior communications system on a ship. So named because it's normally used to bitch at another watch station.

BLUE ON BLUE: Fratricide. U.S. forces are normally indicated in blue on tactical displays, and this term refers to an attack on a friendly by another friendly.

BLUE WATER NAVY: Outside the unrefueled range of the air wing. When a carrier enters blue water ops, aircraft must get on board—i.e., land—and cannot divert to land if the pilot gets the shakes.

BOLTER: When an aircraft making a carrier landing misses all the wires, the aviator must speed up and fly off the carrier to try it again.

BOOMER: Slang for a ballistic missile submarine.

BOQ: Bachelor Officer Quarters.

BUSTER: As fast as you can, i.e., immediately if not sooner.

BVR: Beyond Visual Range.

C-2 GREYHOUND: Also known as the COD, Carrier Onboard Delivery. The COD carries cargo and passengers from shore to ship. It is capable of carrier landings and also operated in coordination with CVBGs from a shore squadron.

CAG: Carrier Air Group Commander. This is an obsolete term since an air wing rather than an air group is now deployed on carriers. However, everyone thought CAW sounded stupid, thus the original acronym is still employed.

CAP: Combat Air Patrol.

CARRIER BATTLE GROUP: A combination of ships, air wings, and submarines assigned under the command of a rear admiral. Also known by the acronym CBG.

CDC: Combat Direction Center. This replaces the old term CIC for Combat Information Center. All sensor information fed into the CDC, and the battle is coordinated by a tactical action officer on watch there.

CHERUBS: Hundreds of feet above ground. Cherubs five is five hundred feet.

CHIEF: Term used to denote chief, senior chief, and master chief petty officers. On board ship the chiefs have separate eating and berthing facilities. They wear khakis as opposed to dungarees for lower enlisted ratings.

CHIEF OF STAFF: The COS in a battle group staff is normally a senior captain who acts as the admiral's executive officer or deputy.

CIA: The Central Intelligence Agency.

CIWS: Close-in Weapons System, pronounced *see-whiz*. Gatling gun with built-in radar that tracks and fires on inbound missiles. If you have to use it, you're dead.

CNO: Chief of Naval Operations.

COD: See *C-2 Greyhound*.

COLLAR COUNT: Traditional method of determining the winner of a disagreement. A survey is taken of the opponent's collar rank devices. The senior person wins. Always.

COMMODORE: Formerly the junior-most flag rank, now used to designate a senior captain in charge of a bunch of like units. A destroyer commodore commands several destroyers, a sea control commodore commands the S-3 Squadrons on that coast. Contrast with a CAG who owns a number of dissimilar units.

COMPARTMENT: A room on a ship.

CONDITION TWO: One step down from General Quarters, which is Condition One. Condition Five is tied up at the pier in a friendly country.

CRYPTO: Short for cryptological, the magic set of codes that make a circuit impossible for anyone else to understand.

CV, CVN: Abbreviation for an aircraft carrier, conventional and nuclear.

CVIC: Carrier Intelligence Center located down the passageway from the flag spaces.

DATA LINK, THE LINK: The secure circuit that links all units in a battle group or in an area. Targets and contacts are transmitted over the link to all ships. The data is processed by the ship designated as Net Control and common contacts are correlated. The system also transmits data from each ship and aircraft's weapons systems, e.g., a missile firing. All services use the link.

DDG: Guided Missile Destroyer.

DDI: Digital Display Indicator.

DESK JOCKEY: Nonflyer who drives a computer instead of an aircraft.

DESRON: Destroyer commander.

DICASS: An active sonobuoy.

DICK STEPPING: Something to be avoided. While anatomically impossible in today's gender-integrated services it has been decided that women can do this as well.

DMZ: Demilitarized Zone.

DOPPLER: Acoustic phenomena caused by relative motion between a sound source and a receiver that results in an apparent change in frequency of the sound. The classic example is a train going past and the decrease in the pitch of its whistle. When a submarine changes its course or speed in relation to a sonobuoy, the event shows up as a change in the frequency of the sound source.

DOUBLE NUTS: Zero-zero on the tail of an aircraft.

DPRK: Democratic People's Republic of Korea, i.e., North Korea.

DSCS: Defense Satellite Communications System.

E-2 HAWKEYE: Command, control, and surveillance aircraft. Turboprop rather than jet, and unarmed. Smaller version of an AWACS, in practical terms, but carrier-based.

ELF: Extremely Low Frequency. A method of communicating with submarines at sea. Signals are transmitted via miles-long antenna and are the only way of reaching a deeply submerged submarine.

ENVELOPE: What you're supposed to fly inside if you want to live to fly another day.

EPA: Environmental Protection Agency.

ETA: Estimated Time of Arrival.

ETS: End of Term of Service.

EW: Electronic warfare technicians who man the devices that detect, analyze, and display electromagnetic signals.

F/A-18 HORNETS AND SUPER HORNETS: A combination fighter/attack aircraft.

FAMILYGRAM: Short messages from submarine sailors' families to their deployed sailors. Often the only contact with the outside world that a submarine sailor on deployment has.

FBC: Flag Battle Center.

FF/FFG: Fast frigate and guided-missile fast frigate.

FLAG OFFICERS: Admirals.

FLAG PASSAGEWAY: The portion of an aircraft carrier that houses the admiral's staff working spaces. Includes the flag mess and the admiral's cabin. Normally separated from the rest of the ship by heavy plastic curtains, and designated by blue tile on the deck instead of white.

FLIGHT QUARTERS: A condition set on board a ship preparing to launch or recover aircraft. All unnecessary persons are required to stay inside the skin of the ship and remain clear of the flight deck area.

FLIGHT SUIT: The highest form of navy couture. The perfect choice of apparel for any occasion as far as pilots are concerned.

FLIR: Forward-Looking Infra-Red.

FLTSATCOM: Fleet Satellite Communications System.

FOD: Foreign Object Damage, or loose gear or debris that can cause damage to an aircraft.

FOX: Tactical shorthand for a missile firing. Fox One indicates a heat-seeking missile; Fox Two an infrared missile; and Fox Three a radar-guided missile.

FROG: A member of the catapult and arresting crew, i.e., Green Shirt.

FTX: Field-Training Exercise.

G-4: Logistics/supply staff section of a brigade or higher.

GCI: Ground Control Intercept. This is a procedure used in the Soviet air forces. Primary control for vectoring the aircraft in on enemy targets and other fighters is vested in a guy on the ground rather than in the cockpit where it belongs.

GIB: See *Backseater.*

GMT: Greenwich Mean Time.

GRAPE: Member of aircraft refueling team, i.e., Purple Shirt.

GREEN SHIRTS: See *Shirts.*

HANDLER: Officer located on the flight deck level responsible for ensuring the aircraft are correctly positioned—"spotted"—on the flight deck. Coordinates the movements of aircraft with yellow gear (small tractors that tow aircraft and other related gear) from maintenance areas to catapults, and from the flight deck to the hangar bar via the elevators.

HARM: Antiradiation missile that home in on radar sights.

HOT: Reference to a sonobuoy holding enemy contact.

HSDA: Home Security and Defense Agency.

HUFFER: Yellow gear located on the flight deck that generates compressed air to start jet engines.

ICS: Interior Communications System. The private link between a pilot and a RIO or the telephone system internal to a ship.

IMC: The general announcing system on a ship or submarine. Every ship has many different interior communications systems, most of them linking parts of the ship for a specific purpose. Most operate off sound-powered phones. The circuit designators consist of a number followed by two letters that indicate the specific purpose of the circuit. 2AS, for instance, might be an antisubmarine warfare circuit that connects the sonar supervisor, the USW watch officer, and the sailor at the torpedo launch.

INCHOPPED: A ship entering a defined area of water, e.g., inchopped the Med.

IN RNG: When this appears on the HUD or DDI it indicates that the selected target is in range.

INTELREP: Intelligence Report.

IR: Infrared.

ISOTHERMAL: A layer of water that has a constant temperature with increasing depth. Located below the thermocline where increase in depth correlates to decrease in temperature. In the isothermal layer the primary factor affecting the speed of sound in water is the increase in pressure and depth.

JBD: Jet Blast Deflector. Panels that pop up from the flight deck to block the exhaust emitted by aircraft.

JTFEX: Joint Task Force Exercise.

KAMIKAZE: Japanese for "Divine Wind". It refers to suicide attack aviators of World War II in the Pacific Campaign.

LEADING PETTY OFFICER: The senior petty officer in a work center, division, or department, responsible to the leading chief petty officer for the performance of the rest of the group.

LOFARGRAM: Low-Frequency Analyzing and Recording Display. Consists of lines arrayed by frequency on the horizontal axis and time on the vertical axis. Displays sound signals in the water in a graphic fashion for analysis by ASW technicians.

LONG GREEN TABLE: A formal inquiry board.

LSO: Landing Signals Officer.

MACHINIST'S MATE: Enlisted technician that runs and repairs most engineering equipment on board a ship. Abbreviated as MM, e.g., an MM1 is a petty officer first machinist's mate.

MAD: Magnetic Anomaly Detection equipment.

MCAS: Marine Corps Air Station.

MDI: Mess Decks Intelligence. The rumor mill aboard a ship.

MEZ: Missile Engagement Zone. Any hostile contacts in the MEZ are engaged only with missiles. Friendly aircraft must stay clear.

MIG: Russian Mikoyan line of aircraft designation.

MRE: Meals Ready to Eat, i.e., field rations.

MWB: Motorized whaleboat. These are lifeboats and shipboard utility boats powered by diesel. They are usually around 25 feet in length and are steered by a tiller.

NATIONAL ASSETS: Surveillance and reconnaissance resources of the most sensitive nature, e.g., satellites.

NAS: Naval Air Station.

NATOP: The bible for operating a particular aircraft.

NCO: Noncommissioned officer (corporal and above in enlisted ranks).

NFO: Naval Flight Officer.

NOMEX: Fire-resistant fabric used as material for shirts. See *Shirts*.

NSA: National Security Agency. Primarily responsible for evaluating electronic intercepts and sensitive intelligence.

NUGGET: Rookie aviator.

OOD: Officer of the Day. Responsible for the safe handling and maneuvering of the ship. Supervises the conning officer and other underway watchstanders. Ashore, the OOD may be responsible for a shore station after normal working hours.

OTH: Over the Horizon. Usually refers to shooting at something you can't see.

P-3: Shore-based antisubmarine warfare and surface surveillance long-range aircraft.

PHOENIX: Long-range antiair missile carried by U.S. fighters.

PIPELINE: A series of training commands, schools, or necessary education for a particular specialty. The fighter pipeline for example includes Basic Flight then fighter training at the RAG (Replacement Air Group—a training squadron).

PLA: People's Liberation Army (Red China).

PUNCHING OUT: Ejecting from an aircraft.

PURPLE SHIRTS: See *Shirts.*

PXO: Prospective Executive Officer. The officer ordered into a command as the relief for the current XO. In most squadrons, the XO eventually "fleets up" to become the commanding officer of the squadron, an excellent system that maintains continuity with an operational command. The surface navy does not use this system.

RACK: A bed or bunk.

RAF: Royal Air Force (United Kingdom).

REDCROWN: The ship in the CVBG that coordinates air defense.

REDOUT: This occurs when an aviator goes through a negative force field of gravity and his vision reddens from blood forced into his head.

RED SHIRTS: See *Shirts.*

RHIP: Rank Has Its Privileges. See *Collar Count.*

RIO: Radar Intercept Officer.

ROK: Republic of Korea, i.e., South Korea.

RWR: Radar Warning Receiver.

RWS: Range While Searching radar.

S-3: Command and control aircraft. Redesignated as sea control aircraft with individual squadrons referred to as torpedo-bombers.

SAM: Surface-to-Air Missile.

SAR: Sea Air Rescue.

SCIF: Specially Compartmented Information. On board a carrier, used to designate the highly classified compartment next to TFCC.

SEAWOLF: Newest version of the Navy's fast-attack submarine.

SENSO: Sensor Operator on board an S-3B Viking aircraft.

SERE: Survival, Evasion, Rescue, and Escape.

SHIRTS: Color-coded Nomex pullovers used by flight deck and aviation personnel for rapid identification of their functions. Green: maintenance divisions. Brown: plane captains. White: safety and medical. Red: ordnance. Purple: fuel. Yellow: flight deck supervisors and handlers.

SIDEWINDER: Antiair missile carried by U.S. fighters.

SITREP: Situation Report.

SIERRA: A subsurface contact.

SLR: Self-Loading Rifle.

SONOBUOYS: Acoustic listening devices dropped in the water by ASW or USW aircraft.

SOP: Standing Operational Procedures.

SPARROW: Antiair missile carried by U.S. fighters.

SPETZNAZ: The Russian version of SEALs, although term encompasses a number of different specialties.

SPOOKS: Slang for intelligence officers and enlisted sailors working in highly classified areas.

SUBANT: Administrative command of all Atlantic submarine forces.

SUBPAC: Administrative command of all Pacific submarine forces.

SWEET: When used in reference to a sonobuoy it indicates that buoy is functioning properly.

TACCO: Tactical Control Officer; the NFO in an S-3.

TACTICAL CIRCUIT: A term that encompasses a wide range of actual circuits used on board a carrier.

TANKER: A fuel-carrying aircraft for in-air refueling.

TEU: Twenty-Foot Equivalent Unit. Capacity of cargo containers used on a container ship.

TFCC: Tactical Flag Command Center. A compartment in flag spaces from which the CVBG admiral controls the battle. Located immediately forward of the carrier's CDC.

TOP GUN: Advanced fighter training command.

UNDERSEA WARFARE COMMANDER: In a CVBG, normally the DESRON embarked on the carrier. Formerly called the ASW commander.

UNREP: Underway Replenishment—the resupply and refueling of ships at sea.

VDL: Video downlink. Transmission of targeting data from an aircraft to a submarine with OTH capabilities.

VX-1 Test pilot squadron that develops envelopes after Pax River evaluates aerodynamic characteristics of new aircraft. See *Envelope*.

WHITE SHIRT: See *Shirts*.

WLCO: Will comply.

WINCHESTER: Out of weapons.

XO: Executive Officer. The second-in-command.

YELLOW SHIRT: See *Shirts*.

"Fasten your seat belt! *Carrier* is a stimulating, fast-paced
novel brimming with action and high drama." —Joe Weber

CARRIER

Keith Douglass

**U.S. MARINES. PILOTS. NAVY SEALS.
THE ULTIMATE MILITARY POWER PLAY.**

The Carrier Battle Group Fourteen—a force including a
supercarrier, amphibious unit, guided missile cruiser, and
destroyer—is brought to life with stunning authenticity and
action in high-tech thrillers as explosive as today's headlines.